Vestal

ASHLEY SCHWELLENBACH

For Colin, Jack, and Cat Cat.

CONTENTS

ACKNOWLEDGMENTS

For all the solitude required to write a book, actually putting one together requires skills I could not hope to possess. To Lena Rushing for once again allowing me to use her artwork and to Mignon Khargie for her counsel and for once again creating a stunning cover image, thank you, thank you, thank you. To Bryce Wilson for advice and shop talk, to Kristi Elkins and Lindsay Wilcox for bravely reading what no one else had, and to Colin Rigley for a little of everything, thank you for enabling this ridiculous passion of mine.

PROLOGUE

When I was 16, I was inducted into the College of Vestal Virgins, after spending 10 years studying the sacred rituals and ultimately kneeling before the emperor on a cold, white, marble floor to swear an oath of chastity.

At 17, I met Nesreen.

I never made it to 18.

But that was ancient Rome—a time and place with little relationship to Livingston, New Jersey. Without sounding self-important, the only connection, really, is me: Rhea. Me and the film reel lodged invisibly and resolutely in my cerebral cortex, playing vivid scenes of feminine faces piously framed by infulas preparing *mola salsa*, collecting water from the sacred spring, watching the tawny sands of the Coliseum floor blossom with freshly spent blood, and—always! always!—guarding the sacred flame.

When I turned 16 in New Jersey, my father started giving me driving lessons, directing as I took the Hyundai to neighboring suburbs and patiently practiced left turns, while he yelped every time another car came into view.

At 17, I turned down two dates for the prom—no

need for vows of chastity in Livingston, not when the only achievement anyone my age can boast is tackling an ungainly youth while wearing 50 pounds of foam padding.

And at 18, I graduated from high school and my parents insisted that I visit *nostra patria*, our ancestral home in Rome.

I fear I won't make it to 19.

I

It didn't come as any great surprise that they ambushed me practically the moment the high school band finished playing "Pomp and Circumstance." Their arms were full of flowers, and my mom—whom I sometimes call Abri because referring to my parents as Mom and Dad still makes me uncomfortable—kept dropping envelopes with graduation cards sent from various limbs and branches of the family tree. And their faces couldn't contain their pride. Even varnished in a cynicism that was half teenage birthright and half wariness from my past life, I couldn't help but observe that it really looked as though the smiles would lift right off their faces with the energetic force of their delight in my accomplishment. In me.

My younger sister Emeline trailed behind them, seemingly indifferent to the ritual hugging and exchange of Mylar balloons accompanied by buoyant prophesies for the future. She was only there to see off the male specimens of the Class of 2016 anyhow.

My father, Fedele, was the first to broach the subject. We were home by then, and I was at least no longer wearing a voluminous black gown; ceremonial attire had a tendency to trigger bad memories.

"Well, Rhea, what are your plans for the summer?" he asked, in a tone that was meant to pass for casual.

I hadn't made any plans—not for the summer, nor college, nor any other season or milestone for which a recent high school graduate is expected to prepare. Fedele might not have known this. Within my family, I had a reputation for being secretive and—while my family conscientiously never spoke the word in my presence, using it only in whispers on nights when the darkness fed by an anorexic moon obscured their words—*different*. They worried the word was a kind of charm that, once spoken, would seal my fate as one of those droll, physically indefectible girls who for no seemingly good reason watches people live from the wrong end of some unseen barrier.

When Emeline waxed poetic on the subject of volleyball tournaments and the senior hockey player in woodworking class, they nodded dutifully, not because they shared my sister's sincere belief that the fate of the world hinged on the outcome of a high school volleyball tournament, but because they had tacitly agreed to live by the sitcom code of family life. And that code dictated that they empathize with whatever my 16-year-old sister had to say. If they ever found the subjects of her gripes petty, they never offered any indication. Emeline's world was exactly as they expected it to be, and so the three formed a perfect nuclear unit, unfettered by unusual thought or inconvenient preoccupations.

I was a different story.

"We thought you might spend the summer in Rome," Fedele ventured.

"It's time, Rhea," added Abri, whose words were punctuated by the violent sound of glasses clashing as she rummaged through cupboards for vases to house my graduation bouquets.

"Long past time, in fact."

She clipped a lily down to size, and I winced.

"Your sister's already been four times," she added.

"But you've been away so long, Uncle Basilio wouldn't even recognize you after all these years."

"It's not an unreasonable request," Fedele said, already sounding rather desperate. This argument had been played out dozens of times over the course of my adolescence, and, despite outnumbering me, my parents never won. An ordinary teenager might have been bought with promises of a car or a new wardrobe, but not me. My parents had no leverage. There was nothing I wanted or needed or required of them, and I think they resented my perverse independence even more than my perverse refusal to travel to Italy and find myself a charming Italian *ragazzo* and finally get my heart broken like a normal teenage girl. All against the romantic backdrop of … .

"The Coliseum. Trevi Fountain. Palatine Hill. The Vatican. The palazzos—"

"The Pantheon," shouted Emeline, from the living room judging by the sound of her frantic, violent typing.

"You don't have to go alone," Fedele assured me. "We're willing to pay for two tickets. You can bring anyone you want. A friend … ."

He seemed to recognize his mistake, even before Abri put her hand on his shoulder as if urging him to take back his words. I had no friends. Studying associates, a few. I was on friendly terms with the guy at the zoo who fed the tigers, and with the woman who taught me new drops at my tri-weekly aerial fabric dancing classes. But I was fairly confident that the zoologist—if not the employee at the fabric dancing gym—was married, and even with my limited grasp of contemporary interpersonal relationships, I understood that asking a near stranger to spend the summer with you in Rome was unpardonably desperate, at best.

"It's just … you love history so much. You'd love the Coliseum and Palatine Hill," my father fumbled.

"What, so I can gawk at history with the other *turistas*?" I asked, incensed. "History is not alive in those places—not to people who buy a ticket and click, click photos of everything they see. One photo per square foot of the

Coliseum, ten for each of the pope's fingers and toes, three for each of the heathen gods the Christian church drove out of the Pantheon!"

My father drew back, unable to summon a suitable response to my scorn. Unlike Emeline, I kept a tight rein on my emotions. It was likely for the best that I had only one sibling to throw into stark relief my otherness, the complete wrongness of my being.

We might have many lives, but only properly belong to one. But some sins are too tectonic to be confined to a single life. We must keep paying for them again and again. I suspected that was what Rome was for: an entire city littered with nuns and leering tourists just so I could pay for my sin of 1,500 years.

Past lives are tricksome: what you remember, how you remember, and the exact integer of enemies and loves who recognize you through the veil of long centuries best forgotten. For some, time is a cobweb that can be brushed aside and ignored. To others, it's more like hurtling rapids; if you are big enough, you can navigate time—float through, unscathed, to the other side. And if not, it will ensnare you and drag you along in its path toward a long and inevitable sleep.

Strangest of all, to me, are those who march on with their lives as if they don't see it, this foul crust of age overtaking them, eroding their painstakingly landscaped civilizations, reducing every mighty empire to a footnote in a history textbook or travel guide. *Imperium sine fine.* An empire without end. What I once believed, what I once lived—and lost my life—for. Some people might find a way to balance their many lives with a measure of grace. For them, time could be a beatific veil to be worn as an honorific.

I had yet to decide.

Common wisdom holds that a contemporary 18-year-old is incapable of making a decision of any great import, though at 18 I'm two years older than I was when ordained as a vestal virgin, and one year older than when I was buried alive in Campus Sceleratus—the Evil Fields—for violating the oath of chastity taken by all girls sworn to the keeping of the eternal flame.

I am older, though somehow not yet wise enough to manufacture a plausible excuse for my desire to avoid Rome. Fedele and Abri simply won't hear of it. Over the years, I've shown them pictures of Russia and Greece, conjured in .76 seconds through a single Google search. But they remain firm. I can visit Greece and Russia and any other country I like, but first I must visit the land of our heritage, and specifically its capital. Where our ancestors lived long ago.

When I was in eighth grade, my family went to stay at my uncle's villa in Rome, and I instead visited my grandmother in Cape May, forever ingratiating myself with my adoring Nana and baffling my parents. Even Cape May, with its stillness, its endless capacity for reflection, was too close to the magnet of Rome. I felt its tug while boating across a perfect blue lake with one foot trailing in the water and chaos in my mind, a knot of memories I'd made 1,500 years ago and the strange certainty that at 13, I was dangerously close to the end of my line. It made me unlike the other girls, however I tried to hide it. Having only one sister makes it difficult to deflect my parents' scrutiny. And a trip to Rome is, to them, an entirely reasonable request—and one they feel they shouldn't have to make, given my passion for history.

But if time really is a veil, there are those who could lift it easily, recognize me for who and what I once was. Passion—whether love or hate—can cross the threads of time as easily as a hungry spider dancing across its own line. Time exists to unite sworn enemies and lovers, again and again, to link them across the centuries and ages. If I had known then this essential detail about the function of time, I might not have committed the mortal sin.

Or I might have done it sooner. The same threads that bind me to my sworn pursuers also tie me to Nesreen. Another pull I've successfully resisted, for I had learned a lesson in the Evil Fields, dirt filling my mouth to satisfy my hunger, darkness pouring through my hair, slipping through desperate fingers. Nobody wants to die, especially a 17-year-old who has just discovered love.

The fact and reality of death were not new or startling to me. My seat at the Coliseum adjoined the emperor's; it was one of—and some argued, the principal—privilege of being a vestal. I had seen many things die: naked, hunted, defiant, foolish, clad in the armor they stockpiled in the *hypogeum* beneath the Coliseum. It was merely the final signature on the contract unwittingly created at your birth. You live. You die. Nobody bothered to pretend otherwise.

And I appreciated the simplicity of such frankness. My people bargained with gods all the time, beseeched on bended knee all manner of favors. But they never bargained to cheat death. Such an act was cowardly and downright unRoman. And stupid.

I shook my head. Now, all people can think of is cheating death, forsaking realism and the beauty created by its finality.

I'd abandoned my parents and their lost cause in the kitchen, walked away without a word of apology or explanation, and made it as far as Emeline's room, which was just a few yards down the hall from my own. We hadn't shared a room since I was 10 years old and in the years since, we'd practically never entered one another's sleeping quarters. There was no active dislike between us, simply a lack of understanding that prompted us to interact like alien beings. Which was why I was surprised to hear Emeline call out as I passed on my way to my own room at the end of the hall.

My sister sat cross-legged on the floor, throwing a hair dryer into her suitcase. The combination of her pose, the rapid motion of her arms as they darted to and fro with the routine of packing, a particular strain of beauty that flourishes in the shade of the commonplace, and a self-assurance that usually belongs to an older woman suggested the grace and wisdom of a Hindi goddess.

Looking at Emeline had always been uncomfortably like staring into a mirror. We both had the same dark hair:

black and thick as ink and, under the right conditions—when we were happy with a barely perceptible but rich undercurrent of melancholy or caught in the beam of a full harvest moon—a rainbow shot through the contours. When Emeline's first high school boyfriend—a dreadful, lanky creature named Yurin—compared her hair to a raven's plumage, he did so not because of the color, but because he was convinced her hair had the ability to transmit secrets in motion. And he wasn't very far off. Emeline's hair (and I suspected mine as well, though mine had never been given the test of young love) was perhaps closest in kin to the vinyl record, burnished and lustrous to behold, though it would confide its revelations only to a select few.

My features were narrow and delicate, framing gray eyes and waggishly arched eyebrows that gave anyone put off by my sternness hope that I nevertheless harbored a sense of humor somewhere deep in my core. I had an altogether otherworldly look about me, I had been told, which was at odds with landscapes that featured tract housing, strip malls, beige paint, and disinfected walls.

Emeline's hair was perhaps a shade of a shade lighter. And her eyes were a bright, innocent blue not haunted by past lives—the same blue the women of my family had used to bewitch helpless men for countless centuries. It was a blue that called my own gray eyes into question. Other than that (and Emeline's chin, which was the tiniest bit wider than my own), we might have passed for twins.

If one twin hogged all the attention, I thought, uncharitably. Because the truth was, people had always been drawn to me, since I was a tiny child. But I deliberately shied away from them and cultivated a personality that people found off-putting. That's what happens when you're buried alive by an entire city after being paraded through the streets while your family and friends mourn as if you're already dead. It tended to make you something of an introvert.

But Emeline erred in the opposite direction. She yearned to be the center of everyone's attention and was rewarded by often achieving this ambition.

"You wanted something?" I asked. I suspected my sister knew I was there, hovering in the doorway.

"I'm going to Rome. And you're coming with me." Emeline didn't look up or pause from her task.

"Why aren't you going with Soren?"

"We broke up a month ago." She was matter-of-fact.

"I'm sorry. He seemed ... ." *Like a loser.* I left the thought unfinished. "It's sweet of you to offer, but I can't go with you to Rome. Maybe we can take a trip to Cape May to visit Grandma instead. Or New York."

I tried to leave the room, not wanting to prolong the conversation. But Emeline—varsity volleyball player, B student, longtime admirer of soulful brown eyes, and underappreciated little sister—was packing heavier emotional artillery than I ever could have credited.

"*Propter vitam vivendi perdere causas.*"

I froze. Thus far, this second life had managed to produce few surprises. Maybe that was how people felt during the second half of their own single lives—disenchanted, bored. Though my alienation stemmed from another source as well: I spoke the language of the dead, and therefore felt barred from the living.

Until now.

"What did you say?"

This time, Emeline put down the shampoo she had been about to toss into the suitcase and looked up at me.

"Squandering life's purpose merely to stay alive."

"That's not what you said," I accused.

"That's what I meant."

"Well, that isn't what you said. And you know it. I don't have time for games, Emeline."

"Why? Because you're so busy getting ready for college? Or polishing your résumé for your dream career of doing nothing?" Emeline shot back.

The notion that my little sister viewed me as some sad species of slacker with no plans and no future—however accurate a portrait that was—was more than I could take. I left the room, fully planning to ignore Emeline for a month at least. A difficult task now that summer was upon us and we were both at loose ends.

"I'm sorry, Rhea!" Emeline called. "*Propter vitam vivendi perdere causas.*"

"Since when do you speak Latin?" I asked. Emeline and I were not so very close, but I knew my sister had never studied the tongue of my first life.

"I learned Latin around the same time you did," she replied coyly.

"You didn't take Ms. Jordan's Latin class, Emeline." There were only five students at my high school who had enough interest in a dead language to sign up for Latin, and I knew them all fairly well after sitting next to them in class for four years.

"And you knew Latin long before you took that class," Emeline said, standing with some difficulty, amid the pile of clothes and duffel bags strewn across her room. She faced me dead on: "Admit it."

"What exactly are you implying?" I spoke carefully, leaning on 18 years of carefully concealing memories and training myself to speak slowly and infrequently to prevent any stray Latin phrases from escaping.

"You're afraid of the dark and terrified of enclosed spaces."

The dank, moldy air of the tomb they'd buried me in filled my nostrils.

"You speak Latin fluently. Much better than that quack Ms. Jordan."

A thousand responses sprang to my lips, but they were all in a dead language and in the time it took me to sort my thoughts into English, Emeline had already spoken.

"You had five sisters—Liviana, Junia, Hortensia, Decima, and Aemilia—who you hardly ever saw after you were 6."

"How do you know this?" I whispered. A younger

sister would reasonably know that I struggled against an incapacitating fear of the dark. She might even believe that my preternatural grasp of a difficult language was somehow miraculous. These were things I could logically explain. But Emeline's sudden ability to conjure names long dead to everyone except me was a blow I could neither account for nor defend.

"You fell in love with a *venatore*, violated your oath of chastity, and allowed Vesta's flame to extinguish. And for your crime, at dawn on the fifth of *Iulius*, they buried you alive in an underground chamber with a loaf of bread, a bowl of milk, a bucket of water, a lamp, and two days' worth of oil."

"How do you know all this?" I pleaded.

"And the day the Pontifex Maximus led you away from your family, your sister Aemilia cried inconsolably and refused to partake in the feast Father ordered to celebrate his daughter's honor."

"Aemilia?" I'd never thought of myself as crazy when I was alone on a ledge with 17 years' worth of memories of an ancient city, but my little sister was rapidly changing that assessment.

"Did you really not recognize me, all these years?" Emeline sounded frustrated, and maybe the slightest bit hurt.

"Are you truly telling me you're my sister Aemilia? The little girl I grew up with thousands of years ago?" I couldn't see any reason for Emeline to play this kind of joke on me, to claim to recall a life I had long since resigned myself to remembering in isolation. But I also couldn't imagine where she would have learned the name Aemilia—or Liviana, Junia, Hortensia, and Decima, for that matter. Maybe I believed her too quickly, but if I did it was because I had so longed for someone with whom to share that life.

"Fifteen hundred years ago." Emeline was matter of fact. "I always suspected. Those weddings you used to stage with your dolls: 'I take you, *Amata*, to be a vestal priestess.' Those were the only vows you knew, the ones you swore. Mom and Dad thought you picked it all up watching television, but you never could be bothered with the TV. I knew after that incident in your Latin class, and Mom and Dad were so confused. I knew then."

My first Latin class was a disaster. My teacher had called home, demanding to know where I'd learned to speak it. As if a woman who took three semesters of Latin at a community college could possibly be certified as fluent in a foreign language, and especially one as complicated as Latin.

"That was two years ago."

"Well, the subject never came up." Emeline returned to packing, as if the issue was already decided. "We can talk about it more in Rome."

The part of me that loved Rome, that wanted to see it one more time, one final time, lashed out at her.

"The empire is dead! They extinguished the holy flame. Rome is nothing more than a tourist trap run by a homophobe in a funny hat who took a vow of poverty and now lives in a palace!"

"Actually, you're thinking of the previous pope. Go there," Emeline urged. "With me. It took me so long to recognize you, Rhea. It took me years, because every time I thought I caught a glimpse of you, you shuttered yourself away like a hermit. You've been bound and gagged every day of your life, only you did the binding and gagging all on your own. Do you really want to spend the rest of your life in the shadows?"

"Do you even understand what you're asking? You know the penalty a vestal virgin pays for violating her chastity oath—you watched me pay it! All I want this time around is to survive, and if I keep my head down, I think I can accomplish that."

"Not forever," Emeline pointed out. "Just because you were buried alive once doesn't mean it's going to happen again. It took me 16 years to recognize you, and I knew you better than anyone."

I thought of Nesreen. "Not *anyone*."

"Maybe not *anyone*." I could tell from the tone of Emeline's voice that she knew where my mind had gone. "But most. And Rhea, you weren't born to live with your head down. Not in the last life, and not in this one. You were one in a million, literally, chosen to serve as a priestess, to guard the eternal flame."

"Yeah, but Emeline … Aemilia … I let the flame go out." It was really the only thing I regretted. Of being found with Nesreen, of being stripped naked and whipped when I was declared guilty of incest against Rome, of being hoisted through the streets by my terrified, enraged countrymen, the only thing I would undo—were it in my power—was forgetting Vesta's flame.

"You defied Rome. You placed your own pleasure above the well-being of the empire. It might not be noble, but it was the bravest thing I've ever seen a 17 year old do. And look at you now. You can't even bring yourself to go on a date. Or apply to college. You're so afraid someone will see you that you've faded into the walls."

Emeline wrinkled her nose, and I realized that my periwinkle-blue linen dress really did match the paint, which Emeline had always been characteristically vocal about hating. I'd never bothered to issue an opinion about the walls or the carpets or the bathroom tiling or anything. And why shouldn't I? I had opinions. As many as Emeline, I dare say. And as much a right to them. As monstrous a capacity for joy, or anguish. But such treacherous thoughts, ambitions of any kind, are poorly suited to a teenager who has retreated from the world.

"*Vincit qui patitur*," I sighed.

She conquers who endures: my survival plan this second time around.

"Life is not meant merely to be endured, Rhea. Life cannot be conquered through passivity. It requires something more substantial: whimsy and passion and folly. *Vincit qui se vincit.*"

She conquers who conquers herself.

I smiled wistfully. It felt good to argue in Latin again.

"Maybe we'll find your ghosts," Emeline offered.

"Maybe we won't. Maybe we'll defeat them if we do."

"And worst case?" I had to ask.

Emeline cocked her head. "Maybe next time you'll make it to 20."

"You really are Roman!" I recognized her at last. "No American would speak so casually of her sister's death."

Emeline shrugged. "I was a Roman. I'm an American now."

And I realized that Emeline had been playing her own game of survival. She'd just gone about it differently.

Emeline was quiet, for a change. I suspected, given her confidence, that she'd believed all along that she could manipulate me into going to Rome with her, but I doubted that she'd accurately reckoned the strength of my longing for the world I'd left behind. If Rome retained even a fraction of its former glory, if I could warm myself before the hearth fire I'd sworn to protect, I'd return in a heartbeat. I'd let them strap me to a litter and relive the funeral procession and live burial all over again, just for a last, heartbreaking view of the city as my bier passed through it.

But if it was no longer my Rome?

Then, I supposed, I could go on living. Or perhaps begin.

"*Quidnunc*," I sighed, and Emeline knew she'd won.

"Please. You're the busybody," she accused, and happily returned to her packing.

II

We were on a plane within three days. Aemilia—I had started thinking of (and calling) her by her old name, and she didn't seem to mind—didn't want to give me time to back out. And anyway, she'd already purchased the tickets using the credit card Fedele had foolishly given her to shop for a graduation dress.

The fact that she had not, in fact, graduated was not mentioned. The fact that I had, and had not bought new clothing for the occasion, was also left unspoken.

The subject of my vestiary was particularly painful to Abri, who, until Emeline arrived, felt deprived of certain key maternal privileges. A daughter is meant to be born in her mother's image—not merely to look like her, but to imitate her habits and tastes. But from my earliest infancy, I exhibited a sad tendency toward independence when it came to my dress.

By high school, I had settled on a uniform of sorts: long linen dresses with hems that hovered at my calves or ankles. Abri once accused them of being identical, but, besides my partiality toward wild bursts of color, each had something that made it special. A bunched and padded collar that belonged on the neck of a nomadic Mongolian tribesman. A careful row of pleating down the bodice, or a soft gray diagonal wave across the shoulders—such tiny warps in the fabric, but they made all the difference. It was almost always the same dress, though sometimes austere, sometimes whimsical, always timeless. Aemilia accused me of wearing these dresses to set myself apart, but I never saw it that way. I wore my dresses with soft leather boots and flats delicately folded into organic shapes, though often dyed as vividly as my dresses.

And, almost always, I wore a belt buckle with a vintage map of St. Paul. The frame was pewter and heavy, and I wore it almost every day, though I never could pinpoint why it first attracted me. I'd never been to Minnesota—and didn't find it likely that I one day would. Nor did I have any particular attachment to Dayton Bluff or the Mississippi River. But somehow the crowded grid of lines—which the shopkeeper estimated dated back nearly 100 years—appealed to me. I could appreciate the knowledge that the city in the buckle would likely be unrecognizable to anyone who inhabited it today, that a place could be reduced to a series of squares around a hipster's waist.

Aemilia didn't mind the belt buckle, though by the time I was a junior and she was a freshman, she'd come to loathe the linen dresses.

*   *   *

Our plane touched down at 12:30 a.m., thanks in part to a two-and-a-half-hour delay, and by the time my feet first made contact with Roman soil, I was almost too tired to care. The air was oppressively warm, and the transition from 12 hours trapped in a pressurized cabin to an air-conditioned airport terminal to a curbside pick-up lot that reeked of cigarettes and sun-baked concrete was dizzyingly abrupt. Honking taxi drivers competed with the self-important click-clack of suitcases trailing behind smartly dressed travelers who somehow did not look as though they'd been living out of suitcases.

Emeline took the lead in finding us a taxi, throwing out Italian phrases with an ease that distinguished us from the other American tourists.

"What is this place?" I demanded when our taxi pulled in front of a raucous bar.

"The Mauve."

Two shirtless men in their early 20s crawled along the sidewalk, and a woman sat astride the tallest of them, yelling, "Yaw, pony! Yaw!" and clutching the remnants of a ripped collar in her fist.

"The Moth?"

A woman emerged from the bar, passed the cowgirl a day-glo plastic trident, and disappeared inside.

"The *Mauve*."

There was no point in arguing over the fact that Aemilia had clearly booked us at a party hostel, if not *the* party hostel. She would simply plead ignorance, and I had no desire to start our first night in Rome with an argument.

We stepped carefully over the cavorting trio and straight into a bar I was pretty sure Aemilia was not legally old enough to occupy. But she exhibited some sense, for a change, leading us past four tables of revelers speaking three languages and making straight for the front desk.

Remembering, at last, that I was the older sister (at least in theory), I offered my version of a friendly smile—more of a half-hearted twist at the corners of my mouth—and addressed a man in his 30s who was intently flipping through his iPhone.

"I'm Rhea, and this is my sister Aem—Emeline, and we should have a reservation for seven nights."

"Two," Aemilia corrected.

"We're here through the 28th," I corrected mildly, with the patience of an older sister.

"We're spending our first two nights here, and then we're staying with Uncle Basilio at Ilium." Aemilia fumbled with her backpack, dodging my eyes. "Mom thought it would be nice."

Luckily for Aemilia, The Mauve had booked us in separate dorms.

"We find it encourages guests to mingle and meet new people," the man at the front desk sang out festively. I couldn't tell if he was oblivious to, or merely amused by, the big sister death rays I was shooting at Aemilia while we collected our keys.

The elevator was technically capable of holding only one person, the receptionist revealed cheerfully, with a doubtful glance at our luggage. When the rickety box first hovered into view, looking as though a trip of any distance was likely to be its last, Aemilia excused herself and began hauling her luggage to the second floor. I had been assigned a dorm on the fourth floor, and stuffed myself into the elevator with more than a little trepidation. A wire gate sprang shut behind me, and I prayed I wouldn't be forced to pry it apart when I arrived.

Of all the Roman gods and goddesses, there is no deity affiliated with elevators. So I prayed to Cardea, the goddess of the hinge, figuring that her penchant for safeguarding doorways could reasonably carry over to include elevators. In New Jersey, I'd sometimes been self-conscious about praying to my multitude of gods, but not here, firmly on their territory. Innumerable threats lurked through the Rome of my imagination, malevolent beings that wanted to punish me for my broken vows, but my first encounter with danger was with an outdated piece of hostel machinery. What a golden age I had found myself in.

Despite my exhaustion, or perhaps because of it, I found myself in the top bunk of an otherwise empty dorm, wide awake and fearful.

My uncle—Abri's brother—visited us in New Jersey just once, when I was 6 years old. I don't remember much from the visit, just a big face with thick black eyebrows, and cheeks with loose flesh that creased into downturned lips that did not seem to approve of anything. His hair was just starting to show silver then. He found me playing in the garden, and all

I remember of the visit was my uncle asking questions, lots of questions, his Adam's apple moving up and down, frightening me, before Abri came and led me away with the injunction that I must not bother *Zio*.

My memories of that afternoon are a golden-green haze, slicked over by a more recent fear that made my stomach feel oily.

"What is that?" he interrogated.

"*Canis*."

Dog.

"And that?"

"*Papilio*."

Butterfly.

He smelled strongly of black licorice.

Flos. Flower. *Puella*. Girl. *Caelum*. Sky. *Capillus*. Hair. Until I wearied of his ceaseless game. And then … .

"*Abire*."

Go away.

That was before I understood that most American children weren't born speaking Latin. Before I knew what Latin was, that a harmless word—papilio, butterfly—could set me apart and endanger my second chance at life. Because even if no one in New Jersey connected me to the 17-year-old vestal virgin buried alive in ancient Rome, I could still be branded as different. And 22nd-century America is not a safe place to be different. They may have done away with the Coliseum and ritual sacrifice, but they still had their microscopes and asylums. The American Psychiatric Association would have a field day with me, and all it would take was one word: papilio.

My own personal butterfly effect.

I made a point of avoiding my uncle after I realized my potentially fatal youthful blunder. He probably didn't remember, so why remind him? And if I had to visit him in Ilium—as it seemed I did—there was no point in panicking until absolutely necessary. And if it did turn out to be necessary, I gave myself permission to utterly freak out. Let Aemilia be the cool and dispassionate sister for a change.

At some point during my internal ramblings, the door had opened, and a slight shift in the cheap bed frame indicated that it was my bunk mate.

Two bunk mates, actually, I realized when the frame continued to quake, and I deciphered the suggestive murmurs fighting through the peace of darkness. I remembered the bar downstairs, and the incontrovertible truth that hormone-driven impulses were more difficult to fight in a city like Rome. Hopefully, Aemilia was settled in a quieter room. I thought about checking on her, but that would require stepping within inches of the impassioned couple below me, which seemed unhygienic. And the truth was, in this life and the last, Aemilia was far better equipped to care for herself. It was another incontrovertible truth that my performance as a big sister could use some work.

So there I was stranded on a bunk bed with two drunk—I assumed—strangers beneath me. If they were aware of my existence, they seemed unfazed by it, as the tempo and range of their sounds increased and multiplied. At the sight of a pair of jeans sliding gently across the floor, my already thin resolve seemed to snap. I pulled the covers tightly around my chest and let my left hand linger just below the waistband of my pajamas.

When in Rome … .

*　　　*　　　*

To be chosen as a sacred vestal, a girl must be between 6 and 10 years of age, the daughter of a patrician family, and flawless both physically and mentally. Those were the minimal requirements, anyhow.

I was the fourth of six daughters, and as I grew, people often quipped that the family would surely produce at least one vestal virgin—six being the number of active vestal priestesses at any given time. At least, patrician families without daughters—or without daughters lovely enough to become vestal virgins—made these jokes. Other families pretended not to understand why the Pontifex Maximus might find it auspicious to choose a sixth daughter as the sixth vestal.

I was not the most beautiful among my sisters, but Hortensia and Liviana, at 14 and 11, were already too old to guard the sacred flame. Junia, who was a year older and the closest to me in age, had eyes the exact shade of the purest pump from Rome's most sacred spring, and Decima, the youngest, was destined for the emperor's bed.

A vestal virgin requires more than perfect beauty and the rare patina of presence that inspires great artists to pit will and chisel against great pillars of marble. To be a vestal, they said, required a spark from the gods themselves to help keep the fire burning.

The choosing ceremony, or *captio*, took place in 180 AD, when I was 6 years old. On our way to the gardens where the ceremony was to take place my mother leaned in close despite the spaciousness of our carriage and whispered instructions for how I was to behave. Her commands were vague, but she repeated the word "chaste" seven times, more than any other word, including my name. Purity, as it turned out, was to become a major condition of my success, if not happiness.

But my absolute faith in her quelled my nerves so that when the time came, and 20 patrician daughters of Rome stood side by side, I hoisted my shoulders back and tilted my chin ever so slightly upward.

"You must be proud but not haughty, approachable but not common, chaste but not spiritless." It was a lot to remember, but my mother made it sound important, and with five comely sisters competing for her attention, I wanted to please her. Junia stood to my left, shaking so hard she resembled a stray olive tree caught in a powerful gust. She stood in danger of being stripped of her dignity, as surely as any tree had been harangued into loosening its grip on its fruit.

I wanted to grip her hand, but was fairly certain my mother would disapprove, and besides, Junia stood a few inches beyond reach. Many of the other girls standing at my side were familiar to me as well. We had chased each other across our parents' estates playing hide and seek, and huddled in spare corners of our homes tossing knucklebones.

Our families were gathered in a tense cluster at the edge of the room. Liviana twisted her *stola* in clenched hands. She was far too old to participate in the captio, and resented that it was Junia and I who now stood the chance of becoming Rome's highest priestesses, so trusted that we alone would be required to swear no oath when bearing witness at a trial. So beloved that the penalty for inflicting harm upon our persons would be instant execution. Inculpable, the vestal virgins, the first daughters of the greatest empire in the world.

While neither of us could compete with Junia, Liviana and I both knew that she was undeniably the prettier between us. People tended to use the word "striking" rather than "beautiful" to describe me. But Liviana could be—and had been—mistaken for a living, breathing statue of Juno. Liviana reminded me of this often, particularly as the captio approached, applying the memory like a balm to her wounded ego. It would not be fair to fault Liviana for her ambition; with five breathtaking sisters—even barely squeaking by with the term "striking," people still tended to sweep me into the attractive dust heap, if only for consistency's sake—a senator for a father, and a mother who defied tradition and hired tutors for each of her daughters, Liviana was thoroughly justified in expecting great things of herself. A position as a religious leader of the Roman empire would have suited her admirably.

Hortensia, who was three years older than Liviana and eight years my senior, was staring intently at the Pontifex Maximus. He loomed directly before us, studying us each for minutes on end, sometimes silently, sometimes speaking harshly to himself and causing the candidate nearest him to shudder.

His eyes fell on Junia, who quaked and averted her eyes. My mother's face remained stoic, but she placed a hand on Hortensia's shoulder, and my eldest sister flinched. I understood that I was not to look away when my turn came.

My father seemed to relax when Junia turned her head, though his expression was as stern as my mother's. Either he disagreed that Junia had ruined her chances, or he was pleased that Junia would not become a vestal virgin. It was difficult to tell. In accordance with Roman law, my father was head of our household and wielded *patria potestas*—the power that made a man owner and master of his family. But his absolute dominion blurred in practice, and I had learned to fear my mother's disapproval more strongly than my father's. Her hand was the first to whip me, and it was at her insistence that we were rigidly educated in history, philosophy, music, and rhetoric.

Suddenly, my father was tense again. The Pontifex Maximus stood before me.

He was a handsome man, which doesn't really matter when you're the emperor of Rome, though I suppose it was good for whichever of my sisters would grow up to become one of the emperor's mistresses. My tutor made me memorize his full name—Caesar Marcus Aurelius Commodus Antoninus Augustus—and each of his titles: Caesar, *princeps senatus*, consul, Pontifex Maximus, Augustus, and about a dozen others. It was sometimes hard to keep track, as Commodus had already changed his name five times and added a half-dozen or so honorifics besides. But showing the emperor proper respect was the most basic rule of survival in Rome. And that was the ultimate goal behind my mother's educational campaign.

"What's your name?" He was big, but spoke softly.

"Rhea." By comparison, my own voice was bold and clear.

"The daughter of Senator Aetius Equitius Regilla?"

"Yes. And Quinta Equitia." I was more my mother's daughter than my father's, whatever the law said.

"And you have five sisters?"

"Hortensia, Liviana, Junia, Decima, and Aemilia." I nodded toward Junia, to indicate that she was my sister. It felt strange to discuss them when they stood nearby, watching the exchange.

He turned toward my family, gathered in a tight, unhappy knot with all the other mothers and fathers who had brought their daughters here to become brides of Rome. He even looked back at poor Junia, who was no better equipped to withstand a second round with the Pontifex Maximus. She froze so rigidly in place that I could no longer discern the rhythmic rise and fall of her chest.

"I'm the fourth oldest," I ventured, hoping to recapture his attention so that Junia could resume breathing.

"How old are you?" He spoke to me as though I were any other adult.

"Six."

"Do you understand why you are here?"

"You need to choose a vestal virgin."

"Why?"

"To protect the flame of Vesta."

"Are you willing to pledge a 30-year oath of chastity and minister to the sacred fire?"

"Yes. If I must."

"Your sister is willing to do the same."

I looked toward Junia, who was staring so hard at our sisters that I knew she was wishing they could exchange places.

"Yes."

"Would you make a better priestess than Junia?" He spoke loudly now, so everyone could stop pretending they weren't listening.

"I do not know," I admitted. "I've never guarded a sacred flame before. Junia is taller than I am, and she sits very still during history class."

The Pontifex Maximus hadn't exchanged more than two sentences with the other candidates, but I wasn't very optimistic about my chances of being chosen. I knew I should be presenting an argument for myself as vestal virgin, but I wasn't entirely clear on what the position entailed, and that made it difficult to craft an argument. Lying seemed foolish, like stealing a paddle for a boat when I didn't even know which direction I wanted to travel.

"And she has the most beautiful eyes of any candidate here today," he added, still speaking in a voice that carried across the room.

"She does," I agreed, curiously more disappointed than relieved that Junia seemed to be the Pontifex Maximus' choice. I didn't know what it meant to be a vestal virgin, but I knew what it meant to be chosen first among my sisters, first among the women of Rome.

So I added, "Rome has many beautiful women, and my sisters have always shined brightly among them." My entire family approved of that comment, exchanging proud smiles. Except for my father, who now scowled at the Pontifex Maximus.

"But not all are chaste. And few among the blameless can blaze to complement Vesta's fire." I wasn't certain whether he spoke to me or himself, and I was still formulating a response when he extended his hand to me.

"I take you, Amata, to be a vestal priestess, who will carry our sacred rites which it is the law for a vestal priestess to perform on behalf of the Roman people, on the same terms as her who was a vestal on the best terms."

I didn't take his hand. Instead, I looked back at my family. My mother was supposed to look proud, but she was weeping quietly, and I was unhappy because she hadn't told me what I was supposed to do when I was chosen. I might have succeeded in this first phase only to fail her at some later and far more important juncture.

Hortensia and Liviana clutched each other's hands, wearing identical expressions of grief, while Junia wilted with what I could only assume was relief. None of the other families present could express outrage at the decision—not when it was made at the sole discretion of the Pontifex Maximus. But they did not look terribly surprised either, and it occurred to me that I was the only person in the entire room who had not anticipated this outcome.

Gently, the Pontifex Maximus took my hand and led me away from my family. With the exception of 4-year-old

Aemilia, who followed me everywhere when we were at home and now clawed to be free of mother's grasp, my family watched quietly as I walked away. Aemilia's howls were the last sounds I heard from my family as the Pontifex Maximus led me to my new life.

*   *   *

"You want me to go where?"

My first day back in Rome was not off to an auspicious start. Aemilia had slept late and missed breakfast. Not only was she holding me responsible for failing to wake her in time—never mind the fact that I didn't have access to her second-floor room—but I was pretty sure she was punishing me by insisting that we visit the last place in the world I would want to see.

"The Vatican is one of the top sites visited by tourists in Rome," Aemilia explained patiently. "You know Mom expects it. It's best to just get it out of the way and save the really cool stuff as a reward. Besides, we can't go today anyway. It's Sunday, so the Vatican is closed for ... Vatican business. So I booked us tickets for tomorrow."

Aemilia had no idea what went on at the Vatican on Sundays, but I kept this thought to myself. I did not respond, but merely stubbornly resolved not to go within 100 yards of the Vatican. Its floors were lava to my pagan feet. Its air was poison to my pagan lungs. For every crucifix that adorned the walls, 100 heathens had suffered a fate more barbaric than crucifixion.

"Oh, c'mon Rhea. Aren't you the slightest bit curious? It doesn't matter that—"

"But they extinguished the flame," I interrupted before my sister could enlighten me on the subject of things that didn't matter. There was no relief from the anguish I'd felt when I learned that under the orders of Theodosius I, the Christian savages had smothered the fire and disbanded the College of Vestals in 394 AD. I breathed a prayer of thanks that I hadn't been forced to endure that particular nightmare—the intrusion of Christianity into our sacred rites.

"That was 2,000 years ago, Rhea." Aemilia's voice was less patient, and she stole embarrassed looks at our fellow hostel dwellers, concerned that the fact of our reincarnation might diminish our social cache. Or hers, at least. I'd never had any to begin with.

"It was 1,619," I muttered, not caring that I sounded petty. *"Christianos ad leones."*

Throw the Christians to the lions.

"And anyway, it's not the first time the sacred fire went out."

My hand must have registered the meaning behind Aemilia's words before my brain, because it tightened into a fist that connected with her cheek before I even had time to consider her words or my reaction. It was the first time I'd ever hit my sister—or anyone, for that matter. I felt embarrassed, and a little gratified, and then a little more embarrassed at feeling gratified. A stinging cheek for stinging words.

The bar's earliest occupants gaped through the window. Clearly they mistook us for barbaric Americans. Not that they seemed to mind.

"Hit her back!" suggested someone with what I thought was a Scottish brogue.

Would she hit me? I shifted. In a soft gray halter dress and tank top, I probably didn't look like anyone's idea of a warrior. But I had the strong, lean shoulders of a fabric dancer. More importantly, I had devoted my life to the fine art of survival, and that required that I must excel at whatever was necessary of me. If that meant flattening my younger sister in a Roman street just outside a hostel ... .

Reason somehow asserted itself, and I began to realize how badly we had behaved—and maybe me in particular.

"I'm sorry, Aemilia ... Emeline." It didn't seem genuine unless I apologized to them both, the sister who'd cried when the Pontifex Maximus led me away 1,834 years ago and the one who never felt entirely real to me. "Impulse control—"

"I know all about your impulse control," Aemilia muttered.

"If I could go back in time … ."

If I could go back in time, I knew I could find a way to be with Nesreen and protect the fire. But I couldn't go back in time. I could only go to the Vatican with my sister. Tomorrow.

*   *   *

My inauguration took place the day after the captio. All the residents of the House of the Vestals emptied into the atrium to watch as I swore to perform my sacred duties. There were the six adolescents who served as active priestesses; six acolytes, counting myself; and six teachers who had served 10 years as acolytes and 10 years as priestesses and were now in their final decade of promised service. The Pontifex Maximus was also there, though he seemed distracted, and the servants whispered that he had just come from the Coliseum.

Marcus Aurelius was more interested in affairs of state and winning military campaigns than in the frivolity of staged combat at the Coliseum, but it seemed to hold great allure for his son and successor who saw in its brutality and power a reflection of his own temperament and rule. Even I knew that one of the privileges of being a vestal virgin was a prime seat at gladiatorial combats and hunts.

There were rumors of modern displays deemed too lewd for the chaste eyes of the empire's flame keepers. But when I asked Hortensia to describe them to me, she would only answer, "Our emperor, in his infinite wisdom, has deemed the slaughter of animals by other animals, the slaughter of animals by man, the slaughter of man by animals, and the slaughter of man by man appropriate spectacle for your tender eyes. Whatever it is that he doesn't wish you to see must be weighed against the fare permitted you. Though you are young, you are not foolish."

Sometimes Hortensia took her responsibilities as eldest sister more seriously than I would have liked.

They began by shearing my hair, reducing the black wave that my mother carefully brushed and oiled to a fringe that barely reached my chin. I watched as the swath of black was bound with a ribbon and secured to a branch of *Lotus capillata*, which teemed with delicate pink flowers that spent all their color at the heart and bled a pale white at the tip of the petals. I didn't mind the loss of my hair, not when I saw it hanging high in the tree where it could catch breezes and reflect sunlight while I tended to my vestal duties. Perhaps it would metamorphose into a butterfly or some other graceful tree-dwelling creature.

As if I had spoken the thought aloud, the Virgo Vestalis Maxima—greatest of the vestals—approached and instructed several of the students to remove my tunic, which was a brilliant saffron, the color my mother most liked to see me wear. They replaced my toga with a white stola, draped and pinned a *palla* over my left shoulder, and placed a red *infula* on my head, followed by a white *suffibulum*. The final garment draped slightly over my forehead and fell to the small of my back, about the length of my hair before they severed it and offered it to the lotus tree.

I was allowed to keep my *lunula*, a crescent-shaped amulet presented to me on the ninth day after my birth, though the Virgo Vestalis Maxima said that when I came of age and was no longer a student I would have to put it aside.

From that day forward, the only color I would ever wear was white, a symbol for the vow of chastity I swore before they trussed me in the palla.

"Honor Vesta with your purity and devotion to her service," the Virgo Vestalis Maxima instructed when the inauguration concluded.

And I knew she was right. I had left behind my mother and father, and had no one else to please.

III

Rose sangria: The color of the lotus flowers in the *Atrium Vestae*. Papaya crème: my palla, floating over my shoulders. Chocolate coconut curry: Nesreen's cheek, her wrists. Chocolate orange saffron: a giraffe loping across the Coliseum floor. Limoncello: Sol's nebulous sphere.

"Rhea." The voice was firm, and concerned rather than annoyed. Aemilia handed me a squat plastic spoon.

"I ordered for you. I couldn't get your attention."

I looked down the endless column of blended milk, cream, and sugar, then offered my sister an apologetic smile.

"Too much," I murmured. "Impossibly beautiful."

"It's gelato. We must have passed 50 works of architectural genius on our way here, and you didn't say a thing," Aemilia commented wryly, but at least she was smiling.

"But those buildings are dead and rotting where the emperors left them." I was insistent.

"They weren't built by emperors," Aemilia argued. Except today she seemed more like Emeline, more like a girl viewing the city through a contemporary lens. She didn't understand that the city itself was once electric, daily extending its own boundaries, whatever the risk, whatever the cost. And now all it could do was look back on itself and carefully polish its relics from centuries gone by—not terribly unlike myself, when I really thought about it.

A deluge of raspberry, followed rapidly by lavender chocolate chip. The human tongue has, on average, 2,000 to 8,000 taste buds. I decided to let it go, my prejudice against this new Rome.

"Who were you talking with when I went downstairs?" I asked. I'd returned to my dorm after forgetting my camera, and in the two minutes it took to return, my sister had made a friend.

"Adam, from Australia." Aemilia had the smug expression of the proverbial cat full of proverbial canary. Better still, the handsome, slender Australian canary with green eyes and lush lashes. "He wants to go sightseeing with us tonight. And to the Vatican tomorrow."

I groaned in dismay, and Aemilia grinned.

"I have *you* to thank for that, actually," she said. "He was approaching you while you were looking for your camera, but you spun away so abruptly you didn't even see him."

"So you swooped in."

"I knew you wouldn't want him." Now it was Aemilia's turn to lose herself in thought. Which was fine with me. Gelato was considerably less dangerous than romantic entanglements. Given the prevalence of diabetes, some doctors might disagree, but I'd never been buried alive for getting caught with a cup of gelato.

"I was half expecting to find Valens after I recognized you," Aemilia mused after several minutes of silence.

I searched my memory and surfaced with a vague recollection of a boy following me through olive trees on my father's estate.

"Why Valens?"

"He was in love with you. After you'd been found guilty, after the funeral, Commodus' guards caught him trying to dig you out of the pit. They spared him because they knew he wasn't your paramour." She lingered over the last word, and

I wondered how much Aemilia had guessed about the identity of my accomplice. She paused and seemed to be expecting me to say something.

"What happened to him?"

"I married him." Aemilia had waited 1,600 years to reveal this secret triumph, how she had slowly lured Valens from his all-encompassing fog of loathing and depression and into her bed. It had taken five years, and during that time she'd fended off no fewer than six highly eligible suitors, but she'd managed it. Aemilia was 19 when she finally wed Valens. She'd been old, by Roman standards, but very, very happy.

"Did you have children?" I asked, disliking the flare of envy that raged through my gut.

"Three," Aemilia said proudly. "Two boys, one girl. Gratianus, Otho, and Rhea. I miss them sometimes."

"How did you die?" My own death—execution, really—had been so public, so shaming, that I didn't feel all that guilty asking Aemilia about hers. Instead, I felt somehow vindicated, knowing that ultimately the same fate had awaited us both. My executioners didn't change anything, really. Just the time stamp on my passport. But the destination was out of their hands.

"Malaria. I was 39."

My sister looked sad, remembering her death. Or, more likely, remembering the people she had left behind. Her three children. Her husband, Valens—the neighbor boy, more faithful than my own shadow, which followed me only by day. I realized how rarely my sister visibly mourned the life that had passed before. It was utterly gone, with no chance of return, and yet she lived as if this passage was her one and only. When really, she'd lost so much more.

"I'm sorry," I told her. And I really was. I had been self-indulgent and judgmental, wrapped in a cocoon that segregated me from the living as efficiently as the funereal linens they'd used to bind me to my bier. Meanwhile, Aemilia-Emeline—I really would have to sort that out, eventually—was simply making the most of a second chance. Suddenly, most—

if not all—of my past behavior was called into question.

The year before, the fall of my senior year, I was approached by one of the more socially active girls at my school. Prisca wasn't quite homecoming material, but close. She was carrying a clipboard and a box that jingled ominously as she strode through the halls. She couldn't remember my name, and seemed baffled to discover that I, too, was a senior.

"Rhea Artuso?" She frowned. "Are you Emma's sister?"

I'd nodded. Emeline and I shared a strong physical resemblance that people often failed to notice, mostly on account of the fact that they failed to notice me entirely. I preferred it that way. Still, I sometimes forgot not to be irked when people like Prisca looked right past me day in and day out.

"That's your sister?" she asked again. And I'd understood. Emeline was always finding something to giggle about in the most inviting manner. And she always had somewhere to go, and half a dozen people to join her. More importantly, she understood that it wasn't the fact of having somewhere to go that was important; it was the fact of having people to go with. Emeline lit up a room. It was all superficial, of course. That's what I told myself at the time, anyway.

"According to my parents," I replied.

"Oh. Good. She's nice." I couldn't tell if she really meant it.

"I'm on a mission on behalf of Campus Crusades for Christ. We're trying to get 200 people, half the student body, to sign a chastity pledge."

"Oh." Now it was my turn to be awkward. "That's kinda a lot to ask, don't you think?"

"Well, we're not asking people to remain chaste forever," she said, as if that were obvious.

"Of course," I replied apropos of nothing.

"Just until they're married." Prisca nodded and smiled as she talked, leading me to conclude that thus far in her campaign no one had the temerity to tell her to rot in the underworld. Unfortunately, my survival plan did not involve riling up the entire school by embroiling myself in a debate about the merits of abstinence.

"I'm ... not sure." That seemed like a safe response.

"Well, give it some thought." Prisca nodded to the clipboard tucked under her arm and placed a pewter ring in my hand. It was cheap, but the metal circle scorched my palm, and my hand sagged with the weight of it. There wasn't enough oxygen to counterbalance my hypocrisy, and I knew that as long as I held onto the ring, there never would be.

"Prisca! Here, I made this promise once before, and it didn't work out so well." My lips quirked in my imitation of a smile, an impish sneer that either frightened or charmed. Prisca rolled her eyes, and I could see her mentally confirming all the rumors about my weird behavior. She probably regretted talking to me, but at least she got a good story out of it.

What I remember taking away from my conversation with Prisca-I-don't-know-you-but-I-want-you-to-sign-my-chastity-pledge was resentment toward Emeline for being the Artuso people remembered and liked. But the girl sitting across from me, thoughtfully scooping *stracciatelli* gelato from a cup, was not as vain and out of touch as I had made her out to be.

"Well, there was nothing you could have done. You were gone," Aemilia said in a light tone meant to mask the fact that a heavy subject was under discussion, in a tone that made it clear my apology had a lot of ground to cover.

"Yeah, but that was my fault, too."

"Yeah. It was." There was no softening of blows between daughters of ancient Rome. Clementia willing, one day Aemilia would forgive me. I just had to stay alive long enough to see that day come.

"What made you think of Valens?" I asked in a change of subject that was about as blatant as a rhinoceros charging through the gelato shop.

"I just think of him sometimes. And ... Adam reminded me of him, a little. Don't you think there's a resemblance?"

"I don't know. I didn't see Valens all that much after I was chosen. It would have been frowned upon, a vestal virgin fraternizing with a man."

We both smiled at the irony. Valens had been no more a threat to my chastity than the silly boys in Livingston who asked me to the prom without knowing my name.

"Well he does … look like him a little. There's something about the eyes, and he stands the way Valens used to stand. Very still. But he moves quite suddenly."

Her fond description sounded, to me, like some kind of feral animal. But it was nice to know that Aemilia and I would probably never set our hearts on the same person, unless Venus took it into her head to play some loathsome trick. With great reluctance, I dropped my last bite of gelato onto the curb beside me as an offering and issued a silent prayer that she allow us to follow our disparate courses of affection. It wasn't a sow or ram, but given the setting—and the fact that I was now a vegetarian, and wholly incapable of animal sacrifice—it was the best I could do.

"I really don't remember," I reminded my sister.

"I just think it's strange, that he showed up here so quickly, and that they look so alike."

A knot of dread and fear tightened in my stomach. "What are you saying?"

"It might be him."

"How could it be? And even if it was, how did he find us?"

Aemilia really wanted to believe that she had found Valens, wished it with an impractical longing that put little children's faith in the Easter bunny and tooth fairy to shame. Which made me feel all the more cruel for hoping that Adam was merely some Australian guy, and not my little sister's reincarnated husband.

"Relationships complicate everything." I'd meant to keep the thought to myself.

"Reincarnation complicates everything," Aemilia retorted. "And besides, you're the one who's supposed to be hiding, not me. Maybe he's been waiting in Rome all this time because he knew we would turn up eventually."

"Maybe." I didn't want to be committal, but I wanted the conversation to end.

"He might have it too, you know." She lowered her voice.

"Have what?" My mind raced through the list of ancient artifacts someone like Valens might have come to possess: the Palladium—a wooden statue of Athena, which shielded Rome from attack. Perhaps one of the vases we had used to carry water from the spring. It seemed unlikely, as I couldn't recall anything extraordinary about Valens. Now I was the one grasping at straws.

"The tug! I know you've felt it!"

I gave Aemilia my best skeptical look.

"The impulse, the feeling, the urge. The fact that you can be totally lost, but you always know which direction Rome is. It's some kind of instinct, a magnet that wants to draw you there, always." Aemilia's mouth curved into a wide, blushing smile as she spoke, and I knew that she loved this city as I had.

"I always thought that was the result of some spell to trick me into coming back so they could kill me again."

"Well, if it is, then they want to kill me too," Aemilia said. Again, her voice was forcibly light.

"So, do we really have to go clubbing with this Australian guy tonight?" I asked with a playful smile. This time Aemilia laughed and let me change the subject.

As we stood to leave, I stole one glance back at the gelato display guarded by a surly middle-aged Italian in a white apron.

Pistachio. Thick and mossy green, like … .

*　　　*　　　*

The Tiber flooded the year I finished my decade as a student and was finally inducted as a vestal virgin.

The year I met Nesreen.

Annus mirabilis. Wonderful year.

Annus horribilis. Horrible year.

The river hastened through the city in a thick, mossy column that couldn't wait to spill into the Tyrrhenian Sea. On *Maius* 15, one month before I was to be raised to active vestal, I was finally allowed to participate in the ritual of the Argei, for which the raging river played an integral role.

We gathered at Porta Carmentalis and marched clockwise, stopping at each of the other 26 stations along the Servian wall. It might sound dull—walking around giant blocks of *tufa*—but this was the edifice Hannibal could not conquer, and even if we had outgrown its boundaries, it had protected us through our first youthful whimpers. And with a parade of praetors and 11 residents of the College of the Vestals, we made a merry procession, all very conscious and proud of being charged with the city's ritual cleansing.

The figure I carried was made from straw and fit perfectly into my hand, not like the sloppy dolls impatient mothers or servants gave to their daughters. Each straw was carefully measured and placed, and the finished result was clearly the work of a craftsman. Any priestess would have been proud to carry such a figure, but the responsibility was mine, and I took it as an omen of great things to come. I would be chief among the vestal virgins one day, first among the women of Rome, Vesta willing.

We gathered at the center of the bridge and mounted the scaffolding that separated us from the long plunge into the Tiber below. I bent my knees to brace myself against the updraft of air that battered at my trunk and brought a heady rush of life to my cheeks. I made a solid figure standing above the Tiber—lithe and strong with a self-assurance that comes from being predestined. At the cusp of 16, I was now my full 5 feet, eight inches, and 10 years of religious training had instilled in me a sense of religious piety that could not help but combust in expressions of fervent joy and severity. I was energy rendered visible by the intersection of my intense faith and perfect youth, standing at the edge of the Tiber, but also my future.

Many of the more cautious praetors stood alongside the barrier and leaned over the edge to face their city's most crucial artery, the chariot that bore the infant twins Romulus and Remus to the she-wolf who took them into her care. But we vestals needn't fear the Tiber, nor any other force of nature or man, when in the service of our people. Vesta watched over us, and granted us godly powers.

"Cast the Argei into the waters!" instructed Fulvia, our Virgo Vestalis Maxima. Typically, the order would have come from the Pontifex Maximus, but an army of slaves had marched into Rome two years earlier with the intention of assassinating him. Several months later, the emperor's brother-in-law was caught plotting against him. These were hardly the first attempts to kill him, but after that, Commodus retired to his personal estates and rarely appeared in public, with the exception of the Coliseum, where he was heavily armed at all times.

When I heard Fulvia's command, I didn't hesitate. The figure was feather-light in my hand one moment, my fingers working their way around its contours, familiarizing themselves, briefly, with its features; and the next it was gone. I flung the miniature as if it carried the plague. The impassioned frenzy of the gesture nearly swung me over the edge of the bridge, but a divine hand stayed and steadied me.

Out of the corner of my eye, I saw Alberico, Domitius, and Teofilo—three magistrates chosen by Commodus to participate in the ritual—gingerly release their Argei and watch with relief and wonder as the effigies slowly, peacefully meandered toward the river.

Caecilia caught my eye and shook her head. Among the vestals, we were nearest each other in age, and we sometimes decried the use of secular men in religious ceremonies. Privately, of course. We believed that dangling the opportunity to partake in sacred observances as political rewards diminished our own roles as lifelong servants of Vesta.

I could almost hear Caecilia's low, confident voice

insisting, "Profane hands have no place in priestly worship."

It was exactly the kind of thinking my mother feared I would one day indulge, but without her to humble and ground me, and under the influence of constant adulation, my natural self-confidence had grown as brash as Jupiter's lightning. Still, I retained enough of her teaching to refrain from giving voice to these immoderate views—except to Caecilia, who encouraged and shared my brash streak.

My hair had grown considerably since the captio ceremony, falling unbound below my waist in a determined black wave. Or it would have, if unbound hair weren't considered immodest for a woman of patrician birth, and especially a virgin priestess wed to Rome. Every morning, two servants came to my chambers to help me dress and arrange my hair in a labyrinth of braids called *seni crines*. After years of practice, the four deft hands could sweep across my head with lightning speed, weaving my hair into seven braids that left my face unfettered by even a single stray strand.

Anyone who looked at me would know I was a virgin, even if the bulk of the servants' efforts was concealed by my infula. I sometimes wanted to ask whether they were ever bothered by the fact that they spent no fewer than 120 hours braiding my hair each year. But they might have fairly countered that I spent almost an equal amount of time transporting water from the sacred spring. Ultimately, the truth of our lives was the same: precise gestures that, when repeated often enough, became details. Enough details, perfectly executed, become an empire.

Besides, it didn't pay for a vestal virgin to become overly friendly with the servants. Everyone knew their real purpose was to spy on us and report our activities to the Pontifex Maximus. It was a lot like having little sisters, except that you were rarely condemned to death after your sister tattled on you. There were few instances of a vestal virgin being brought to trial on charges of incest, but when it happened, servants were almost always called to testify against her.

On *Iunius* 9 of the year 189 AD, the day of *Vestalia*, I completed my service as a student in the Atrium Vestae and quietly made the transition to full-fledged service. On that morning, I awoke long before the sun even considered rising and began baking the sacred cakes using holy water Vibiana and Septima collected for me while I set about my preparations. One of the first and most essential lessons of my training was preparation of mola salsa, the special flour used in religious ceremonies.

The inner chambers of the temple were open to all women during the week of Vestalia, and they crowded our home in their eagerness to make an offering to the goddess of the hearth.

My mother arrived early in the morning with Decima and Aemilia in tow. Hortensia and Liviana were now married, and Liviana had recently fulfilled her early promise by becoming the emperor's mistress. Junia died eight years earlier when the plague swept through Rome with such malice that my parents counted themselves lucky to be left with five children, even if I was no longer their daughter in the eyes of the law. Many parents were left without a single child to carry on their legacy, and many children were left without parents to help them navigate and survive the empire's tempestuous political waters.

I attended both my sisters' weddings and visited my family as often as I was allowed, but I nevertheless occupied a strange no-man's-land in the family hierarchy. Hortensia and Liviana settled into lives befitting Roman matrons, but they had not quite forgiven me for eclipsing them by being made a vestal. Decima hardly remembered me. It was only Aemilia who followed me like an adoring puppy, though her affection was often tempered with a sadness I did not understand.

Valens, the neighbor's son, somehow always found an excuse to intrude on my time with my family, and I had become so accustomed to the sight of him at my family's estate or by my mother's side when she came to visit the temple, that I had unconsciously begun to regard him as a sort of cousin.

While my mother relinquished the basket of homemade bread and salt cakes she had brought to curry favor with the goddess of the hearth, Aemilia and I chatted about her plans to leave Rome during Iulius and *Augustus* when temperatures—and outbreaks of deadly infection—climbed uncomfortably high. After Junia's death, my parents insisted that their unmarried daughters clear out of the city come summer.

"I would prefer to stay," Aemilia revealed unhappily. "It's an ill-favored time to leave." She hesitated, and I stroked her hair. I would always be her big sister, but my status as a high priestess gave me an authority that exceeded any my parents could claim, and a gravity that encouraged people to confide in me. There was only one Roman whose words carried more weight than my own, and he was engaged in a near-constant struggle for power with the Senate. One that would likely claim his life.

"Aemilia, tell me what is troubling you," I urged. "And I will counsel you."

"No."

With a single glance, I could reprieve a man sentenced to death. But I could not make my 14-year-old sister speak, nor banish the monsters that robbed her of her peace of mind.

"It is impossible. *As astra per aspera*." To the stars on the wings of a pig.

"Nothing is beyond the reach of Rome's fairest, best-educated daughter," I encouraged. "I will find you your pig, and you will sail it to the stars, if that is your wish."

I believed I could do it. The gods favored me. I was essentially Vesta's bodyguard. But for all their power, my gods were not omniscient, and I suspected that Aemilia's woes did not fall under Vesta's sphere of influence.

"Unless this is a problem best resolved by Venus? We can visit her temple, and present an offering on your behalf. If you would like, we can even—"

The rest of my plea went unspoken. Aemilia became stiff, gripping my hand so tightly that I wanted to pull it away, but her grasp was too strong. I wasn't accustomed to being touched by anyone but the servants who prepared my hair and dressed me. The penalty for harming a vestal is death, and a man accused of dallying with one received the same fate. I doubted Aemilia would be whipped to death for bruising my hand, but knowing the mortal consequences of excessive physical contact made it difficult to accept any at all.

Suddenly Valens was beside me, beaming as though he'd fallen into a vat of sacrificial wine. He almost always smiled, which seemed unnatural for an 18-year-old whose task of the past few years had been to convince the empire that he was fit for political and military service to Rome. I doubted that his father was pleased that his son spent so much time in the company of a family of daughters.

"Congratulations, Rhea." He stepped between Aemilia and I, his brown eyes fixating on my face while he spoke. "You really are a vestal."

He had a habit of leaning forward and lowering his voice when we talked. I was sure he was not aware of the intimate tableaux our conversations presented, for if he were, he would have understood the danger they presented to me. It was a trait that always annoyed me—the fact that he locked onto something and became oblivious to all else, including others' conventions and expectations.

Aemilia was gone, and I knew that she would rebuff me if I attempted to follow her and resume our conversation.

I smiled at Valens, suddenly and surprisingly grateful for his simplicity. He required nothing of me beyond my presence. And how many people can you say that of over the course of a lifetime?

"Ten years is quite a journey," I told him. "I wish I had their measure in miles. I might have crossed the entire empire, trekked north to Hadrian's wall, and sailed the Mediterranean along the African coast."

I didn't often speak fancifully, and something about my words triggered his interest. His smile disappeared, and his face assumed an expression of intensity that rendered him nearly unrecognizable.

"Twenty years of service, and you can leave this temple. You could see all of it: Egypt, Macedonia, Mesopotamia. You could marry ... ."

I shook my head. "Most vestals remain at the temple after their 30 years are done."

"But it is their choice, and it will soon be your choice," he insisted. "Twenty years is but the blink of an eye. Consider how quickly the past 10 years have gone."

"Stop trying to blink away my youth," I replied sternly. "I have not thought about what I will do when I leave here. *If* I leave here. But it can never be more important than these 30 years, so do not try to hasten them away from me."

A passing servant—Cloelia, who often came to my chambers late at night to ask if I needed anything—caught Valens' eye, and he apologized for interrupting my time with my family and left rather abruptly. Cloelia, who had touches of white at her temples despite being in her early 20s, gave me a friendly, knowing look, and I realized that she had probably chased Valens away as a favor to me. Maybe I had found a servant in the House of Vesta who didn't want to watch me climb down a ladder and into a sealed tomb.

IV

I first saw Nesreen during a hunt at the Coliseum. We occupied a specially reserved box a mere three yards from the emperor—Septima, Vibiana, Maximiliana, Nona, and myself. The five vestal virgins.

Caecilia stayed behind at the temple to protect the flame, and in six hours I would have to return for my shift, whether the entertainment had concluded or not. It was not a long journey: through the Arcus Constantini, a triumphal arch built to commemorate Constantine I's victory over Maxentius; beyond the Temple of Venus; and through Archus Titi, which was built to celebrate Vespasian and Titus' conquest of Jerusalem. The Temple of Castor and Pollux was our neighbor to the west, the Roman Forum to the north, and Domus Tiberiana—a palace built by Caligula and Nero—lay to the south. We were Rome's beating heart, setting the pulse for the entire world.

Our podium in the Coliseum provided the best view of the hunt—save the emperor's box, of course. The senators sat several yards back and took pains to behave very respectfully when we were present, but the tension between the emperor and Senate was as visible and deadly as any beast that entered the Coliseum that day.

The previous month, enraged by rumors that the Senate intended to limit his powers—which everyone was aware the Senate wanted desperately—Commodus proclaimed that all coinage released from that day forward would read "*Populus Senatusque Romanus.*" The People and the Senate: a reversal of the "*Senatus Populusque Romanus*" emblazoned on coins since long before my birth. Three little words conveyed a world of insult.

And the best part—for anyone who took the emperor's side in all this, at least—was that the Senate couldn't fully express its outrage, not when the people were madly in love with the message: The people before the Senate. A Senate in service to its people. This had, of course, always been the ideal behind the Senate, but when did any politician—the emperor included—put the people before himself? If that were really the point, 60,000 Romans would sit in the Coliseum's sumptuous boxes, while 600 senators would take their place on the wooden seats in the third or fourth tier.

My role was to mediate their disputes, to guard their confidential documents, to protect the flame as a source of hearth fire for every Roman household. Vestal virgins are not above politics, but neither were we supposed to publicly slop around in the mud with the professionals. I sometimes wondered if we weren't a panacea, a lullaby without end to allow the people to sleep peacefully at night. But we couldn't plod brashly into every battle without diminishing our numbers so severely that there would be no one left to serve the important religious functions. We served emperor and senator alike, as well as the *populus*, and that was the real source of our power and respect.

Most *venationes* were themed, and among the most common displays was an exhibition of a conquered territory. Its people—trained like gladiators in the *ludi* and armed with weapons whose business was to tear through flesh with ease— pitted against whatever beast their native land had to offer. Teams of craftsmen spent weeks transforming the Coliseum into the conquered territory. I'd seen hunters stalk their prey through lush jungles, across seemingly barren desert scapes, into dense forests. Sometimes, the humans were the hunters, but not always. If the hunters were lucky, Commodus just wanted to see as many animals killed as possible, and their task was merely to build a mountain of carcasses. I'd seen 100 animals felled in a day, 1,000 in a week. If the hunters were lucky.

Commodus understood that people want a story. Sure, they'd cheer as a Transvaal lion ripped apart an unarmed criminal or a specially trained hunter brought down a herd of 50 zebras. But if the carnage had a proper plot and setting, and characters the crowd could learn to love or hate, well, those were the venationes people talked about for weeks.

On that day, the Coliseum was an arid desert, painted varying shades of beige with outcroppings of rock to match. Clumps of aromatic bushes like African wormwood, which stood no more than two feet tall, would provide little in the way of cover for the hunters or prey, but they did save the setting from being entirely stark.

The senators were fond of calling Commodus crude, but he was the first emperor to truly comprehend the Coliseum's potential. To merely watch something die was an injustice to the other senses. You must also recognize the sound of iron making its home in a man's skull, which was altogether different from the crack of a neck or spine. Smell the fear and the blood and the excrement and—because Cyrene was a coastal settlement—the sea. Commodus imported thousands of gallons of seawater so that 60,000 Romans could understand what it really meant to die on the Libyan coast. It was my first intimate encounter with Neptune, and I savored the strange, liberating sting of it.

The air was so thick with salt that my nose burned, and a primitive longing set my thoughts aloft with the breeze. I did not belong to Rome, but to something more vast and lonely and savage.

"I could fancy one of those apples," Septima said,

nodding to a small bush in the Coliseum. Wide fan-like leaves tried to conceal corpulent green growths, and failed miserably.

"It would not make a very flavorsome final meal, but if you command it of me, I will ask one of the venatores to present you with one after the hunt." We had captured the attention of the emperor, who now held Septima's gaze with a focused, unblinking stare. Whatever divine or verbal powers she had once possessed fled, and she stared at him shamefully, fearfully.

"They are poison?" I asked. Since attempting to shield Junia at the captio, I had found that Commodus did not terrify me as he did so many others. Then again, I was one of the few vestal virgins who had not felt the misery of his leather scourge upon my back. We were bound to secrecy if we committed the grave sin of letting the fire go out, but any vestal who would not leave her bed for two days and could not bear the slightest weight upon her back had clearly suffered the wrath of the Pontifex Maximus. Most of us believed it was too small a price to pay.

"Toxic." He drew out the final hard consonant, savored it. "A metaphor for our conquered territories. In Cyrene, a giant apple can kill. Imagine what a beast with fangs or claws three inches long could do to an unprotected woman."

He hooked a finger and ran it along Septima's cheek, but his eyes never left mine. I could feel the hot gust of air as the senators behind us gasped and decried the emperor's unnecessary contact with a vestal virgin.

The senators fell silent as the *bestiarii* entered the stadium in a tight pack, warily avoiding the foliage lest it conceal a trapdoor with a hungry tiger at the opposite end. Two hunters carried swords. The third and fourth each wielded a spear in the right hand and a sword in the left. The final two were armed with a bow and trident, respectively. All but the two carrying double weapons clutched shields, which were already angled defensively before them, though the animals had yet to appear; Commodus took special delight in catching the venatores unaware. The hunters gleamed with sacrificial luster, and I could swear I heard 60,000 Romans licking their lips eagerly.

The floor to my left split open, and a pair of caged wild boar appeared where there had been nothing but sand before. Directly across from where I sat, the floor vanished once again and the hypogeum below spat out more beasts from Cyrene: eight striped hyenas, slinking and snarling in their prison. Clockwise right: one rhinoceros. And at the emperor's feet: two leopards. With exquisite choreography, the cages flew open.

The venatores formed a tight circle. They were outnumbered two to one, but most hunters in the Coliseum had faced far worse odds. At least they now knew their enemy.

Before the animals could leave their cages, the audience cried for blood. Every meal they could not afford and therefore did not eat, every injustice, every illness, every child lost in the wake of a new sickness was in their cry. The senators finalized a near-infinite variation of bets: How many, and which venatores would die. Who would die first, and by which animal. Which beast would fall first, and which last. The duration of the hunt. Some even bet *denarii* over which weapons would fall to the arena floor.

When the rhinoceros scored the first kill by trampling one of the hyenas, Commodus ordered slaves to spatter the plebeians in the fourth tier with buckets of fresh blood—all part of his sensory immersion campaign. They howled with rage and delight and bloodlust. They wouldn't be content to watch animals killing other animals for long.

Vesta's handmaidens watched impassively. I did not allow myself favorites in the Coliseum. To show preference to a gladiator might be viewed as moral weakness, even a willingness to betray my oath. Anyway, it was often impossible to tell who would live and who would die, and I would not shed tears over the lifeblood that wetted the sands of the arena floor

It was the fashion, of course, to choose a champion in

each contest and to align your sympathies so closely with the fate of your warrior that each death was greeted with a stormy bout of weeping and thunderous applause. The Coliseum was a machine, a meat grinder, and most of what entered—everything, in the case of animals that appeared in the hunts—had an expiration date. If I knew the great white lion stood a chance, that the bounding deer were headed anywhere other than the barbecue pits set up outside the stadium for cooking and feeding the noble beasts to the hungry Romans—

But I was Rhea Equitius Regilla, priestess of an empire that suffered no fools, and neither did I.

My stoicism was out of fashion, but I believed in the games for what they were: lessons in the might and triumph of Roman rule and law. To view them as anything less seemed frivolous. And though I had a knack for discerning comedy in life's unconventional folds and hideaways, I had no appreciation for the trivial.

As a group, the venatores attacked the boar.

"Risky, turning their backs on a horn-mad rhinoceros," Vibiana tsked. "They likely hope the rhinoceros cuts a swath through the hyenas, and that the leopards are too battle-shy to go on the offensive. It all depends on how hungry the leopards are."

The answer, it turned out, was hungry enough to eat an armed venatore. The leopards must have longed for grasslands as they slunk with deadly eloquence after the venatore chosen to protect the hunters' flank. The Cyrenian—bearing a shield carved with a stalk of silphium, indicating the hunter hailed from the conquered territory—appeared unaware that the two exquisitely patterned blurs intended to make a meal of the hunter.

Then, as the first leopard flung his paws forward to embrace his prey, the hunter spun out of the feline's path and thrust his sword into the animal's exposed belly. There was no time for surprise or regret or fear; the leopard experienced the kindest death the Coliseum could offer. But its mate, who circled to the left while the now-dead beast launched its doomed attack, shied away from the hunter.

Rome was astonished. We had watched these hunts hundreds of times, but each one was still a revelation.

Instead of rejoining the pack of hunters worrying the wild boar, the lone venatore followed the leopard. Crouched in a feral survival position equally suited to fending off and striking a fatal blow, the hunter appeared inappreciably small.

"If he lasts five minutes, I am a monkey's mistress," announced Bruttia Crispina, feigning boredom to annoy her husband. The emperor appeared not to hear her.

"Somehow I don't think the emperor would mind," Septima replied boldly, but not loudly enough for Bruttia to overhear.

The emperor's wife was required by law to sit with vestal virgins when attending public events, which meant we were treated to two spectacles: the one playing out in the Coliseum and the one playing in the theater of marital discord. From my perspective, it would have been more humane had one of the pair picked up a spear and stuck it through the other and been done with it.

Emperors and their wives have been killing one another for centuries. And Romans have become experts at seeing nothing. But mutual respect called for subtlety: poison or ordering a lover or subordinate to carry out the assassination. Subtlety, like honesty, comes in degrees.

"That was clever," Septima sighed, and I knew by her exhalation that she, too, believed the venatore was about to die.

"He certainly is a nubile young specimen," Bruttia said, continuing her commentary. I assessed her thoughtfully. She had pale hair, likely lightened with quicklime, wood ash, and old wine, which was an increasingly common fad among respectable matrons. The city's prostitutes had been doing it for decades, imitating the Germanic women Roman soldiers brought back from their travels. The empress had a wide face and distinct cheekbones that made pockets of her cheeks when she smiled. Her eyebrows were so light they were difficult to distinguish—which did not really matter because the empress almost never smiled, and when people spoke to her, they always reacted to her position rather than her expression.

The empress had as much right to her dissatisfaction as anyone. Commodus' tastes ran to male and female, young and, well, mostly young, willing and unwilling. At some point in their 11 years of marriage, the couple had struck an unspoken agreement, in accordance with which they largely ignored one another—only occasionally rattling the peace with a vicious barb. Bruttia was never quite certain whether she appreciated her husband's mistresses for diverting his attention or loathed them for usurping her political clout. But she knew her husband loved the Coliseum, almost childishly, and derived perverse joy from undermining his enjoyment of a battle or hunt.

The venatore cornered the leopard against the wall just yards below the emperor's feet, and the senators and my fellow vestal virgins tensed and instinctively moved to put distance between themselves and the battle unfolding below. Only Commodus leaned over the rail, his fingers straying to the sword at his hip. If he could reach, he would take a few swings of his own, and he did not much care whether he struck the leopard hunched and snarling near the wall or the venatore who took cautious, measured steps toward the prey.

The animal was just within reach. I was grateful I couldn't see the creature's face, and eager for this particular encounter to reach its predictable end. But on the last step, the venatore faltered, and the shield engraved with a large silphium stalk fell to the ground. Two things happened in that moment—three, if you count the gasp of the crowd, which had come to admire the petite venatore aiming to singlehandedly dispatch the most dangerous of the Coliseum's game. But that was merely a reaction to the hunter's fatal error in allowing the shield to drop.

The leopard sensed its advantage and plunged toward the venatore, who raised dazed eyes upward to follow the feline's path. I caught the hunter's eye and was so startled that

I smiled accidentally. The venatore, in turn, merely arched an unimpressed eyebrow, as if to suggest that the timing of our strange intercourse was ill favored. It is true that the venatore was about to be skewered by a leopard, but it was precisely this detail that made the strange moment between us all the more urgent. The venatore was about to die, not I.

Before I had time to worry that someone had witnessed my exchange with the venatore, or turn my head from what would surely be the gory sight of the hunter mangled and bloodied, something extraordinary happened. The hunter crouched to reclaim the fallen shield, hefted the guard to deflect the brunt of the leopard's charge, and thrust the sword upward in a second motion to cleanly and quickly dispatch the large feline.

They reposed together in their tragic, magnificent tableaux—the leopard atop the shield, and the hunter all but invisible at the bottom of the pile—for mere moments while the crowd noisily tried to decide how it felt about the last 10 seconds. On the one hand, they hoped the venatore would never rise from the Coliseum floor so they could mourn the deceased's heroism and spread tales of the hunter's courage to anyone who had the misfortune of missing the day's games.

But before a lackey dressed as Charon, the ferryman of the dead, could collect the Cyrenian's corpse and parade it through the death goddess Libitina's gate, the silphium stalk on the shield began to shudder. Everyone—striking, indifferent Bruttia included—stared at the basin of red gathering almost directly below the emperor's feet, wondering whose blood they were watching as it coursed through the arteries of the Coliseum.

One of the hunters broke away from the main pack and trotted toward the site of the leopard—and possibly the venatore's—death. The trident he clutched in his right hand, and sometimes waved warily behind him as if to ward off the agony and death that were the Coliseum's twin exports, was larger than the hunter lying beneath the silphium shield. Without setting his weapon aside, he thrust an arm into the confused pile of death and withdrew a small figure with blood caked across the face and smeared through long strands of dark hair.

Despite my proud vow not to grunt and squawk and applaud along with the mangy populus, I gripped Vibiana's hand and gasped with the masses. The wounded hunter had lost all head coverings during the scuffle, revealing a Cyrenian woman with rich brown eyes that locked onto our box until the bestiarii led her back to the other hunters.

At the sight of her, I was struck by a bolt of nonsensical recognition, and part of me fled forever to be with the hunter. This emotional flight didn't conform to any of the laws or logical tenets my tutors had patiently drilled into my memory. When it comes to love, few things will. Most things we do because we are told we must and have seen them done in precisely this fashion a thousand times. Loving Nesreen was my first original act, and the only thing I had ever done entirely without guidance.

*　　　　*　　　　*

After two and a half hours of staring at frescoes and statues of pagan gods and Christian martyrs, Emeline took pity on me. She could have spent an entire year perusing every detail of the Vatican's massive hoard of artwork, entirely skipping her junior year of high school, but I had already exhausted my small store of patience, and the comments I muttered to myself were starting to get louder.

"So this is where they stashed the gods they drove out of the Pantheon," I announced after catching a glimpse of Juno defiantly clutching a shield and spear.

"I've seen enough," Emeline announced cheerfully. "And we have to check out from the hostel in an hour anyway. Let's grab some gnocchi to go and pack our luggage. Gnocchi's on me."

"I don't know why you're pretending you don't recognize her." My gray eyes threatened a tempest. And though Emeline and I had heard and swapped stories about people being kicked out of Disneyland, marched through an underground network of tunnels and permanently banned from the Happiest Place on Earth, Emeline wasn't sure how an ejection from the Vatican would go down—and she wasn't anxious to find out.

"There's truth to what you're saying," Emeline said, mostly to shut me up. "But this isn't the place to discuss it. Unless you're planning on asking a docent why the Vatican exhibits statues of gods and goddesses it deems pagan and excommunicates people for worshiping … and please don't do that!"

"Fine."

Emeline would have been justified in taking me to task for my terrible attitude. Instead, she said calmly, "For someone who vowed never to visit Rome because you were afraid of attracting the wrong kind of attention, you seem hell-bent on creating a scene in the exact place people might be waiting for you. It's weird, because you're smart, and you're normally so careful. It's almost like you want to be found out and dragged back to the tomb."

I knew, from photographs my sister had taken that day, that the angular plains of my face were unforgiving as stone, and the set of my chin communicated at least one lifetime's worth of defiance. I looked scared, but not as scared as Emeline wanted me to be. So she drew closer, so close that the smell of her shampoo shut out the stale, sweaty tang of old artifacts and far too many tourists.

"And Rhea," she said softly, "I fully believe they're out there waiting for you. Here, too."

She knew I would be angry. Frightened people always are. And my fear had nearly nine centuries to steep and fester. On the plane, Emeline had said that she pictured my terror as a vine that strangled and felled its host by blocking all access to light and oxygen. Except that Emeline wouldn't allow me to succumb to so loathsome a fate. I'd already paid for my sin. I deserved to live now, Emeline insisted, even if I didn't realize it.

There was always the risk that, in trying to save me, Emeline would lose me altogether. We were just beginning to understand one another, just starting to form memories that we could talk about and share, a future I actually wanted a place in.

I had danced. At the club, when it was so packed that the revelers didn't dance so much as jump into the air and tumble where the crowd left space to fall. Emeline had never seen me dance. And even with Adam's green eyes and light-hearted smile waging a very successful campaign for her attention, Emeline admitted that I'd held her attention that night as well, shooting out of the crowd like a spark.

Somehow Adam knew that I was not a viable candidate for affection or romantic advances, and Emeline knew that Adam would have pursued me if he'd been given the chance. But nobody could be bothered by who was attracted to whom, and why, and what would possibly come of it. Not on a hot night when your clothes stuck to your skin and the excess energy the brilliant summer sun left behind at the end of the day seemed to linger in the city's youth, and the only possible outlet was to dance, dance, dance and scream, caterwaul, curse until you were so hoarse you needed your body to do the screaming.

Emeline and Adam.

Me.

Aemilia and Adam.

Me. Leaping, ascending in a hot, red strobe to Italian techno music that sounded exactly like its American counterpart. Luminous. With everyone watching me out of the corners of their eyes, waiting for the right moment to approach and congratulate me for no reason in particular in a language I didn't fully comprehend.

But I was wily. I was the moon—everywhere the dancers looked, and on everyone's mind, but just beyond their reach. Even when I allowed gravity to return me to the wet, greedy dance floor, I somehow managed to hover beyond their reach, attracting and repelling them until they went mad.

This is all according to Emeline, and would have been easy to dismiss; what little sister didn't look at her older counterpart and think of the moon, hovering wisely and chastely just beyond her reach? But something about her description of that night haunted me.

It was the same conundrum that plagued the celestial figures chosen to serve Rome as vestal virgins. The city's coffers were glutted with denarii, but its streets teemed with the empire's real pride: sprightly stalks, fresh as dew, following their parents hither and thither, promising to marry the glory of the past with the promise of the future. A girl must shine very brightly to distinguish herself.

And yet, from that moment forward, she must be above suspicion, positioned directly in the public eye but as a remote figure sworn to repel even the simplest of embraces. It was true that I had failed spectacularly, but the rules of the game were not made with our well-being in mind.

I

Basilio's villa was a cavernous ellipse situated 10 miles outside Rome at the base of a small hill where craggy rocks allowed very little vegetation to trespass. He had commissioned the house 15 years earlier, with a simple phone call to his closest friend—a Jesuit priest turned architect— explaining exactly what he wanted. Five years later, he spent his first night there, in the house he'd called Ilium in that first phone call.

Ilium was a fortress that forgot its purpose somewhere along the way and contented itself instead to astonish and confound. The architect credited divine inspiration with helping him conjure the dizzying effect of spiraling concrete and sunlight rebounding in all directions. The house kept Basilio sharp and reminded him that appearances are often deceiving. It also impressed his houseguests, of which there were many. Basilio had always chosen to live alone, with a single houseman to run his errands.

Basilio's work often called him away from his retreat. Though he served several clients in Rome, he was most popular among wealthy families of Venice and Genoa, and he had published a theory attributing emotional instability to constant proximity to vast bodies of water. The sea, Basilio believed, stirred unrealistic expectations and unrealized desire. It called people to a life that was always somewhere else. Ilium was the antithesis of the sea: solid and finite and just comfortable enough to keep him rooted there forever.

There was no possibility of preparing me for Ilium, so when our taxi pulled into view—the driveway didn't extend fully to the house because Basilio preferred the illusion of seclusion—Emeline leapt out before the vehicle could come to a full stop, leaving me to pay the driver. It was late afternoon, and the house loomed and smoldered against the sun's last light.

Emeline was already inside, unloading her luggage in one of three cozy guestrooms. I was apprehensive as I circled the monolith, trying to find the entrance. I had always been wary of structures with obscure exits, and I was so wildly fearful of becoming trapped inside the house that I considered bedding down by a nearby pine tree and camping until morning, when I could call a taxi and catch a plane home.

As if alerted to my possible flight, Basilio materialized from a gap in the wall and beckoned me inside with a warmth I did not remember from our previous encounter. He was smiling, genuinely, from the eyes, but he never stopped watching me and assessing as I sniffed discretely around the cavern where he lived, ate, and entertained. He had the advantage; though I was an introvert and prone to observing and dissecting a person's every word and move—as shy people often have the habit of doing—my attention had been wholly appropriated by Basilio's strange castle. It stirred my claustrophobia. Never had I been in a space that so closely resembled the prison and tomb of my last life.

Had I been a rabbit, I likely would have burrowed a safe house deep in the earth's soil. But I was, sadly, a human, and etiquette—and an abiding fear of being committed to a lunatic ward—dictated that I behave as though Ilium were just any other home.

"Welcome, Rhca." Basilio spoke only after he sensed I

was finished with my first assessment. Despite the strength of his expression, his voice was quiet. "You are Rhea? It's been quite a long time, hasn't it? You've never even seen my home. Or my country! I must say I'm very proud of Ilium, but Italy! To ignore Italy is practically a sin! I'm confident the Pope would agree with me. He's probably working on adding it to the list of cardinal sins."

Aemilia appeared before I was forced to make any reply beyond, "Thank you for welcoming us into your home," and we disappeared to the second floor. She helped me settle into my room, which was really a loft above the main living room. I hadn't seen any doors in Ilium, but before I could panic, Aemilia discovered that the guestroom bathroom had a sliding door and latch.

Long before she'd bought the plane tickets for this trip, Aemilia knew Ilium would be difficult for me. With the exception of the sunlight pouring in from all directions, Basilio's home was a very near approximation of the crypt where Romans disposed of the vestal virgins who failed to live up to the latter half of their title. But Aemilia gambled that Basilio's home might serve as a form of therapy where I could confront and claim victory over my fears and return home as a whole person, rather than the fragmented being I had allowed myself to become. But she only acknowledged her plan after I had already guessed it, and by then the information was of little use to me.

While I finished unpacking, Aemilia snuck downstairs. She found Basilio chopping mushrooms in the kitchen and felt obligated to at least attempt to explain my antisocial behavior.

"Rhea's just settling into her room," she confided casually. "Might take a while. She's not terribly comfortable with confined spaces."

When Basilio made no reply, she leaned on the counter and spoke a little louder.

"She's terrified of them. Always has been."

"That's an odd fear for an 18-year-old American girl."

"Well, Rhea's an unusual girl," Aemilia said calmly and

not a little proudly.

"It's something of a recent conceit, putting a high premium on unorthodox behavior," Basilio observed. "This notion that some people are just born special, with an irrational fear already rooted deep in their psyche or just happen to be misanthropic despite being born to two friendly, normal parents. It's exceedingly rare for a phobia to develop without a catalyst."

"I dunno, Uncle Basilio. It kinda sounds like you just haven't spent a lot of time around teenagers." The summer before eighth grade, Aemilia had perfected the art of dismissing a person's words without actually voicing any insult. She understood that the bulk of communication was subtext: body language, tone, eye contact. And she could communicate more with a relaxed slouch and bored expression than most adults could accomplish with a thoughtfully crafted lecture about respect.

Aemilia's biggest secret was that she always listened— to everyone and everything—but she believed that not all information was equal. There are some tidbits that are more valuable if nobody realizes you possess them. Like the fact that Uncle Basilio was clearly concerned about my mental well-being.

Well, that line had been forming for quite some time, and Aemilia figured she and our parents had dibs on concern for her big sister. The fact that Basilio was a well-respected psychiatrist meant very little to Aemilia, unless he'd specialized in reincarnation adjustment disorder, which wasn't really the type of question it's safe to ask a mental health professional. Still, it made for a pretty good joke, and Aemilia mentally filed it away for later, when we were alone.

If Basilio believed he was on to something, then Aemilia decided it might be best to spirit me away for a few days, explore the lake in Bracciano. I clearly wasn't ready for a triumphant return to the Coliseum, and Aemilia knew I'd be thrilled to escape the cave Uncle Basilio insisted on calling his home. She also had to admit that I deserved some reward for visiting the Vatican—and moving into Basilio's house—without inciting a riot.

Without ever meaning to, I somehow inspired powerful emotion in those around me. But I never recognized this tendency in myself, and therefore never learned to channel it toward some useful purpose. What might have been a skill instead became a weapon that I turned against myself as often as not. Aemilia believed that if I ever honed my power, it would be my enemies who fled Rome and the reincarnated vestal virgin who hunted and tried them for their crimes against humanity.

*   *   *

She came to Rome in the winter, when the light from the sun is always slanting and dying and you have to catch it and hold it to your face in just the right spot to feel any warmth.

The journey took 54 days, long enough for Nesreen to convince Traianus—ship's captain, slave trader, and philosophical dabbler—that she could better serve Rome as a free woman than slave.

She told me this story, in bits and pieces, over the course of our nights together in Atrium Vestae, speaking softly out of respect for the sharp, jealous ears of nearby slaves, but she always forgot herself and grew increasingly animated until I was forced to silence her in the most pleasant manner possible.

On the first day, Nesreen distinguished herself from the others by refusing to cry as the Libyan coast shrank until it was swallowed entirely by distance and water. She assisted the ship's crew with an air of helpfulness, reasoning that the vessel was making its way to Rome. Whether she'd climbed aboard willingly or been tossed on the deck bound and gagged with less care than the casks of water that followed, she'd rather confront the strange circumstances of her new life than languish unhappily on a ship.

The third day, while the captain's second in command

expounded on the merits and torments of strong winds at sea, Nesreen fluttered her hands into the air and spoke authoritatively on the contents of Claudius Ptolemy's *Almagest*, the world's most comprehensive treatise on astronomy:

"The Earth lies still in the center, and all the stars revolve around us in their own fashion. There are 1,022 stars placed among the constellations, which he ranges in magnitude from one to six according to their brightness."

She was gazing upward, hoisting her arms toward the heavens like sails to catch her meaning and direct her audience in their thinking.

"You'll finance this trip on your own, my fine Cyrenian star-gazer," the captain predicted gleefully. "There's not a patrician household in Rome what can afford to be without an exotic slave girl who understands their stars better than they."

"So I'm to pay for this crossing?" Nesreen asked curiously.

"Keep talking about Ptolemy and the stars, and you may pay for three," Traianus predicted. "Though the market shifts faster than the emperor changes names."

"Riches do not exhilarate us so much with their possession as they torment us with their loss," Nesreen said, speaking with such confidence that the captain laughed instead of slapping her into silent submission as he had done to other slaves before, and would do again to slaves who did not yet know that was what they were.

"You and Epicurus may have a point," he agreed heartily. "But I can not prove him right by regretting my lost riches until I have first acquired them."

Perhaps it was because they mutually surprised one another—the Cyrenian slave and student of philosophy, and the slave captain who knew Epicurus and tolerated a startling degree of familiarity from a slave—but by the end of their journey, with the lighthouse in Portus beckoning them into the harbor and a surge of sudden awe and fear and homesickness and courage threatening to overcome Nesreen's stalwart stomach, the two struck a deal.

Nesreen was meant to be free. Specifically, she was meant to be a free denizen of Rome. But the captain had already paid her captors in Cyrene, plus the cost of her voyage in food and the manpower required to propel them to Rome. Therefore, Nesreen would have to work for her freedom, repaying Traianus—and to a certain extent, the empire of Rome—for the privilege of her citizenship.

"Thracius will see to your well-being," Traianus assured Nesreen when the time came for them to part. "He will serve as my proxy in this. Obey him. Learn quickly, and you will live to see yourself as free as any woman can be who belongs to Rome."

"The gladiator?"

"He survived 36 matches. I believe you will be offered your freedom well before that."

And Nesreen realized she had neither understood nor gotten the better of her deal with the Roman ship captain. Still, she waited until she was completely alone that night before purging her fear, and dinner, onto the floor of the cell where she was being held until Thracius could have her placed in a *ludus*.

*   *   *

Bracciano was old and blue, just the way I liked it.

"The key to eating gnocchi," I informed Emeline with a self-importance that was only partially feigned, "is to always order twice as many as you think you're going to eat. You see, I've already eaten four, and I've no intention of stopping anytime soon."

I illustrated my point by popping another dumpling into my mouth as soon as I'd finished speaking, marveling that a tuber with a reputation as a bland staple crop could dance so eloquently with ricotta and truffle.

Day one in Bracciano we discovered a lakeside trattoria with outdoor seating that served the best gnocchi I'd ever tasted. We returned every day, sometimes more than once, even though the *anziana* who ran it always scowled at us, and the first time we tried to eat there she pretended to misunderstand us for more than an hour—despite Emeline's nearly flawless Italian, which improved by the day—before letting us order. She always wore the same black blouse, and Emeline wanted to believe that her unfriendly demeanor could be attributed to some recent loss.

I couldn't agree with her, not when I saw the pleasure the old bat derived from trying to stare us down. If I ever made it to her age, I resolved to be just as curmudgeonly, only I planned to wear the very worst thrift store cardigans I could find with spandex biker shorts just to see what people would say. No, because they couldn't say anything at all—not to an infirm old woman whose every minute might just be her last.

The lost years—the zenith of exuberant, unretreating youth that would, if all went well, be forged by time into something more singular and stalwart—had made a connoisseur of me. I studied the effects of those years on people, the ones they tried to poison, iron, hydrate, bleach, starve, tuck, and exercise out of their skin. An old woman's crosshatched hands held more meaning for me than the surprised, fledgling confidence of a fawn preening at its reflection. I had everything that was necessary to sit in a trattoria and growl at American tourists while my hands cajoled potatoes into perfect spheres of culinary goodness. I just didn't have the years.

"Isn't it interesting that we talk about discovering this place the way we talk about Columbus discovering America, even though neither is true?" I asked, gesturing to the restaurant.

From Emeline's expression—not quite dreamy, but certainly not fully present—it was apparent that she had not heard my question. "I could get married here," she said absentmindedly. Which was fine. I'd only asked it to distract myself from the hands of the battleaxe conjuring gnocchi in the kitchen.

"I may even invite you this time," she added playfully.

"You mean there?" I gestured to the Orsini-Odescalchi castle lording over my lakefront haven and looking exactly like every castle in every story that had the gall to promise "happily ever after" at the end. "You'd be in good company. The tour guide said Tom and Kate got married there."

"Well, you can't hold that against the castle," Emeline insisted. "It's 600 years old! Not as old as you, perhaps, but it still deserves some respect."

"Could you really? Get married here?"

"I don't know. Probably not." Emeline wrinkled her nose and raised it to the wind for a tentative sniff, as if that were the deciding factor.

Knowing Emeline, it might well be. We were bloodhounds when it came to our noses. Bracciano might be beautiful enough to float the postcard industry on the strength of its castle, but if it didn't smell right—if Emeline caught a whiff of the wrong plant or person—she might decide to set neither heel nor designer sunglasses there again. I was the same. It was our version of trusting our gut, except that we were relying on olfactory receptor neurons instead of whatever package of intellect, desire, courage, fear, and experience comprised our instincts.

It was not lost on us that smell is the sense most closely linked to memory. Perhaps our intense reliance on olfaction could be called upon to explain the fact that we remembered our reincarnation. If everyone could smell as we could, my junior year history teacher would remember selling spices in a Moroccan souk three centuries earlier, my fabric dancing teacher would recall her unpleasant years building the pyramids beneath an unforgiving sun, and my parents would remember something that would allow me to finally connect with them over something more substantial than piddly DNA. Perhaps.

Hyperosmia. Acute sense of smell. The reason I loathed ants and black licorice and wouldn't set foot in our neighbor's backyard owing to the presence of a noxious plant with a celery-colored stalk and seemingly innocent lavender petals. The reason Emeline suffered a migraine for days after entering any store that carried perfume.

"Who knows?" Emeline said, and I gathered that the results of her smell test had been inconclusive. She rifled through her purse, producing a pen branded with the name of a prescription drug company in purple letters, followed by a stack of postcards.

"Mom and Dad." She handed me the pen.

I withdrew my own packet of postcards from the pocket of my horizon-blue linen halter dress, which that very morning had produced a generous "That's not terrible; I think Italy becomes you, Rhea" from Emeline.

"Already got 'em." I brandished my own pen, a basic instrument with blue ink that tended to find its way onto my knuckles and into the crevices of my canvas tote bag.

A glass tumbled across the table, and Emeline dabbed guiltily at the soggy green tablecloth. Fortunately, the guardian of the gnocchi was occupied in the kitchen. It was difficult to imagine what penalty she might exact for spilling a glass of water, but I was fairly confident the dungeon in the nearby castle might finally find contemporary employment.

"I'm sorry … I just didn't realize … You bought postcards! For Mom and Dad!"

She hugged me harder than she ever had, and the embrace conveyed the extent of my failings as a daughter and sister. Shouldn't I, as the eldest, have been the one to remind her of our filial responsibilities?

"And please don't address it to Abri and Fedele," Emeline pleaded.

"I wasn't going to," I retorted. There was already a trash can outside our hotel room with a postcard addressed to Abri and Fedele, and I prayed that Emeline never found it. "I don't call them that on purpose. It just sort of slips out."

"Yeah, well, you should see Mom's face when it just slips out when your back is turned. It's beyond unfair—"

"I know." And I really did. When I was younger, I would sometimes catch her watching me, studying me, willing the emotional distance between us to disappear. By my junior year of high school, I knew it never would, and she did too, because that's when she started to avoid looking at me. She gave up, which I didn't acknowledge, because that first would have required me to demonstrate that I was aware of her incredible grief and longing.

So I wrote the postcard I knew they wanted from me, the one they couldn't talk or even think about because they were so sure they would never receive it:

Mom and Dad (Mamma and Papá, as you are called here),

This country is beautiful, and feels very much like home to me. I suppose it's because Italy is in my blood, which I am very grateful for, and grateful to the two of you for helping me to see it. Right now we are in Bracciano, and Em fancies she will be married here at the castle one day. This unveiling of the past has got me thinking a lot about what's to come. I hope you'll help me figure it all out when we get home. I love you, and am so very thankful for this opportunity.

Rhea

Emeline read the card with a disdainful sniff and silently pushed it back across the table.

"Did you mean it?" Her voice had a deliberately hard edge to it, like an eggshell that could crack at any moment.

"Most of it. Enough," I assured her. "I don't know if 'grateful' is the most honest word I could have chosen to describe my relationship with this country."

Emeline nodded and seemed satisfied. "Then it's a good card. They'll like it."

"I have an idea," I said, as if swept up in the moment, when really I had planned this conversation during the train ride from Rome to Bracciano. "What if we stayed here a couple of extra days? We could give you some time to prepare a seating chart, give me enough time to go up a pants size or two." I twirled a ball of gnocchi on the end of my fork.

"Yeah, that would be nice. But we're expected back in Rome tomorrow."

"Come on, Emeline! Three more days won't kill us."

"I already went out on a limb for you with this trip. Uncle Basilio was not pleased that we disappeared as soon as we arrived."

"I didn't come to Italy at Basilio's pleasure, and I don't much care whether he approves our itinerary or not." I put down the gnocchi. I couldn't savor it properly while discussing Basilio.

"Well, he did technically pay for this trip." Emeline wore the same expression she'd had the first night at our hostel in Rome, when she'd been forced to confess we were staying with him.

"What!" I made a four-letter word of that "what." It was pure indignation and disgust. And a little bit fear that Basilio had gained leverage over me, cleverly disguised as paternal interest.

"I don't know why you've decided he's your enemy, Rhea, but it isn't sound logic on your part. In fact, it isn't any kind of logic at all."

"You told me you paid for this trip with Fedele's credit card."

"I was all set to, and then Basilio swept in and offered to cover everything. It's not as though he has kids of his own."

I snorted, and threw my copy of *Middlemarch* to the sand.

"Dorothea Brooke may have tolerated this sort of behavior from Edward Casaubon, but I will not!"

Emeline stole a glance at our fellow diners, who appeared blessedly indifferent to my outburst. In fact, Italians on the whole seemed a lot less offended by what Emeline referred to as my "temper tantrums." I preferred to call them expressions of moral indignation. In any case, the last time we'd argued publicly I'd used a fork to illustrate my point and, rather than calling the police, I was pretty sure the waitress just tipped the bottle a little more heavily when pouring my second glass of wine.

"You're absolutely right, Rhea." For a brief but blessed moment, I thought Emeline had seen reason. "Shall we call the *polizia* and report that some monster, some dreadful villain had the audacity to buy us plane tickets to Italy?"

I waved my hand at the waitress. There was a tempest in Emeline's eyes—the eyes she'd somehow inherited from the women of our family, despite the fact that she was as much a reincarnated imposter as me—and I knew from the incidents that passed for high tragedy in our household, namely lost volleyball matches and poor test scores, that the spark in those eyes indicated everyone nearby ought to take cover. I did not come all the way to Italy to get bludgeoned by my little sister. I could just as easily have accomplished that in New Jersey without the discomfort of a 14-hour plane flight.

"But why leave it at that?" she continued. "Let's find someone who can sympathize with your plight! Does anyone have a phonebook? We need to call some poor people to help my sister throw a pity party. *Scusi!*"

Emeline managed to catch our waiter's eye, but before she could ask him to recommend a local calligrapher to help write out the invitations, I gestured enthusiastically for wine. Emeline could rant us all the way back to Basilio's creepy den if I could just have one glass of Prosecco.

Bacchus bless the waiters of the world who give us the strength to endure our nagging younger sisters and uncles who overstep their rightful boundaries.

"No, Rhea. You're right. A fictional character in a novel written a century and a half ago might tolerate this sort of heavy-handed behavior, but you will not!"

The wine sparkled and snapped, much like Emeline's eyes, but its sweetness tempered the bitter truth that we were to return to Rome the next day.

Suddenly Emeline was laughing her full, deep gust of a laugh that always took people by surprise. I'd known Emeline across two lifetimes, but I still didn't have any idea what made her laugh. How she could transition from full-on rant to delighted hysteria in the space of two sips of Prosecco. My sense of humor was dry, much like my father's on my past life side. Much like the wine balanced on the back of my tongue.

But nothing like the sacrificial wine we drank the night we danced and imbibed to honor *Bona Dea*, the Good Goddess. The night honorable matrons and pious virgins alike cried, "*Non sum qualis eram!*"

Nobody dances sober.

VI

That was the night I met Nesreen. Inebriated, adorned with an impudent wreath of vines and flowers. Over the slaughter of a sow.

Some things are just meant to be. We might not will it, but the gods do.

We celebrated Bona Dea twice a year: the first time in Maius at her temple on Aventine Hill, and the second in December at the house of the senior magistrate. Of course, the magistrate could not be present for any of the festivities. Bona Dea was a night for the women of Rome only—the two lone evenings in the entire year when we were permitted to drink and offer blood sacrifice. Severina, honorable wife of Consul Dulius Silanus, acted as host. But, really, it was a night for the vestal virgins to shine.

We scoured the house of all masculine presence—every male, whether human or animal, was forced to leave for the night. Fulvia, our Virgo Vestalis Maxima, even ordered us to remove all portraits of the magistrate's male relatives. It wasn't so terribly different from the way I lived, shuttered away from the polluting influence of the masculine gaze and presence. But I took special care on that evening. It was my first Bona Dea, and Fulvia reminded us all, in the sanctuary of Vesta's temple, that this was the only night of the year our sisters of Rome had the honor of serving as priestesses on the empire's behalf. And there were members of the Senate—conservative alarmists who doubted the moral strength and intellect of my sex—who believed the sacred worship of the good goddess had been transformed into a tawdry excuse for the women of Rome to drink and carouse.

They cited the occasion when Publicus Clodius Pulcher disguised himself as a woman and snuck into the festivities, intent on seducing Pompeia, who was both the hostess of the evening and Julius Caesar's wife. Publicus was discovered before he could commit any harm graver than rendering the sacred ceremony profane, thus requiring the vestal virgins in attendance to repeat the rituals. But Julius Caesar divorced Pompeia under the logic that his wife must be better than blameless; she must be above suspicion and gossip.

More than two centuries had passed since Publicus' adventures in cross-dressing, and we were still enduring the consequences. But Fulvia was highly creative and not easily deceived: No man would cross the threshold of the magistrate's house on that night. Everything would be perfect.

Bona Dea—her statue, at least—reclined on a couch with a banquet table before her and serpents at her feet.

The house was essentially one giant bouquet, endless garlands of vines and flowers extending to the wreaths encircling the crowns of the evening's honored guests. No myrtle, of course, on account of the fact that Faunus had thrashed Bona Dea to death with a rod of myrtle after finding her drunk on wine. There was to be no mention of the word, and I could sympathize with the goddess' antipathy toward the instrument of her death—though not half so well as I would in six month's time.

We had a vessel at the center of the room filled with the evening's "milk;" the word wine was forbidden, even if the actual beverage was not.

And there was a sow waiting in an adjacent room.

Fortunately, she did not seem to realize that she was to play a central role in the sacrificial segment of the festivities.

The moon retreated from Rome that night, and hung obscure and distant. It was easy to believe the sun would never rise again, and—with the "milk" flowing freely and practiced fingers coaxing magic from the lyres and shepherd's pipes— easy not to care.

I was careful not to overindulge in Bona Dea's milk. Already, Bruttia Crispina was behaving as though her odds of remembering the night's festivities were low. But she was there, and would likely relish the opportunity to denounce a member of the House of Vesta. If Caesar's wife must be above suspicion, a vestal virgin must not set foot within a mile of it.

But the cloying fetor of flowers and blood was having much the same effect as the milk continually replenishing the vessel in the middle of the room. My cheeks were hot, as if with fever, my palms damp with a sweat that discredited my station, and my head both clouded and confused. Caecilia swept by with a cup in her hand, golden hair whipping rebelliously with each turn, but a militant, alert look in her eye. Caecilia understood that a ceremony, even a religious one, was really just a show. We always had eyes on us—especially Caecilia, with her full, stunning face and quick mouth—and she would not be found wanting.

A tangled knot of women, their wreaths brushing one another and snaring, paid thorough homage to the pitcher of milk, neither abandoning it nor suffering revelers who fell within its orbit to depart without paying tribute. The color and motion just served to confound my head, which had begun a desperate pounding. I could not bear to look at them for long, and I especially could not allow my thoughts to linger on the libation that fed and sustained their frenzy. My stomach would not allow it.

I sought out a skylight at the opposite end of the room, beyond a series of pillars that obscured my view of Bona Dea's sober faction—at least, certainly more sober than those who opted to camp mere feet from the distinguished pitcher.

Maximiliana hovered near the first of the pillars, looking as though she would have liked to move nearer to the wine. Twice I saw her step forward with a determined expression, but then her eyes darted around the room to where Fulvia stood addressing a circle of senators' wives, and she retreated back to her pillar. It was her first Bona Dea as well, and we were all having a difficult time adjusting to the fact that indulgences previously forbidden to us were now encouraged.

I wanted to talk to her, and would have, but before I could reach her I realized what was happening beyond the pillars, and I could not make myself care about talking to Maximiliana after that.

She was there: the woman from the Coliseum, who had so immediately captured my attention and imagination. She might have been there all night, for all I knew, and simply did not recognize me with a crown of flowers on my head and hair flowing freely about my shoulders. Or she had recognized me and did not find me interesting enough to address.

I did not understand why women swarmed her, their bright eyes determined and a little bit desperate. I did not understand, because a vestal virgin was not expected to have any understanding of, or need for, silphium, the plant we imported from the gladiator's native country. Rome had recently suffered the pangs of a silphium shortage, something about overharvesting and possible extinction, but what that meant for the women of my country was utterly lost to me.

I could only see a mob of patrician women hanging on the words of a slave as though they were honey. If I was brutally honest—which only a fool or an emperor can afford to be—I wanted to be among them, chief among them, the only among them. Which perhaps doesn't make a great deal of sense, but the pain in my head strangled my last reserve of logic, and I could not reconcile the presence of a gladiator at Bona Dea, much less the sight of the sister of the emperor's favorite mistress clutching her arm and softening her lips in what was supposed to be a beguiling smile.

There was nothing wrong with Arvina, technically

speaking. But there was nothing right about her either. She was a thickset woman with uncomprehending green eyes and hair that couldn't decide if it was blonde or brown. She had a habit of being sly in her interactions with people, but always in a harried manner, as though afraid she would be caught behaving improperly. Also, I had noticed that she smacked her lips, which did not indicate any moral deficiency or physical flaw, but I found it annoying nonetheless.

Her sister Marcia had the same green eyes, which were rather stunning, actually. At least Commodus seemed to think so, because Marcia had been his mistress for several years, and she'd been given the final say in more than one execution. Most importantly, Marcia was a Christian, and therefore one of the dangerous elements who might one day make or raise an attempt on the eternal flame I was sworn to protect. Arvina did not share her sister's religious persuasion, else she would not be present at a polytheistic ceremony. I also doubted Marcia would approve of her widowed sister pawing the gladiator like some animal from the Coliseum.

For the briefest of moments, I was disgusted with the entire affair and wished the conservative senators had voiced their opinions on Bona Dea with more potency. Of course, the shame that followed this self-indulgence was so overwhelming that it almost knocked me to the floor. Even then, I knew I could not excise all human failings. So long as I drew breath, I was flawed, and so were Fulvia and Maximiliana and Caecilia and Nona. Our gods were jealous, and so were we. But wanting to deprive my sisters of their only night of worship and celebration because I had succumbed to an errant fancy was a low I had never before experienced.

If I could just bathe my face in the fresh air exposed by the skylight, I could cool my head—and hopefully the thoughts within it. A painting of Diana guarded the aperture, and though naked with the exception of the crescent moon that graced her brow, her arrow was nocked, with two careful fingers drawing tension in the bow. I could not see her enemy—she reclined behind a rock, and gazed expectantly outward to some point beyond the wall—but I wondered whether the goddess herself knew what she hunted, and why.

Sacrilegious thoughts from a virgin priestess! What would I do next, use the wrong kind of wheat when preparing the mola salsa? I longed for my bed and fire, and wished I had volunteered to remain behind at the temple with Septima.

I believed myself alone until a phantom hand tilted my wreath, and I had to free my own clasped hands to restrain it. Diana aimed her bow in the direction of my assailant, and I turned to discover the gladiator's impudent, happy face. She reached out a hand—the color of coriander, but infinitely richer, softer—and dismembered a floral plait that linked the entrance of the room to a statue of Mercury adorned with no fewer than three sets of wings.

"These should be yours." Her voice had a lilt that would have placed her origin outside of Rome, even if I hadn't seen her brandishing the Cyrenian shield at the venatio. But there was nothing labored or slow in her words, and I found myself wondering whether she'd learned to speak Latin before she left her home. If she had, it would place her as someone from a wellborn family, raising all sorts of questions about the circumstances that found her hunting wild animals in the Coliseum in Rome.

She'd selected a gladiolus. They came in yellow and pink, and white trimmed with yellow and bashful pink. But she ignored these, choosing a long stalk with lusty incarnadine blooms. I should have known.

Without asking my permission, she slid the stem of the flower through my wreath, gazing at her handiwork with intent brown eyes. She ruffled my hair repeatedly with her ministrations, and a petal brushed the tip of my ear.

No one touched me without first asking my permission. But mostly, no one touched me.

"Thank you." I didn't often get to thank people. The servants didn't expect to be thanked, and didn't much appreciate it, and there was never any cause to thank the other vestals when we were all just doing a service we had sworn an oath to perform. Ours wasn't a society constructed on frivolities like the will of the individual, and there's no call to applaud a person's actions when they're merely following a script written out for them by one million Romans.

She smiled and made no reply, but I caught her eyeing the garland framing the portrait of Diana and knew that if I did not distract her, there was a reasonable chance my head would soon resemble a hedge. And I feared that if I were forced to endure the amount of physical contact that would require, I would collapse to the ground, forever shaming myself in the eyes of the two huntresses now watching me. Diana still marked her prey, but her form invoked courage in all maidens by virtue of her fine example.

"*Salve.*" I clasped the gladiator's right hand with my own, a gesture that brought our arms together from wrist to elbow. A far more appropriate greeting than twining flowers in one another's hair.

"They suit you," she replied, gesturing to the gladiolus she'd placed in my hair. "I saw you at the Coliseum."

"I am impressed that you managed to take note of anything with a pair of leopards stalking you," I replied lightly, hating myself when she frowned in displeasure at my response. This exchange was harder than I had thought it would be.

I thought I had a solid understanding of the world, grounded in the finest education that could be made available to a young Roman woman. But when this gladiator spoke, a new world of possibility and fear opened to me.

"You seem to have a following." I tried again, gesturing at the women I wished didn't exist, now circulating nearer the wine. I was capable of summoning an awful stare, comprised of disdain, authority, superiority, and threat in equal measure. And I would happily employ this skill to repel any of them, should they decide to return.

"I do not think so," she said thoughtfully. "They are not interested in the Coliseum. They want to know if I can help them obtain silphium."

"Can you?" I did not reveal that this was the first I had

heard of the plant. I mostly just wanted to keep her talking for as long as possible.

"Possibly. The captain who brought me here … . But you are not in need of silphium—" She appeared confounded, as if suddenly realizing that contrary to the messages from her primitive subconscious, insisting that she knew me, that she'd always known me, she did not know my name. And I realized that I was in the same predicament.

"Rhea."

She did not smile as most people do when introducing themselves to someone new. Instead, her face took on an intensity that many women in Servina's house that night would have read as anger. But I had never been the sort of person who confuses fervor with madness, fire with peril. In fact, it had always been the absence of passion that frightened me the most, possibly because I had come to associate extinguished flames with a long and painful beating at the hands of a mad emperor.

"I am called Nesreen."

I hoped she was saying it didn't matter that we hadn't possessed that information about one another, that what they called her and who she was were not necessarily one and the same. There were more important things to know and understand about her, and these things could not be shared in a single word.

But it was possible that she was just telling me her name. It was also possible that she'd just approached me because she knew a vestal virgin was a guaranteed refuge from the deluge of questions and demands about a plant used as a deterrent against that most desired and undesired condition among women.

Silence. Seconds of it. Hours. Centuries, even. I might be exaggerating, but what is the harm if the dampening effects of seconds of silence are the same as though they had in fact stretched into months or eons or centuries? I began to catalogue my deficiencies as the moments stretched by, certain that my thoughts were so loud that Nesreen could hear each and every one of them.

At any moment she would walk away. I wanted to stop—desperately, in fact. But my mind—which heretofore had been my greatest weapon and ally, the source of my keenest pleasures and pride—was not my own.

"Would you like some wine?" She had turned bravely toward the urn at the other end of the room.

"You must not call it that!" Suddenly, I was no longer a 17-year-old girl battling an onslaught of hormones and impulses that violated the terms of my marriage to the world's greatest empire. I was a priestess. And I had just grabbed a gladiator's arm, just below the shoulder, without considering the possible consequences.

Now she smiled. "But that is what it is."

"Tonight it is milk." I maintained my grip on her arm.

"Just for tonight?"

"Just for tonight."

"But on the other nights, I would have spoken correctly?"

"Yes. But on other nights, it would have been forbidden us, and you could not have offered it."

She nodded, and I suspected this had already been explained to her. I let go of her arm.

"I was not making fun of your festival."

On the one hand, I did not believe her. But on the other, I knew it was not her fault that Roman women were not allowed to drink wine. And that using the word was dangerous because it reminded men that they were uncomfortable with women drinking.

I had to wonder what the gladiator's true feelings were. About me. About Rome. But mostly about Rome, because she could not truly care for me if she despised Rome.

Nesreen was not Roman, but she was forced to risk her life for the entertainment of its citizens. And I still did not understand how she had wound up there. We stared at each other, as I tried to assess how much damage she could accomplish, and she—well, all I could do was project my own emotions and hopes and pretend I knew what she was looking for in me.

A cool hand grasped mine.

"Rhea, it is time to leave." The voice was Vibiana's, but the girl holding my hand had rich brown hair that stretched to the small of her back, and her face was flushed with milk. I wondered whether I was not perhaps in some sort of trouble for talking with the gladiator, for touching her arm, but Vibiana's hazel eyes were guileless and content.

"Fulvia has been chatting up Arvina for information about Marcia. She realized we should not have left Septima alone at the temple. There is a *carpentum* outside, and a *lictor* to accompany us."

I was not sure why Vibiana felt it was necessary to mention the carpentum. We never traveled in anything else, and were always attended by a lictor. But she seemed anxious to assure me that everything was proper, and I attributed her interest in excessive details to the milk I had seen her consume that night.

I turned to leave—both regretful and relieved. But Vibiana was not finished, apparently.

"You are the gladiator from the Cyrenian venatio! You were superb. Deft. Courageous. Your timing when you dispatched those leopards—" Vibiana paused, overcome by the memory, and I hoped she had exhausted herself. The Virgo Vestalis Maxima was talking with Severina, but I felt her gaze on us. On Vibiana, actually. I relaxed. Vibiana was drunk, and Fulvia trusted me to take her home. I was not in trouble.

"That was your first hunt, was it not?" Vibiana was staring at Nesreen with big hazel eyes filled with admiration. The gladiator was looking at Vibiana with a mixture of wariness and guarded amusement.

"We have to go," I said. "Septima is alone at the temple." I could not bear to see Nesreen look at Vibiana as she had been looking at me before Vibiana arrived. Neither could I stand to see a sister priestess treated with anything less than perfect respect. That left very little territory I considered safe, so I gently turned her toward the entrance.

"*Vale*," I said to Nesreen, because I could not make myself depart without saying anything at all.

"You must come to the house," Vibiana said, over her shoulder. "We would like to hear more of your exploits, and we have never had a gladiator come to visit us at the house before."

Against my better judgment, I, too, looked over my shoulder to see Nesreen's reaction to this offer.

"I will." She was looking not at Vibiana, but at me, as she said it.

*   *   *

The motion of the train lulled me into an agitated rage nap, which was my body's rather ingenious solution to the fact that I often couldn't risk sounding my every emotion as so many of my peers had the luxury of doing. Of course, this had also resulted in Abri consulting a nutritionist and purchasing protein shakes to combat my flagging stores of energy.

I didn't need energy. I needed a cork to stopper my anger. But I wasn't alone in this. I'd observed that the most wrathful beings I knew—specifically, domestic cats—were also the sleepiest. Imagine the extent of the carnage if they weren't unconscious 20 hours of each day! Of course, I also could have done with one fewer sister and uncle. Maybe that was the real reason I slept so often: too many relatives. Emeline accused me of trying to hibernate through this second life. There may have been some truth to that.

I awoke with half an hour left in our trip.

The train was nearly empty, and Emeline occupied the seat ahead of mine. Her dark head was bent over a notebook, and she was talking to herself, which was a very unEmeline thing to do. If her social success in high school indicated anything, it was that my little sister knew how to attract attention for the right reasons. Talking to one's self is never an appropriate means of attracting attention. Then again, not all crazy people are created equal.

Emeline was wearing her high-rise white pleated shorts—the ones that flared upward like the edges of a petal on the sides, exposing more thigh than anyone properly needed to—with a sleek black vest trimmed in vegan leather at the shoulders and lace-up caged sandals in a color Emeline insisted on calling "cobra gold." She probably could wear a tinfoil hat and loudly proclaim herself Grand Chief Hoopla and Fecal Exterminator of the House of Alien Overlords and no one would think to strap her into a straightjacket.

Because most people would never believe that young, vivacious, pretty teenagers like Emeline have mental problems. They can't. They're too busy getting dressed to accomplish much of anything else, including going insane.

Emeline sighed and cursed, slamming the notebook she'd been reading and consulting her travel guide. The discarded volume had a warm leather cover embossed with a statue of a bearded man who wore only a cloak and shield, hefting a spear in his right hand. There was something familiar about him, but I couldn't … . Emeline shifted her knees and the book tipped backward, exposing the text at the bottom.

"*Aut cum scuto aut in scuto.*" The script was matter of fact, much like the sentiment it expressed.

Either with shield or on shield.

Suddenly, I recognized the face on the cover.

"Is that Mars?" I reached forward for a closer look at the journal.

"Look with your eyes, not your hands." But she shifted the journal to her other hand and tucked it under her arm, preventing me from doing either. She sounded breathless, startled.

"Are you in some kind of weird cult to the god of war? 'Cause that's just what we need." I was mostly joking.

"Relax, Rhea. It's just a journal."

"Why can't I see this 'just a journal?'"

"Because it's private."

Emeline rifled importantly through her purse and

withdrew a vibrant red lipstick, the kind worn by pinups with their hair in roll ups, that trailed insurgent streaks in its wake— that scared the hell out of me. But she kept the journal out of my view the entire time.

"C'mon, Em, I'm way past caring about your latest crush."

I finally noticed the other books scattered across the seat next to her: an Italian-English dictionary and a handful of travel books, most of them boasting an image of the Coliseum, although I thought I saw the leaning tower of Pisa tilting determinedly in the left corner of one text.

"I agree with you. I'd say we're well past that."

She set her lipstick aside and was now smoothing her hair and skirt.

"Em, why does your journal say 'Aut cum scuto aut in scuto?'" I lowered my voice even though we were the car's sole occupants. When it came to ancient Rome, even the poster advertising *Don Pasquale* near the lavatory had ears.

Emeline smiled the predatory smile of a woman with red lips. She looked so much like a grown-up—not a little woman, but a proper adult one—that my heart ached for lost time. Some part of me had refused to recognize that the volleyball camps and dances and studying for Italian midterms she'd busied herself with were all actually subordinate to her real task: growing up, and leaving.

"I also considered *Mea navis aëricumbens anguillis abundant*," she added with a sly tone, and I barked out a laugh before I could stop myself.

"My hovercraft is full of eels?" I faintly recalled my confusion when a rerun of the *Monty Python* sketch aired on television and I couldn't understand any of what was being said.

"Yup. You were the one who explained that phrase to me. Aut cum scuto aut in scuto. I'd gotten in a fight with that boy. The nasty, mean one—what was his name? Well, he would come to our house, and we were always worried father would let his parents draw a marriage contract with one of us.

And the boy—I think I actually repressed his name, of all things!—told me he was going to marry me. I said he wouldn't, and he said he would. So I hit him. And he pushed me back, and soon we were rolling on the floor trading blows until he said we should stop because it would upset our parents to see us fighting.

"Then you came out from behind the couch where you'd been watching. You came out and you said, very, very seriously, 'Aemilia, when you fight, you don't stop just because your enemy asks nicely. You fight, and you only stop fighting when either your enemy is defeated or you are.' And then you explained that when the Spartan sons would go off to war, their mothers would part with them using that phrase. Because if a Spartan soldier died, he would be born home on his shield. And if he didn't, he would return home victoriously, carrying it. And that was how I wanted to fight after that, even though I never thought I'd be part of any battle of any consequence. You were the only one who thought it was important to make sure I knew how to fight."

She was Aemilia to me, once more, even though I only vaguely remembered the incident. I couldn't have been more than 6 if I was living at home, which would have made my scrappy little sister about 4.

"And you just really, really like that phrase and decided to put it on your diary?"

"It's not a diary," Aemilia replied haughtily. "It's more like a blueprint. And I thought it would be good to remember that sentiment, although I suppose in our case, we're either returning home with our luggage or in it."

"Quite a macabre sentiment for a 16-year-old on summer vacation."

"I didn't come here to gawk at the ruins any more than you did. I mean, I wouldn't have minded the opportunity. I actually would have probably enjoyed it. A lot. Italian boys. Some ancient ruins … ." Her thoughts seemed to be getting away from her, and she shook her head.

"But that's not what this is. This is a campaign. And

I've been preparing for it for the last six months."

She withdrew the journal and flipped it open to a random page. Aemilia, Decima, Hortensia, Junia, Liviana— they were all there, and plenty of others besides. Even Commodus and Bruttia and Severina. Everyone we'd had any contact with in our past life, along with a catalog of identifying features. I looked for Nesreen's name, but it was absent. Either my little sister did not know it, or she respected my privacy too much to commit that name to paper. Valens was there, along with a lengthier and more intimate account than the rest of the suspects had been dubiously awarded.

"Are these suspects?" I wasn't asking Aemilia, or myself for that matter, but the universe. As was almost always the case, the universe failed to respond. It was worth a shot, though.

"Yes," my sister answered. "We can't afford to think otherwise. And we're going to be very thorough before anyone leaves this list."

Aemilia swallowed hard, and in that moment her blue eyes were as stalwart as any Spartan shield.

"Even Valens." She held my gaze. "So. We started at the Vatican because I figured that was the most obvious place for them to be. Next on the list are the Pantheon, the Temple and House of Vesta, and the Coliseum. I know the Coliseum isn't as likely as the others, but there's no harm in being thorough. You're not Rhea Artuso on this trip. You're Rhea Equitia, daughter of Aetius and Quinta, and we will draw your enemies out from their musty dens and hideaways, and we will deal with them. And when we're done and we go home, you'll be free to be whichever Rhea you want, all the time. You might even get a date."

"But you made such a stink about my behavior at the Vatican!" My mind could only process so much.

Emeline was kind of a grown-up.

Emeline was Aemilia right now.

Emeline-Aemilia was kind of a badass, more than a little bit crazy, and apparently on a mission to get me killed in

Rome. Or both of us. Who knew how this would play out?

"I knew you'd do it anyway, and it would be weird if I didn't react at all," she said. "Besides, you really were being a brat, and not for the right reasons."

"So even when I behave exactly the way you want me to behave, I'm still a brat? I can't win." I tossed my hands in the air in feigned annoyance. Feigned because the truth was that if Aemilia was difficult to please, I was impossible. Nothing short of a Cyrenian gladiator who had been dead for nearly 2,000 years could put a genuine smile on my face. And with that depressing thought, I silenced the impish Rhea who sat comfortably in my head and who offered a running commentary on everything that happened, unasked.

"I've actually been trying to figure out when to tell you." Aemilia had zipped open her suitcase and was now stacking its contents on one of the seats in full view of anyone. Clearly, we were on red alert.

A pair of polka dot underwear with blue lace trim made its way to the top of the pile.

Followed by something miniscule in a truculent shade of red.

Before I could pester Aemilia about the all-too-public undergarment shower, a boot struck me in the forehead. Or rather, I'd thought it was a boot, but it turned out to be a finely crafted gladiator sandal with laces that ran from the toe to just below the kneecap. And heels.

"Aemilia, these are the most extravagant shoes I've ever seen. They either belong in the Coliseum or some gin joint on the western frontier. Maybe both. How did you afford them?"

I pretended I was asking out of curiosity, even though I knew Fedele couldn't resist giving Aemilia anything she asked for. I suppose I was just jealous. Which was new. I'd been envious of her popularity and rapport with our parents, but never bothered by her extensive closet. It was the old Aemilia I had envied, the Aemilia with freedom to wear whatever she wanted—rich, beautiful color—while I was confined to the same virginal vestment.

"Four months' allowance, and worth every penny," Aemilia said from her position on the floor of the train. "Dad pitched in a little."

Regretfully, I handed them back. Or tried to.

"They're yours," Aemilia said, still absorbed in whatever she was doing with her luggage. "Your graduation gift from me. And your next couple birthday and Christmas gifts. Which you will totally be around for, since we're going to figure out whether anyone from the past truly is hunting you and send them to the underworld in the care of *Dis pater* and Prosperina." I couldn't help but marvel at my sister's interpretation of sweet 16—dealing out high-fashion footwear and death sentences in the care of archaic Roman deities. But that didn't change the fact that I was 18, and had never felt myself to be anything approximating sweet.

"Aemilia, I'd never wear these."

"No, but the Rhea who wanted to attract all kinds of attention would. The Rhea who flipped the bird at Roman conventions and binding oaths for a night of … *stuff* would."

"That Rhea got me killed," I pointed out reasonably.

"True," Aemilia conceded. "But she also got you a coveted role as a high priestess of Rome *and* a gladiator hottie."

Also true.

"I just think *that* Rhea stands a better chance of getting your enemies—whoever and wherever they are—to expose themselves. And that Rhea stands a much better chance of, you know, kicking their—"

"Asses. I know."

"Plus you'd look insanely hot in these. Your feet probably won't be thanking you, but the young men in Rome will. Women, too."

Maybe she knew more about Nesreen's identity than she'd let on.

"Alright. I'll keep them. Not because they're gorgeous and I want to."

"But totally because they're gorgeous and you want to,

right?" Aemilia asked with her sly smile. And, for once, I offered a sly smile of my own in return.

"You know, I didn't really realize it until I started planning this campaign, but we don't really need to do much with your clothes. Those dresses of yours are already a pretty good approximation of your stola—stylistically, at least: the looser draping, the clever twists of fabric."

The revelation that my dull, white weeds might have influenced my present-day finery was decidedly unpleasant, but before I could disagree, she surprised me further.

"I've also been feeling kind of bad for giving you such a hard time about your clothes," she said. "They always looked so boring, but I noticed, on this trip, that they're actually rather sophisticated. They just didn't look right back home, in school, or, well, anywhere we went back home."

"So how much progress have we made?" I asked, gesturing toward the notebook. "Is there anyone we can cross off the list?"

"Maybe. If Adam turns out to be … you know."

She must really have missed Valens.

"I think our next stop will be the Coliseum. Also, I've been thinking: It really is weird that you were Rhea then, and you're Rhea now. It's true that there's not a lot of distinction between Aemilia and Emeline, but there is a difference. It just doesn't seem like a coincidence. Where did your name come from? Did Mom ever tell you?"

"I don't know." Now that she'd said something, it was the most obvious thing in the world, but it felt so natural to be called Rhea, so right, that I'd never questioned it. "I never thought about it. No."

"It might be useful to know. I mean, I find it hard to believe Mom and Dad randomly chose it. And it's not all that common. Maybe we can trace the origin of the name to someone who might know who you are."

I nodded my agreement and resolved to ask Abri the next time we spoke on the phone, which would likely be within the week.

The train started to slow, and a synthetic woman's voice informed us we were approaching *Roma*.

Aemilia hefted her suitcase—once more glutted with an abundance of clothes and footwear—toward the exit, then swung jauntily to face me.

"You and me against the world, Rhea. Personally, I don't think the world stands much of a chance."

*   *   *

I dreamed of her. She was a hawk circling the sky of a country I did not recognize. She was the leopard she had killed, and I was its mate. She was death—inevitable, seductive, omnipresent—and I was everything but myself.

VII

Basilio was waiting for us at the Roma Termini station, sitting patiently in a sleek, black car and reading a Stephen King novel. I wasn't sufficiently familiar with the author's oeuvre to determine whether it was his most recent work, but it was a hardcover, and Basilio's posture seemed unnaturally relaxed for a man reading a horror story.

Emeline—she was almost always Emeline in our uncle's presence—shot me an apologetic glance and muttered something about telling Basilio which train we'd be on last night on the phone. More plans I'd not been privy to.

"Zio!" Emeline smiled fondly as Basilio got out of the car to heft her luggage into the trunk and wave her into the back seat. For me, he opened the passenger door with a genial smile. I made a conscious decision to set aside my discomfort with his heavy-handed behavior and respond graciously to his overtures. I planted a firm smile on my lips and told myself that non-threatening facial expressions were supposed to feel stiff. Step two was a friendly wave—nothing that would have won any prizes in a beauty pageant, but the best I could muster without any advanced notice that I would be starring in the role of well-adjusted, extroverted, and not-at-all-reincarnated teenaged niece.

"How did you find Bracciano?" he asked as we pulled away from the station—and my hopes of escaping Rome for a few extra days.

I bit back several retorts, recognizing that they were ungrateful and that it wasn't fair for me to verbally abuse my uncle on mere instinct. But fighting the impulse to insult Basilio was not the same as stemming the suffocating silence that filled the car. It's important to bear in mind that I was not the sort of person to use the word "suffocating" with the casual disregard many people display toward the proper meaning of things. I fully comprehend the meaning. I had lived it, after all.

The air actually felt thicker in Basilio's presence. I had to work that much harder to dredge oxygen into my lungs, and once I had it there, I was never terribly convinced that it was doing whatever it was supposed to be doing. Was I exhaling the right quantities of carbon dioxide and circulating sufficient oxygen through my bloodstream? Couldn't insufficient oxygen levels account for my inability to think clearly in his presence? And what about the fact that the world tilted just a fraction to the left, forcing me to renegotiate even the most natural gestures and movements?

My nose was off-kilter, too. The world gave off the same fragrances—I was awash in dank, aromatic waves; tumbled by rancid citrus tornadoes; and hounded by an army of ramekins proselytizing the merits of sickly sweet burnt sugar (the smell of burnt anything always managed to make me feel crazy, as if an entire metropolis was ablaze, and I had lit the match)—but it was as if they all wore a cloak when he was around. And even though I'd always considered my overachieving nose something of an inconvenience, I felt bereft without its superpowers.

Without caring what I was saying, without carefully editing my every thought, I began to chatter to chase away the silence. I occasionally caught Emeline's stunned expression in the rearview mirror and laughed, without bothering to explain why. I could be insincere. I could discourse on subjects that didn't really interest me about matters on which I held no opinion. Emeline's agitation made no sense. Hadn't she wanted me to be "normal" all along?

Ilium looked almost normal, too, now that I was bracing myself for the appearance of a contemporary cave. At least I could now appreciate the way the house borrowed its color from the sun, glowing like an egg in its final stages of gestation.

Emeline was out of the car before we had time to come to a complete stop, and she hurried inside without looking back.

"It looks lovely," I said softly, and I caught Basilio's surprised expression as he made his way to the trunk to collect our luggage.

I'd expected that Emeline would not surface until dinner, and possibly not even then, so I was surprised to find her standing perfectly still in the entryway. I gave her a gentle push forward, but she would not budge. Could not, in fact. Basilio was behind us, hovering in the doorway, and I looked beyond her shoulder in an attempt to discover the source of her paralysis.

Standing squarely in the shadows, to the right of the couch, was a slender man of indeterminate height—the scale of the ceiling tended to skew my sense of proportion. There was a familiar air about him, not in his features, which could not be quickly deciphered at the opposite end of a large room, but in the open, friendly expression he directed toward Emeline.

"Adam!" Emeline announced. "Here!"

I spun toward the door at the same moment Emeline took an aggressive step toward him.

"Adam? What are you doing here?" I asked. "What is he doing here?"

Basilio blocked the exit—whether by accident or intent, I couldn't say.

"Emeline! Rhea!" Adam smiled broadly, appearing

neither guilty nor surprised to see us. And it had to be one or the other. Didn't it? Emeline gave me a look that was utterly bewildered, and I could see she was working through the same thought process.

"Wait a minute ... your accent!" I said.

"It's different!" Emeline accused. "You were Australian before!"

"Who are you?" I demanded, and now I, too, was advancing toward him. I was well aware that my moral high ground was rocky at best and incapable of bearing the weight of a hummingbird at worst. He had lied to us about who he really was, but I had been lying to my family about my identity for my entire life. Still, the only other person who knew that was Emeline, and it didn't seem very likely that she'd throw my own falsehoods back in my face. Not right now, at least. Unless he did some kind of smoldering thing with his eyes.

Basilio was apparently satisfied that we would not attempt to escape—or at least, less concerned about an escape attempt than a hostage situation in his living room. He shuffled past us, enjoining us loudly, and with a great deal of hand waving (considering that he was still carrying Emeline's luggage) to remain calm.

"Adamo and I can explain."

"Adamo? So he's Italian?" I was not impressed, but Emeline's expression was just the slightest bit less militant.

"Yes, of course. Adamo is from Rome, and he's been working for me for about nine months now. He really has an extraordinary understanding for how to care for a house as unique and alive as Ilium." Basilio beamed at Adamo. The warm smile became a gesture toward the luggage, and Adamo hurried forward to collect our bags, disappearing with them before I could protest that I wasn't even sure I wanted to stay.

"That's nice for the house," Emeline said, patting the nearest wall to show she really did care. "But that doesn't explain why he lied to us."

"Or what he was doing at the hostel in the first place," I pointed out.

"I felt bad that I was out of town when you arrived and asked Adamo to keep an eye on you until I returned. I have no idea where he got it into his head to adopt an accent and pretend to be Adam from Australia, but I imagine he thought it would be fun to pretend to be someone else. He was in the theater company at his school, you know, and was actually very good. Excellent diction." Basilio spoke with an authoritative air that made me feel I had to ask his permission in order to disagree with him. And why would I disagree, anyway, when he was being so very reasonable? Wouldn't it be simpler for everyone if we stopped being so paranoid?

Centuries ago, on the day of our second kiss, Nesreen told me never to trust anyone who tried to make me doubt my instincts. Basilio had always made me feel like a lunatic. I'd dismissed it at first, his habit of interacting with me as though I were a caged animal that required civilizing, that might lunge and snarl at the slightest provocation—or none at all. But then I remembered Nesreen's watchful eyes, gazing thoughtfully around the corner at a passing servant. Those were careful times, and we were jealous of every moment of contact, even the first, when you're supposed to lose yourself.

"Always trust yourself," she'd whispered to me, without a trace of a smile on the mouth I'd just tasted for only the second time. "Trust yourself, and we may survive this. Loan out your confidence lightly and lose everything."

Despite the perils of our relationship, those were the only words of warning she ever spoke to me. And I was grateful for that. I don't think I would have held her in such high esteem if she had doled out pragmatic admonitions as haphazardly as some young lovers dispense jewelry and flowers.

"Rhea!"

Emeline was now standing on the opposite end of the room, next to Adamo, who had apparently settled our luggage while I was reliving youthful indiscretions from my past life. She had her left arm wrapped around his, and in her right carried her purse and jacket. Sadly, it did not look like a hostage situation. Emeline didn't even have the good sense to be taken hostage. She'd willingly go clubbing with her captor.

Adamo and Emeline. Adamo and Aemilia. Adam and Emeline. Adam and Aemilia. I had to shake my head, which felt like a blue balloon with too much pressure. The one from my graduation, that threatened to get away from us in the car, but then spent the next two weeks at home swaying listlessly in a corner of the living room, dizzy and defeated.

"It's okay, Rhea." Emeline spent half an hour in the car with our uncle, and suddenly she sounded just like him. "Adamo was just playing a practical joke. He knew we'd find out."

They were shuffling toward me. Toward the door.

"Don't worry," she whispered to me. "I'll keep an eye on him."

I remembered our secret campaign. Aut cum scuto aut in scuto. I would just have to trust that she really meant it, and that I could count on Emeline the way I could count on Aemilia.

That left Basilio and me alone, eyeing each other warily in the cavern known as Ilium.

Correction: I had every reason to believe my own expression betrayed my fear and mistrust, but Basilio's face was, as always, that of a man trying to diffuse a situation. Or that of a man telling the world he wanted to diffuse a situation while what he really yearned for was complete control.

We got along well enough at first. He diced and chopped vegetables while I nervously regaled him with stories of Abri's kitchen misadventures—Fedele being by far the better cook of the two. I was careful to refer to them as Mom and Dad, and Basilio seemed thoroughly entertained by his little sister's culinary clumsiness. He was the most Italian I'd ever seen him, and the more Italian—and less like a member of my family—he became, the better I liked him.

I knew enough about normal to understand that there was nothing original in that. No one wants to feel pressured into understanding someone else simply because a higher percentage of their DNA happens to correspond. So I would feel much better about bonding with Basilio if I could forget that he was Abri's brother—the man who'd tricked me into betraying that damned, revealing "papilio" all those years ago.

Perhaps my luck was changing. I ran to the guestroom to fetch some family photos from my luggage. The purse with my passport carrier and travel documents was resting on the dresser nearest the bed, and I didn't even have to hunt for a light switch before my fingers brushed against a glossy surface that felt, to my homesick fingers, a lot like Livingston. My chest and throat tickled with laughter from buoyant bits of my conversation with Basilio. I hadn't yet told him about the night Abri accidentally dosed the entire family with Cool Whip laden with cat sedatives. Was she trying to serve the whipped cream over fruit or shortcake? Humor is in the details.

I was already out of the guestroom and into the hallway when my fingers reminded me of something my brain had failed to register. There had been no thick, bureaucratic skin blocking my access to those photos. No passport.

The No. 1 rule of foreign travel is not to lose your passport. OK, No. 1 is don't get killed by a reincarnated senator or priest from ancient Rome. But not losing your passport is a very close second.

I was back in the guestroom and fumbling for my invisible identification so quickly that I didn't remember moving. Steady breaths. I upended my purse, euros glinting roguishly at me as they hailed down upon a chocolate-colored quilt trimmed with dragonflies. For the second time that day, there were garments flying haphazardly, snagging on furniture and crumpling inconspicuously in unlikely corners, ensuring there would be another frenzy of panic somewhere down the road. But that did not concern me. The only problem in the entire world was the fact that my passport was missing, and if I could just find it, everything would be alright.

And that wasn't just the paranoia brought on by my reincarnation adjustment disorder talking. Inevitably, the thing that is missing just happens to be the cure for everything—

even problems that don't yet know they're problems. And the longer it remains missing, and the more time you have to bargain with god—or, in my case, gods—the more exalted its powers become.

It wasn't there. But Uncle Basilio would probably have some idea what to do, either some insight about his house's habit of stealing travel documents from foreign guests or perhaps a friend at the embassy who could help secure a replacement.

"My passport!" I stormed the kitchen with a formidable combination of the authority of a high priestess and the outrage of a teenager. "It's gone! And I looked everywhere. I checked my purse at least three times, and my luggage just as many. There are clothes all over the bedroom, and euros! But I can't find it!"

Basilio didn't even look up from the stew of eggs and cheese and mushrooms sliding across the pan. I found his lack of tension reassuring. Even the formally informal suit that failed to mesh with my view of what a man should wear while making an omelette in his own home at 10 o'clock at night made sense within the context of his new role as embassy liaison.

A mushroom tried to slip out and onto the counter, but he caught it deftly with the spatula and herded it back to the center of the pan, where the flame burned the hottest.

"Adamo removed it when he took your luggage to the guestroom."

"He took my passport? Why?"

"I told him to. It doesn't make sense for you to race around a foreign country with a document that important. Look how panicked you were when you thought you'd lost it. It's in the safe."

Look how panicked you *were*? Were! As if my heart weren't still racing as if I were being hunted for sport. Or late for a final exam.

"And you didn't think to tell me? Actually, no! You didn't think to ask my permission before rifling through my personal possessions?"

"I didn't dredge through your possessions."

I could feel his satisfaction with the calm, measured weight of his words, knew that, in his eyes, my fear and anger undermined the validity of what I was saying. But he had not been acted upon as I had. We were in his house, in his country. I could not disregard the fact that he had an advantage on me, and I would not distance myself from emotions to which I was reasonably entitled.

"Fine! Your minion! You can twist words all you want, but you know the principle is still the same. I am a guest in your house, at your insistence, but for the time that I am here, that room was set aside for my comfort and privacy. And you know it was wrong for someone to remove things from my luggage without my permission."

"You're a very different Rhea when angry," Basilio spoke with a quiet smile. "Taller. Prouder. Less … lethargic."

"So I've been told," I responded, before remembering that the person who told me that was a fellow vestal virgin. Still, it was disconcerting that there was a consensus among my acquaintances and colleagues—both past and present—that I was at my best, or perhaps simply my most honest, when threatened. It didn't happen often, at least not under what I considered normal circumstances, but my mask slipped, the same as anyone else's.

"Forgive me. I did not realize you would be so bothered by this. I will return the passport at the end of your trip, and it will be safe here at Ilium in the meantime. And perhaps, while you are here, we can begin to address the root of your fear, whatever drives you to react as you just did. Your sister mentioned that you were afraid to come to Rome, though she didn't specify what you were afraid of. I gather it's a person or group of people you fear might harm you. Given that this is your first visit to Rome, I find it unlikely that people are lying in wait to accost you. Such paranoia is unhealthy."

"I'm sorry. You stole my passport, and now I'm paranoid?" My heart rate wasn't quite normal, but close, and I managed an amused drawl.

"How many times have I invited you to Rome?"

"I'd have to consult Ab— Mom and Dad in order to answer that, seeing as how you usually issued the invitations to them."

"Somehow you never seemed to be in the house whenever I spoke on the phone with your parents. And sister."

I shrugged. Damn Emeline for being the outgoing type and making me look insular and sullen by compare!

"Social withdrawal is a common symptom of a schizotypal personality, Rhea," Basilio said as he slid the omelette onto a plate and set it on the counter in front of me. "You're never going to achieve your potential in this life while carrying the burden of the past. You're already lost. Worse than lost, for you have no path. Socially, you've suffered. Academically—"

"I hardly think that's fair," I protested. "I was salutatorian. And I would have been valedictorian if I hadn't received a B+ in Latin. Which was one of the better grades that sorry excuse for an educator gave out."

"That's a respectable grade," he assured me. "For someone who doesn't speak Latin."

I directed a sigh at the mottled yellow half moon sitting patiently in front of me. I was now certain that this was bad, and hoping it wouldn't permanently prejudice me against eggs—assuming I lived long enough to suffer permanent damage of any sort.

"I don't know if a B+ in an advanced high school Latin course in New Jersey would qualify me as a Latin speaker, but I sure do appreciate the compliment." I wanted to sound jaunty and unaffected, but wasn't certain I'd hit the mark.

"You spoke Latin when you were 6 years old, long before you confounded your high school teacher by knowing more Latin than she did."

Merda. Shit.

"It's all right, Rhea. There's no shame in needing a

little help sometimes."

He withdrew a translucent brown-orange bottle from his pocket.

"About half of your countrymen suffer from mental illness over the course of their lifetime."

"I'm not suffering from mental illness," I was quick to inform him. I picked up my fork and took a bite of the omelette, as if an appetite for unfertilized chicken eggs was some kind of evidence of my sanity.

"Of course, most of your fellow Americans still manage to attend college, get a job, function at an age-appropriate level. But there's no reason we shouldn't be able to get you there in a few months."

I realized we were no longer having a dialogue, and I wondered if we ever had been, or if he had spent the entire evening evaluating and deliberating, looking for evidence to substantiate whatever it was he already believed about my mental state. Basilio was not a man, but an intermediary for some higher power—in this case simple, regulated, clean, rational sanity. There were seven billion people in this world, and this deity had to scrub every one of them clean of its influence. Because I didn't believe it was possible to travel through this world and suffer all its heartbreaks and cruelties without emerging slightly touched on the other side. Different. Less sure, perhaps.

But Basilio was holding that pill bottle as if it were the cure to every errant thought I'd ever had—and there'd been so many, and most of them so alluring and brave. As if it were the cure to Nesreen's soft cheeks and sacred palms.

That's when the kitchen became a merry-go-round, the cabinets swinging drunkenly past, the island where Basilio had been chopping vegetables and whisking eggs twirled and settled, twirled and settled. And I was at the center of this madly careening culinary universe, fighting to keep from being pitched off my stool.

He could take her away from me. Basilio and those tiny yellow pills. (I believed they were yellow, a monochrome of mustard, because that was the color of my fear. Or the way it smelled, anyway.)

"Now, typically, your run-of-the-mill antipsychotic medications require several weeks before they begin to reduce your symptoms. I'm going to prescribe you a slightly stronger dose with the intention of relieving your symptoms that much more rapidly."

It seemed to me that his Adam's apple, rather than his mouth, was talking. It was growing larger, taking up more of the kitchen. He pulled a second bottle from his pocket. This time the terror smelled the squalid green of spinach.

"We're going to start you off on Risperdal to help clear your distorted thinking, as well as a lower dose of neuroleptics. Of course, even with the highest possible prescription dose, there's no guarantee we're going to be able to completely eradicate these psychotic abnormalities. In fact, the odds are very much against it," he said, with a brow that furrowed gravely. "But recent research is heartening! And there's a very reasonable chance we can dramatically improve your symptoms."

"I'm not taking your pills! You must be completely crazy to think I'd go along with something like this!"

"If you refuse to cooperate, I'll have to commit you to a psychiatric hospital for a 72-hour evaluation." His eyes were grave and disappointed, and the lines on either side of his mouth formed parenthesis, but I didn't understand their purpose in the context of our conversation.

"So this is why you had Adamo steal my passport."

I wondered, belatedly, if there had been anything sinister in the omelette he'd fed me, little happy pills ready to ambush me and scramble my thinking the way Basilio had scrambled those stupid eggs.

"I had Adamo take the passport to protect you. Given the advanced stage of your delusions, and the fact that no one has yet taken the time to address them, I feel it is incumbent on me to intervene. As your guardian in Rome, I will ensure you are safe and, more importantly, that your personality disorder is being addressed before you return to the United States."

He set the bottles on the counter just an arm's length away, so close that I could count the pills and read the label, though it remained inscrutable, couched in medical jargon.

"It may take awhile. If it turns out we need to push back your departure, I'm sure your parents will be fine. You have no plans for the fall? College? A job?"

I shook my head, more in horror than coherent response.

VIII

Silphium proved to be as good a friend to me as it had been to many a distressed Roman woman.

It was the servant Cloelia who explained the significance of the Cyrenian crop.

"Drink just one sip of the juice, the size of a chickpea, once a month, and no new life will take hold inside you." She gestured to my stomach, and I stepped back in instinctive horror at being associated with anything concerning intercourse of that nature. Cloelia's brown eyes shone with a playful, knowing smile.

"It also protects against anything that has already occurred."

"I did not ask because ... ."

"If I thought you had, I would not have told you," Cloelia assured me. "Every woman here knows the purpose of silphium because every woman here has an obligation to Vesta, and the women of Rome. Vesta belongs to women first. And any knowledge that assists you in carrying out these responsibilities cannot taint you. Knowing silphium's purpose does not make you impious."

The path we were walking inclined slightly and curved

sharply away from the river, and I didn't dare take my eyes off the ground lest a stray stone should catch my foot. The prospect of sprawling publicly to the ground in a heap of virginal white wool was sufficiently humiliating without the added punishment I would face if I dropped the vessel of water.

But that did not change the fact that I was intently focused on Cloelia's words.

"So have you ever taken it?"

It was an impertinent question, but over the last year Cloelia had taken a particular interest in me that was almost maternal. She watched us all, but I was the beneficiary of her advice. While other servants wooed with flattery, pandering to the fact that someone must appreciate the young priestesses' beauty since the outside world was denied the privilege, Cloelia honored me with thoughtfully arranged bouquets of gossip and information.

I suppose you could say Cloelia and I had an impertinent relationship. And I ardently prayed that Fulvia never learned the extent of my boldness. Commodus, I suspected, was already aware of my capacity for candor, though I doubted he was aware that I had, on occasion, given liberty to these tendencies.

"Of course," Cloelia replied gently. "Servants have … less control over certain things than many other women. And I can be punished for erring, or simply capturing the wrong person's attention. Silphium gives me a measure of control."

"Oh."

It was there again—the fear of being acted upon. But how can you speak out against an intangible colossus when you cannot even find the words to describe it? Julius Caesar divorced Pompeia with the argument that his wife must be above suspicion. But Pompeia didn't dress in women's clothes and sneak into the Bona Dea festival intent on seducing Pompeia. Publius Clodius Pulcher did. And Pompeia was punished.

Maybe there was something to Cloelia's notion of

using my role to impose balance where there was never any hope of it before. It was the first time I'd had any thought about what my life as a vestal virgin might mean beyond carrying water and guarding the fire, beyond the tasks I had been carefully trained to perform. I was finally confident enough in these responsibilities—not careless, not indifferent, but deliberate and capable—that I could now begin to look beyond the daily routines and discern the faintest outline of a higher purpose beyond my higher purpose.

All my new and fine revolutionary notions fled as the other implications of Cloelia's words took hold.

"So that is why all those important women were so eager to speak to the gladiator at Bona Dea!"

Cloelia eyed the sudden, victorious flush that came to my cheeks and pursed her lips.

"I did not know you held gladiators in such low regard," was all she said.

"I do not. It just seemed like an unorthodox place for a gladiator to be. And I found it a little strange how much attention she was receiving."

There. Let her think I was merely envious because I coveted the attention for myself. Though it was the truth: I *was* merely envious. Envious and, as always, wary of the impure presence of a profane mob at sacred ceremonies.

Nesreen is not coarse. Another voice that was just as much my own taunted me. *Nesreen is as rare and constant as that flame you have sworn to tend.* My face burned hotter, and I was grateful I was already flushed from our conversation, lest Cloelia detect my own impurities.

"Silphium is not so easy to come by as it once was," Cloelia admitted. "The guests at Bona Dea likely hoped the gladiator was somehow capable of acquiring more. She is from Cyrene, so it is possible. Perhaps you can ask her when we get back to the house."

"That is nonsense. Why would she be at our house?"

Cloelia shook her head, indicating that she could not account for the strangeness of it any more than I could. But that did not alter the fact that of the two of us, she was clearly in possession of more information, and I was eager to bridge that gap.

"But she is at the house? Today? Right now?"

"The Virgo Vestalis Maxima approved a visit from the Cyrenian gladiator two days ago. I believe we received a request from *Ludus matutinus*, where she trains, directly after Bona Dea, the very next day ... ."

The very next day! The very next day!

" ... But the Virgo Vestalis Maxima was preoccupied with other business and only remembered the request when the gladiator's *lanista* sent a message repeating the query."

"Vibiana requested that the gladiator visit the house ... to regale us with tales from the Coliseum," I said. "I had actually forgotten. That was at Bona Dea, so of course I imagined everyone else would forget too." Hopefully, Cloelia didn't notice that we were walking faster. We were merely well beyond the steepest segment of our route, of course. Traveling mostly downhill, it was natural that we would move more swiftly.

"That was two months ago," I chattered, hoping to distract Cloelia from the unprecedented pace I was setting.

It was *Februarius* and I had all but convinced myself that I, too, was milk-drunk the night of the Bona Dea revelries, and had invented the entire encounter with the gladiator. The statue of Mercury glared conspicuously in my memory and I half-believed that I had passed the night flirting, not with a gladiator, but with a facsimile of the god who guided souls to the underworld. After all, I was a 16-year-old girl who had forsworn romance for a minimum of 30 years. And the gods had a lengthy history of romantic dalliances with mortals. So I was hardly the first vestal virgin to create a romantic fiction where there was nothing but a well-chiseled lump of marble.

We found her in the atrium, staring at a row of statues honoring past Virgo Vestalis Maximas. Her hand rested just above a priestess' knee, her head tilted backward to capture the expression on the statue's face. Her lips were moving, though we could not hear her words, and I knew from the color of her mouth that her prayers tasted of mulberry. It bore the taint of sacrilege to think it, but if I were a deity, I would grant petitions according to their taste rather than sound. Couldn't the messenger outweigh the message?

I was behind her, close enough to touch her, to pull her away from the statue. But I was too surprised at finding her alone and had not yet decided to forgive her for her train of admirers the night of Bona Dea.

The wind masked her words and caught the edges of my suffibulum, threatening to expose the fact that I stood directly behind her, listening. Or trying to.

"I doubt Cloelia approves of the statues receiving quite that much attention. They are sworn virgins, after all."

It was not what I meant to say, nor spoken how I meant to speak. There was a balance between the severe matron and droll clown, and one day I meant to find it. Fortunately, Cloelia was now elsewhere, attending other responsibilities—though she *had* frowned at the sight of the gladiator pawing the feminine form on the pedestal.

"But they are too beautiful to deny any gesture of affection or homage," she replied calmly, her devout face still reading the folds of marble for revelations I did not yet understand.

"Their inaccessibility is part of their charm." I had not given it much thought, but it was true. Publius Clodius Pulcher would not have given Pompeia a second glance if Caesar had not stood between them.

"The sun caresses them, and they are the better for it."

A hand grazed my chin and directed my focus to the figure's neck and jawline, which glowed as if they had been caught in the act of coming to life. The sky was tenebrous and leaden, threatened to wash us all away in the sea forming in the clouds there. But one quick javelin of light and energy had darted through and come to rest here, on Hedia Terentia Flavola.

"What are you doing here?" My question was

considerably safer than obsessing over the possibilities of the unmapped territory between shoulder and jaw.

"I wanted to see where Rome's priestesses live."

"This is it. Well, we do not actually live in the atrium with the statues. But the palace adjacent … that is where we sleep."

"That must be the temple." She pointed to the circular edifice where we lodged and maintained the fire.

"Yes. You know, some people do not consider it healthy to work so close to where you live, but it makes for a short walk when it's my turn to watch the fire between the twelfth and first hour."

"You are not happy to see me."

"I just did not expect to see you here. I am not sure why you are here."

"Your friend invited me. I did not think you would be excited to see me, but I did not expect disappointment either. … Unless this is something else? Nerves disguising themselves as dislike?"

"Maybe," I admitted, not wanting her to leave. "Do you want to see the House of the Vestals?"

"I would rather see your house of worship."

The brief walk to the temple was silent. Nona was guarding the flame, in all likelihood dozing helplessly at her post. She was the youngest of us and, though rarely ill, she projected a feeble, sickly air that ignited our sympathy and protective instincts. When it was her turn to watch the fire, we checked on her as often as our schedules allowed, never fully certain whether we most feared the decimation of the flame or the beating that pale-haired and pale-eyed Nona would subsequently suffer at the hands of the Pontifex Maximus.

The temple's entrance faced east as a tribute to the sun's role in creating the flame and sustaining life. Nesreen did not look at me directly, and only had when asking—stating, really—that I was not happy to see her. Which gave me license to look at her all I liked without getting caught.

The collision with Caecilia—shoulders glancing ribs

abutting hips—was my first clue that Nona was not alone in the temple.

"Rhea! And a gladiator. Under different circumstances, I would say we had a fox in the henhouse." She took in Nesreen's rich blue stola, elaborately draped over her shoulders and across her chest, leaving her arms bare almost to the shoulder.

"Under different circumstances." She spoke quietly, almost to herself. "You came to check in on Nona?"

I nodded. "And to show Nesreen the temple."

No one save a vestal virgin was allowed inside the temple, but Caecilia gave me a warm, wary expression, and when she said, "Enjoy yourselves," her tone was laced with indulgence.

"And do not forget Nona," she warned before disappearing into the rectangular light beyond the temple entrance.

The youngest was, in fact, sitting on a stool beside the altar, but there was no glimpse of the pale blue of her eyes, and her face was propped closer to the flame than was healthy for a priestess swathed entirely in wool. I pulled her away from the fire, catching her by the shoulders before she could fall backward and crack her head on the tile. She woke with a shudder that might have forced me to drop her had she not the figure and heft of a wintertime poplar.

"I am sorry, Rhea." There was no time between Nona's eyes opening and their filling with tears. "You should tell Fulvia that you found me asleep. Again."

She gave no indication that she was aware of the intruder standing behind me, ready to give me a hand should the slumbering virgin prove too heavy a burden.

"Do not be silly. The fire is still burning, so no harm came of it this time. I will finish the last two hours of your shift. Go find Vibiana and tell her that she will be relieving me instead of you."

It was not common practice to alert the other vestals when there was a slight change in the rotation, but if Vibiana knew she was relieving Nona, she would likely arrive early to assure she was not asleep, and I wanted her to know the fire was in secure hands.

Nona nodded her assent and disappeared in the same direction as Caecilia. Except that Caecilia's exit had acted as an eclipse in the temple, but when Nona left, there was no exterior light to block with her tiny figure—just gusts of wind beating at the temple with ever-increasing courage.

I closed the door and returned to the altar.

"Am I allowed to be here?" Nesreen was looking into the fire, and I wondered what she saw there. The first time I visited the temple, a few days after my captio, I saw my family, immolating with passive faces. I sometimes visited the sacred fire late at night when I missed them, and sometimes they were there waiting for me when I did.

"No, but I do not think Vesta will mind." She served women, after all.

"I have to go back to the ludi soon, anyway. But I wanted to see the fire you had sworn to protect."

"We shall extinguish it soon. On *Martius* 1, the Pontifex Maximus puts out the flame, which we renew and protect the rest of the year." I spoke with a sad sigh. It was a terrible thing to witness the death of the fire, even with the Pontifex Maximus standing mere feet away holding the two crucial branches from a sacred tree, ready to reignite the blaze.

We were forced to watch from a safe distance—two years prior, Commodus imposed a ban on what he called our hysterical hovering, and the penalty for coming closer than he deemed appropriate was a beating commensurate with what we would receive for allowing the flame to extinguish on our watch. It was a bold threat, but Commodus was a bold emperor, and the man who was willing to throw the wives of his political enemies into combat at the Coliseum would not balk at whipping his empire's high priestesses.

She took my hand. "Death does not concern us, since when we are, death has not come, and when death has come, we are not."

She was there beside me, mere feet from the flame, and then she was closer even than she had been, and her lips were the flame, and mine, and the magic and wonder of her eclipsed even the allure of Vesta's fire.

"That was from Epicurus," she said. "The idea, not … everything else."

"I saw the Comitium, drenched in blood."

Nesreen was still close, her hand now on my back, while the other gripped the altar.

"The Greek philosopher, not the Beast Master who manages the lions at the Coliseum," she said, staring at me as if the information were vital.

I had no idea what she was saying. So I kept talking: "The Comitium is where they drag the lovers. They bring them there, and then whip them to death. People cheer."

"But I have already told you, death does not concern me," Nesreen assured me. Her face was steady. She regretted nothing. She would regret nothing. She had killed the leopards and was at peace, but she believed there was another sort of peace to be found at the other end of the sword.

"I do not know what I am doing," I confessed.

"*Experientia docet.*" Experience teaches. Nesreen's face was stoic, but her eyes were mischievous. She was still. We both were, until a powerful gust rattled the door, alerting us to the existence of a world beyond the temple—and the concerns and rules that attended such a world as ours.

"I must go. Thracius will be looking for me, and he is not overly fond of volatile weather." The impish smile reached her mouth. She did not try to touch me as she departed the temple. If she had, I would have let her. But I would not have called out to her, as I did:

"I will speak to Fulvia, our Virgo Vestalis Maxima. She will want to meet with you to discuss the impact of the silphium shortage on the women of Rome. Any counsel you can offer will be greatly appreciated, and benefit many. But you will likely have to come here often, as such quandaries are rarely resolved quickly. No matter, though. Fulvia's a patient woman, as vestal virgins tends to be. Most of us, anyway."

My gladiator turned back briefly at the temple's entrance, now with her stoic face, and I recognized it not as an expression she wore, but her very own self.

"*Semper ardens*," she murmured with a nod before letting the world beyond the temple swallow her away.

Always burning.

*   *   *

"You're telling me you're not at all concerned?"

I had let Emeline dress me that morning out of a noblesse born of my victorious certainty that it was to be our final day in Rome, if not Italy.

I was still reeling from the fact that Em chose to put me in my own dress—the same linen tunic design I usually favored, but with a woven top that gave up and simply turned to long strips of fringe that fell just above the breast line and down to thigh-level, with a full, ordinary skirt, all in a powerful shade of violet—rather than one of her own. My sister seemed to have developed a soft spot for my wardrobe, and I'd even caught her trying on the very same garment she'd used as inspiration for a poem titled "Spot of Vomit in the Closet," which so impressed her freshman year English teacher that she'd read it aloud to the entire class. Em took the poem's success as an indication that she was also correct in her judgment of the dress, and I was forced to hide it lest she find and burn it for its crimes against taste.

Of course, she had also insisted that I wear the shoes she'd given me, dismissing my concerns that I looked like a steampunk hooker with a pat on the shoulder and a gracious, "Steampunk hookers are in." I compensated for my discomfort by wearing my favorite necklace: a brown suede leather bolero with red felt butterflies, which Em insisted was distracting and confusing.

But the law of reciprocity was lost on my dearest Emeline, who offered no show of gratitude for the fact that I'd finally allowed her the illusion of control that came with pretending I was her personal Barbie, and she was even showing signs of attempting to derail our escape from our creepy homeland.

"Concerned about what? Zio offered to hold onto our passports for us while we travel around Rome. That's a nice gesture, Rhea. There are pickpockets that prey on tourists, and if one of them stole our passports, we'd definitely be trapped here, and I know how much you'd hate that."

"Zio stole our passports! Frankly, I'd prefer it if a pickpocket took my passport. At least it would be less creepy."

"You should be grateful. Last night, Adamo found my passport lying on the dance floor at the club. Without him, I'd spend our last couple of weeks here in line at the embassy trying to get it replaced."

"Adamo found your passport? How do you know he didn't steal it when he took mine from our luggage?"

It was all so clear. Unfortunately, one person's clear-sky epiphany is another person's Bigfoot conspiracy—especially when that second person happens to be a younger sister who wouldn't agree even if she knew she was wrong … assuming she was capable of recognizing she could be wrong.

"Why would he take it and then pretend to find it? Why wouldn't he just keep it?"

"To gain your trust. And look! It worked! I can try to leave without my passport, but you won't, and he knew I wouldn't leave you here."

"Rhea, we're flying out of here by August 13. Both of us. Together. No one's going to try to stop us." Emeline was starting to sound like Basilio, and I feared I was losing Aemilia altogether.

"I just can't believe that you had this whole campaign planned out, and you're not even willing to consider the possibility that Basilio's in on it," I said. I knew how bitter the words would sound, but they still didn't match the betrayal I felt.

"All right, you want me to take you seriously? You

want me to take Basilio seriously as a potential villain?" Emeline rifled through her pack and withdrew the leatherbound notebook she'd accidentally revealed on our return trip to Rome.

"Basilio—Possible Bad Guy," she wrote in a confident, loopy scrawl. "There. It's in the book. Are you happy?"

"Tell me you're taking it seriously. Tell me it's in the book and you're taking it seriously, or I'm not leaving this house unless it's for the airport or train station."

My bags were already packed, and had been since the night before. They were sitting by the bed, waiting for me to find some means of securing our escape. The longer they sat there, the more I felt that I was failing them.

Emeline gripped my chin, surprising me—and, judging by the expression in her frank blue eyes, herself as well.

"I wouldn't have written it into the book if I didn't mean it. And I'm not taking this lightly. But if Basilio really is our villain, I don't think it makes sense for us to broadcast the fact that we don't trust him. If he truly is that underhanded, then we shouldn't be having these conversations in this house at all."

"Do you think he might have some kind of recording device?"

"Maybe. How are we supposed to know?" I doubted whether Emeline knew if she was placating me or genuinely questioned Basilio's intentions.

"Let's just go. The Coliseum's already open, and if it's half as crowded as the Vatican, it's going to take us an hour per square inch."

Which was partially true, but that wasn't the reason I was anxious to get the visit over with. The Coliseum could be twice its actual size, and it still wouldn't match what people imagined in their heads. They came to the amphitheatre with visions of jeering crowds in tunics and all-powerful men with laurels wreaths around their brow and enormous and deeply troubling sexual appetites. But it hasn't looked that way in a long time. I'd done the calculations in my head and realized the amphitheatre had been out to pasture more than three times longer than it was ever in use.

It hurt.

Instead of venatores and tigers stalking the wooden floorboards below, the hypogeum where the animals and gladiators had been stored before matches was exposed, as though gutted. It didn't look very impressive laid bare by the dispassionate fluorescent bulb in the sky.

These heavens had not known the passing of Apollo's chariot in long and well-documented years. People had drawn the wonder from the sun when they stopped worshiping it, and even now they refused to marvel at its properties and abilities: heating and lighting the entire world. Instead, they had to assign a creator and worship that instead. No wonder the sun was dying, or soon would be.

What life cycle would I be on when it finally happened? Would my hunters find some means of prolonging the chase when we were all the evolutionary equivalent of instant soup?

Aemilia and I had to pause every couple of feet to avoid crossing into someone's photo. Without people in the stands, it looked smaller than I remembered, even as we walked through at a pace that reminded me of a wedding party.

"I gave up counting the languages," offered Aemilia, only halfway around our first pass. She'd been pretending to peruse her guide book, as if for information about the history and purpose of the big, broken circle of rocks. But I'd seen her eyeing the other tourists with undeniable horror.

"It's kind of like coming home and finding strangers using your bathroom, isn't it?" I asked.

Aemilia's answer was delayed by an Argentinian couple who asked her to take their picture. But she had a smile when she caught up with me.

"You know, it's exactly like that, and I'm not really sure why. I never felt all that comfortable here, but I suppose it did belong to us in a way it can never really belong to them.

We were the ones who used it for its intended purpose … ."

"Which was horrific and wrong," I added.

"Of course. It's not like we're some kind of apologists," Aemilia hastened to add.

"Or fetishists," I concluded, catching sight of a couple dressed in what they had clearly mistaken for gladiator garb.

We encountered a roadblock in the form of a long line of people and patiently took our places at the back of it, hoping we had stumbled upon the entrance to the upper levels, or possibly a tour of the hypogeum, which I hadn't been given the opportunity to venture into in my previous life.

I made the mistake of revealing this last thought a little too loudly, and the people directly ahead of us turned warily and began a whispered conversation that was clearly about Aemilia and me.

"We're not weirdos," I retorted, again a little too loudly. Spots of rosy color had appeared on Aemilia's cheeks.

"What?" I pushed. "How do we know they even speak English? They're probably talking about something else." It didn't matter what I had been in my past life. In this one, I was a big sister, and therefore tragically uncool.

"So this spot holds a lot of romantic significance for you, huh?" Aemilia nodded toward the arena, her eyes curious. For one heart-stopping moment, I didn't see her at all, but a tawny, confident face looking up at me from beneath a leopard. The shield was still on the sand. The lunatic Commodus and his blustering, outraged senators hovered somewhere in the background, bickering about coinage. But it was Nesreen. The whole world, my whole world, lying on the ground, prepared to die. The ground where we now stood.

The Coliseum was spinning. I was going to throw up.

"I need to find the bathroom." I clutched Aemilia's arm, trying to stay upright.

"You're in line for the bathroom," retorted the woman standing ahead of us.

"I thought we were in line to see the hypogeum." The world was still a giant Tilt-A-Whirl but I felt somehow misled that the line didn't serve the purpose I thought it had when I joined.

"There's no tour of the hypogeum." The woman waved an informational pamphlet, and I wasn't sure if I couldn't read the text because her arm wouldn't stop moving, or because the Earth wouldn't. Either way, it wasn't helping my condition.

With Aemilia's assistance, I hobbled my way over to one of the few patches unoccupied by tourists' feet and cameras, where I sank to the ground. Aemilia hovered anxiously, without a trace of embarrassment that I was now on the floor of the Coliseum.

"Maybe we should call an ambulance? Do they have ambulances here? Of course they do. But I can't just dial 9-1-1, can I?"

"He drugged me."

"Who drugged you?" Aemilia was spinning around, glaring at everyone. Under drastically different circumstances, I would have laughed. But the weight of my shame was far too great.

"Not them."

"Who, then? Rhea, I know you're sick, but you can't just drop a bombshell like that and not tell me what's going on."

"Basilio."

"Basilio drugged you?" Her face was anxious, but her tone was skeptical. It made everything—my shame; the nausea fighting for control of my stomach and its contents, waging mutiny against reason and public decency; even the blister forming on my left heel—that much worse.

"He gave me pills. He said that they would help with my delusions. If I take them, I get my passport back. And if I don't, he threatened to have me institutionalized."

"*Anseris coleones!*"

I almost wished I were drinking something, so it could spurt out of my nose and arc blithely through the noble, historic ruins.

"Did you just say 'goose balls?'"

"Maybe," Aemilia replied, her lips quirked into a smile. "It was the first thing that came to mind. I'll probably have to pay a therapist a lot of money some day to figure out why."

"I'll bet Basilio has some pills for that." I was beginning to loathe that bitter tone, the one that made me sound like a whiny teenager who was, indeed, suffering from reincarnation adjustment disorder.

"Yeah. Wow. So, I guess this means he knows about your stint as a vestal sorta-virgin." She was serious again.

"Yeah. I think I might have blown it when he came to visit us when I was younger. He was asking all these questions, and I was answering. In Latin. This was before I understood that I wasn't supposed to do that. I dunno how he found out about the whole vestal virgin fiasco though, or whether he even did. I was afraid to ask how much he knew."

"Looks like Zio just made his way to the top of the suspect list." I caught a glimpse of comely ankle and a stalwart shield as Aemilia withdrew the leatherbound journal and scribbled Basilio's name onto a page, then underlined the letters not once, not twice, but three times in thick, black ink. In case we forgot the name of our primary suspect, whose house we were staying at, who also happened to be our uncle, and who also happened to be drugging me.

Was that a possibility? I didn't know what these pharmaceuticals could accomplish—beyond making the world around me sadly inclined to pitch and roll like the deck of some drunk long ship. Would I forget Basilio's betrayal? What about Abri and Fedele? Or even Aemilia?

Could I forget Nesreen?

The floor was orange with the contents of my stomach.

I wiped my chin. Former contents, anyway.

"What if he's right?" A flea at the end of my nose couldn't have heard me.

"What?" Aemilia was still staring at the pool of vomit, but no one else seemed to have noticed.

119

"What if he's right?" That was a little too loud. Not only was Aemilia now looking at me, but I had also succeeded in attracting the attention of a cluster of Irish tourists, one of whom nodded sagely and proclaimed, "Can't hold her alcohol."

"Right about what?"

"You know." I twirled my finger around my ear and crossed my eyes. "That I'm crazy."

She squatted down beside me, folding her arms over her legs.

"You're not. I don't understand why you'd let one person contradict everything you've seen and heard and experienced."

"It's a little different when that one person happens to be a licensed psychologist. Besides, the only reason no one else thinks I'm crazy is because they don't know I think I'm a vestal virgin."

"Well, that's because you weren't," Aemilia replied impishly. "A virgin, at least. You were just a vestal."

"It isn't funny, Aemilia. I'm really starting to doubt myself here."

"Well, that's on you for questioning yourself so easily. How did you ever survive high school if you're this insecure? You know this place, Rhea, better than anybody here. And I do, too. So I guess that means that if you're insane, then so am I."

"I know, I know." Head in my hands, I was the portrait of abject despair. "I keep telling myself that, but there's this other voice in my head, and it's asking which is more likely: That I am a reincarnated vestal virgin from ancient Rome, or that I'm an 18-year-old wallflower from Livingston, New Jersey, who's never had a date and didn't even bother applying to a community college because it seemed too intimidating? You have to admit that anyone with those specs would have good cause to conjure up an alternate-life fantasy."

"I will admit that you were batting a higher average on the first round, but you've got a second inning now and ...

damn, I really suck at sports metaphors. Rhea, you're right. You haven't made much use of this second round … yet. But that's why you're here, and you're doing a great job so far. You've shown a lot of courage. You're more confident. Your outfits are getting way better, and, excuse me, could you maybe try not stepping on my hand? Great. Thanks."

A miffed-looking woman wearing a T-shirt that read "Born to sail, forced to work" clomped past us, muttering about how all the good tourist attractions were too full of tourists.

"She's right about that, Aemilia. I've seen enough. Let's go before one of us loses an appendage." I took one final, appraising view of the amphitheatre. "Although, I suppose it would be fitting the history of this place. If you're willing, they might even pay you to lose, say, a finger on alternate Fridays. You'd make a fortune in tips from the tourists. It might even cover your medical costs."

"Good to see you've recovered from your identity crises," Aemilia replied. "But are you sure you want to leave? Now that we know where the bathroom is and have a buddy in line, we can probably get you cleaned up and finish our tour of this lovely old torture—ewww! What is that?"

She held up an elbow with a piece of gum stuck to it.

"Let's just say, your elbow probably doesn't have any concerns about fresh breath."

"Ugh, I wouldn't be so glib. It was stuck to that wall you're leaning against. OK, it's definitely time to leave. This place was more hygienic when it was filled with thousands of people and giant mounds of tiger shit."

IX

I was trying my hardest to be reasonable—empathetic, even. But twilight was fast turning to night, settling comfortably upon the vivarium like a winter coat. The half-dozen figures lurking in the shadows seemed to grow in direct proportion to the darkness. I had been pleading with them for the better part of an hour, but thus far they had given no indication of understanding, no sign that they recognized me as a fellow being, even. Instead, my pleas were met with raucous laughter.

Their expressions were not those of mindless beasts, which would have unnerved me a good deal less, but rather I could see that there was some calculation taking place. I just did not like the way I factored into their calculations.

A beast master materialized at my side. "There is no point in talking to a pack of hyenas," he counseled, for the third time. "They have not been fed in two days. If they were inclined to listen at their best—and I am not saying they are—the only thing they have profited from your time with them is a desire to feast on your bones. And it would not take long. They eat everything, even the hair. I would not want to encounter this pack without the benefit of three strong men by my side, and some equally powerful weapons."

The hair on the back of the nearest creature—which I

had been calling Valens, because it was the first name to come to mind—stood on end, and he lunged toward us. I sighed.

"That is the fifth time he has tried that. He seems to be forgetting that he is in a cage."

"Or he is hoping that it will not hold, testing the cage for weakness," the beast master offered with a tone of helpfulness. "You might try consulting one of the other animals. They are less—"

Valens threw himself against the cage once more, and this time he was flanked by a second hyena.

The beast master shrugged, a gesture that looked wrong on his Herculean frame, and led me to another cage. Manic laughter followed in the wake of our retreat, and I could not repress a shiver of fear. They laughed when excited, and there was nothing more exciting to them than the hunt. I envied their ability to appropriate control of the encounter, despite being in a large metal corral, and having been captured and hauled here against their will. They surely could not believe their encounter with the Romans would end favorably, and still they did not compromise their instincts and behaviors.

Some would consider them obtuse, and while I had to acknowledge a certain lunacy that made their company untenable for prolonged periods of time, I admired them for being what they were in circumstances as trying as captivity. They were doing a better job of it than I had been, anyway.

"Is everything well, Rhea?" asked Caecilia, who accompanied me to vouchsafe for my modesty and decorum when we returned to the house. The further I strayed from the strictest interpretation of my vow, the more consideration I gave my reputation among the other vestals, and especially Fulvia. My standing within the order had never been better.

Cloelia hovered nearby, watching us both with a feigned casualness that marked her as the perfect servant-spy. I had requested to bring her along as well. There had been instances of multiple vestals being denounced as unchaste, but never two vestals and a servant. The presence of a temple servant was the final proof that there was nothing improper about this visit.

And I enjoyed her company. I felt less like a priestess in her presence, and while part of me recognized there might be an inherent danger in allowing myself to forget my principal responsibility to the empire, another shameful part of me reveled in the sensation of being human.

The beauty of our worldview was that I could emulate the gods and sincerely desire to be one of them, while indulging in the occasional deception or ecstasy of wrath. It was only the priestesses who must be purged of all desire, while every night was Bona Dea for the gods we served.

"I know we are entering the first night's watch, and I promise to have my business concluded before it is one-third gone," I assured Caecilia who, by virtue of not needling me about the passing hours, had made me feel guilty about the long stretch of time we had passed in the place.

But if my business was to be well and thoroughly concluded within that time, I would have to ignore my companions and focus solely on the beasts within the vivarium, which tomorrow would make their debut in the Coliseum.

I was being regarded, not impertinently or without intelligence, by a dark snout and pert, petal-shaped ears. The beast's eyes were small, but considerate, even if they were set behind two spired, ivory scythes. The name came to me, from games past, where I had seen them mete jagged, gushing wounds and sometimes execution to those who opposed them. I had seen them die, too, these mammoth creatures.

Boars, I believe they were called. And the one before me possessed all the traits a nobleman of consequence might wish to claim on the final night of his existence. I had never heard the word *dignitas* spoken in praise of anything less than a senator, but felt inexplicably moved by the fate of this creature—and it was not merely brute sentiment brought on by the fact that he hailed from the same homeland as *mea carissima* Nesreen, and would likely die and mix his blood with the same sand. My hunter could do much worse for herself than to be impaled by this august beast. Not all deaths are equal, especially in the Coliseum.

First, he was Roman, for I had been told when I entered the vivarium that all of its captives hailed from Cyrene. Second, he regarded me with the respect owed a conqueror, but without demeaning himself with any indication that he understood himself to be conquered. The third reason came to me as I spied several striped backs, no higher than my ankle, circling a larger figure without tusks.

"They fight more fiercely when defending their young," explained their keeper. "We have never sent them in as an entire family before, so this will be a first in venatio history at the Coliseum."

"I am certain they are very proud of the honor the empire has chosen to bestow upon them," Cloelia said, a touch tiredly. At my startled glance—for I had thought her at the other end of the room, near the cages containing hartebeests and other animals that did not stand much chance of hurting anyone tomorrow—Cloelia smiled and led the beast master away with a question about the purpose of the tortoises doing nothing at all in another section of the vivarium.

She might not know why I was there, but Cloelia understood that I required solitude.

I rested my palm and forehead on the bar of metal nearest the chief boar. It was the least aggressive stance I could assume. Before anyone else could interrupt, I began to murmur.

"I am sorry, so very sorry. But please do not kill her. I am sorry, so very sorry. But please do not kill her. I am sorry, so very sorry. But please do not kill her. I am sorry, so very sorry. But please do not kill her … ."

I stopped attending the games. Not just the hunts, but the battles, executions, parades, sacrifices, torture, wrestling, boxing, concerts, and acrobatics. All I had to do was request a special audience with the Virgo Vestalis Maxima and explain to Fulvia, meekly but firmly, that I wished to volunteer for extra shifts guarding the flame while my sisters attended events at the Coliseum. My greatest desire was to remain close to Vesta's fire and far from anything that might pollute my mind or servant's eyes, for I was Vesta's vassal and any action that did not directly serve her felt wasted.

Of course, the House of Vesta must have representatives at all public functions to remind the empire of the crucial function we served in its well-being, but that role was better suited to my fellow priestesses who felt less strongly about appearing at public spectacles that often featured naked men.

Furthermore, the relationship between the Pontifex Maximus and the Senate had degraded to such an extent that volatile outbursts could be expected whenever they were together. I did not reveal that I was increasingly finding these tantrums comedic, and feared I might laugh in the midst of some intense standoff. My concern, as expressed to Fulvia, was that my mind remained unfettered by prejudice or favor in the midst of their struggle for power.

I talked and talked, deferring immediately to Fulvia when she interrupted my monologue with a query or observation. And when I finally concluded, her cheeks were wet with tears, and she congratulated me for the sincerity and humility of my request. At some point during my speech, I convinced even myself that my motives for avoiding the Coliseum were based purely on my desire to serve Vesta to the best of my ability, and not to avoid the horror of watching Nesreen die there. So I accepted her observations graciously and without guilt.

Routine is the cornerstone of monastic life, and my decision to forswear the Coliseum ushered in a whole new tradition that actually extended the influence of the amphitheatre over the House of Vesta.

Several of the vestals—usually Caecilia and Septima— would return from the Coliseum and immediately seek me out at the temple. One of them would carry a tray laden with olives, figs, honey, loaves of bread, pears, and sometimes fish, and while I ate, they reenacted highlights from the day's battles.

"There is the emperor, brandishing an arrow, which he insists was dipped in deadly nightshade—"

"No Caecilia, he said it was dipped in yew," Septima corrected, in the scholarly tone she only used when referencing activity within the Coliseum. "He used the nightshade on the amputee, just after—"

"What does it matter?" Caecilia demanded with a great deal of frustration. "The point of the story is that Commodus brandished the head of a dead ostrich at the senate in full view of everyone attending the games."

"He did not!" I gasped at the same moment Septima protested, "You are telling it wrong."

"He did," Caecilia insisted, her green eyes wide with remembered horror. "He shot the ostrich, collected its head and the better part of its neck with a dagger, then walked right up to the senators and shook the head at them. Well, he tried to shake the head, but the neck was long and … ."

"Flaccid," Septima supplied.

"Yes, flaccid. So it just sort of flopped when he shook it. Which does not sound as terrifying as it was, but flecks of blood spattered everywhere, and he left the head on Herennius Corvus' lap, and the senator could not move, could not even bring himself to call for a servant to remove the head. He just sat there."

"No, you were right Caecilia. It must have been nightshade." Septima corrected her earlier correction. "Yew takes more than an hour before it kills its victim, and this was over before the senators had time to figure out what Commodus was plotting."

I put the pear I was about to eat back on the tray.

"How do you know so much about poison?" I asked, both curious and afraid. "I can not possibly eat this food you have brought me until I know the answer."

"You are jesting, Rhea," Septima admonished. "Every Roman old enough to swear *sacramentum* knows the names, properties, and antidotes to a dozen poisons, at least. It is the only means of guaranteeing your survival."

"We learned history, Greek, philosophy, music, and rhetoric, but my mother never taught us poison," I replied rather stiffly.

"Your sister is the emperor's mistress, and she was never taught anything about poison?" Septima sounded incredulous, but it was the doubtful expression on rational Caecilia's face that battered through the gossamer sheen of my golden childhood.

"She probably learned after I left. Liviana was only 11 when I was chosen." And it was probably true. If Liviana needed to learn how Romans killed one another without detection or evidence, my mother would have ensured that she had access to that information. It was just difficult reconciling the amount of time that would elapse between ingesting an herb and its juices strangling your heart, and my own tutor painstakingly explaining the founding and history of the senate until I could recite every scrap of information in my sleep.

What was Liviana's Rome? Did I even want to know?

It got worse. On another occasion, they reenacted Commodus' triumph over a 30-headed beast. I had seen many fantastical creatures from my seat at the Coliseum, many of which made me wonder what the gods had intended with their awkward creations. It took some time before I was convinced that the giraffe was not some stunning mechanical contraption invented by the empire's finest engineers. But I had yet to see a creature with three heads, much less 30.

Caecilia's mouth actually quivered and her eyes were downcast when I asked her to explain the origins and appearance of this giant.

"They rounded up people without feet or legs, or in some cases missing a hand or arm. There were soldiers and beggars, and some of them had just suffered accidents. They chained them together and placed them in the arena, writhing and flailing and cowering. Commodus came out, dressed as Hercules, and announced that the mass of people was a giant. Worse, an enemy of Rome."

I moaned. "No, Caecilia, I do not want—"

But what I wanted or did not want was nothing to Caecilia, who had endured the slaughter firsthand.

"He slew the giant," Caecilia announced grimly. "He chopped and sawed at it as at a great tree. Their cries swept across the Coliseum, but that just excited him to the task all the more. He persisted until, until … ."

"Nothing twitched," Septima finished for her.

Several weeks later, he killed 100 lions. In a single day. Another, he slaughtered three elephants.

Through it all, I very carefully never asked whether there were any fatalities among the venatores.

Commodus almost never appeared in public, and when he did, it was almost always at the Coliseum, where he appeared attired as Hercules, with a lion's head on his crown, its carcass forming a train down his back, and a giant club in his left hand, which he swung lazily and almost constantly, the way an irritable cat twitches its tail.

Which made the rest of us his mice, forever watching him warily; in our sleep, he occupied our dreams, even when he was not there at all. Sometimes I thought it would have been better for him to just pounce and get it all over with, but it would not have made any difference. Politics in Rome were sufficiently volatile that not even the most savvy among us could always distinguish between an outright attack and business as usual. It was not about Commodus—it was about all of us and a system we helped to build.

Sic et non. Yes and no. That was how we lived. And the truth was, the only reason any part of me—and not the rational Rhea, who had regarded my mother's counsel as sacred—cried *No!*, screamed it into the silence of the temple while the other priestesses gathered stories at the Coliseum, reluctantly but also with a kind of secret delight because they were people, because they were Roman … it is hard to say, easy to feel, and difficult to speak now, in the blushing dawn, but one day, I knew, it would be simple to speak, even when the emotion had grown dim and possibly absent entirely. So it was best to say it now, when it was as terrifying as anything that had stalked the floors of the Coliseum, but honest at least.

The only reason part of me cried no—screamed it into the silence of the temple—was love.

X

It's difficult to dress appropriately for a homecoming. Selecting the proper attire requires a heightened understanding of the nature of the event. But the true hurdle lies in the brutal dredging of one's intentions, desires, and fears. Before you can select the perfect outfit for going home, you must first understand the true purpose behind your return. And only after coming to terms with this bloody, emotional toll is it possible to confront your wardrobe with clear, focused eyes.

I wanted to convey that I was the same Rhea who had served as a high priestess in the House of Vesta, but also that I was not, having evolved over the lapsed centuries and meager years of my second life; to blend into the pillars and ruins so as to avoid detection and to blaze powerfully enough to ignite the ruins, to incite them to imagine a better life for themselves than as remembrances of things past.

No dress could articulate such paradoxes, but there had to be at least one that could embolden me to make the case for myself rather than slouching in the shadows as I had always done.

I wore white. It was too obvious, and I changed a half-dozen times. I was Sisyphus' neurotic kin, slipping into and out of fresh garments through the late watches of the night, my impulses utterly beyond my check or control. But changing my clothes did nothing to change my mind. Wearing any other color would be a declaration that they had been correct about me: that I was impure and a danger and discredit to the House of Vesta.

The dress was simple, like a linen slip but with asymmetrical petals on either side. The neckline was high, but wide on the corners, so that it barely grasped my shoulders.

They would know me in this dress.

I wore Aemilia's shoes, which no longer excoriated the sensitive skin on my heels. Perhaps she was right. Perhaps the blisters were a test to determine that I was worthy of the statement they made on my behalf, a kind of conditioning.

Aemilia emerged from the bathroom in a billow of steam and light. Her purse was resting on the bed, indicating she was preparing to leave Ilium.

"I didn't know the clubs opened this early," I remarked, unable to ignore the fact that she was wearing an ivory '70s disco revival dress with a ballerina neckline and elastic waist over galaxy leggings, which I'd always secretly wanted to steal.

"Adamo's taking me on a tour of the churches. There's a lot of them, so we're getting an early start. We're trying to set a record. The most he's ever visited in a single day is seven."

"You're going to visit more than seven churches? Today?"

"Yeah. Chiesa del Gesù, Basilica di Massenzio, Chiesa di Santa Maria del Popolo, Basilica Fulvia Aemilia, Basilica di Santa Maria Maggiore, Basilica di San Pietro in Vincoli, Basilica di San Giovanni in Laterano, Basilica di Santa Sabina, Basilica di San Paolo Fuorile Mura, and Basilica di Santa Maria in Trastevere. And Basilica Giulia, if we have time. We have until midnight for it to count." Aemilia looked immensely proud of herself for having remembered and rattled off the list of churches like a native Italian. And well she should. All I could remember was a string of basilicas and chieasas.

"That's a lot of churches." I felt dizzy just thinking about so many vaulted ceilings and crucifixes.

"I thought you'd feel that way," Aemilia replied slyly. "That's why I didn't invite you. Besides, it looks like you're off on an adventure of your own." She said nothing about my vestment, which I believed to be a first in our relationship.

"That and the fact that you want Adamo all to yourself," I replied. "At 5 a.m. … Wait a minute? Why are you leaving so early? I know you want to see them all, but I can't believe there are churches open to the public at 5 a.m., even in Rome."

"Adamo's got friends who can get us into one of the basilicas and two of the chiesas before they officially open. Or is that two of the basilicas and one of the chiesas? You know, it's not easy keeping this all straight in my head." Aemilia offered a wry grin.

"Tell me about it. Be safe, please. It makes me worried to think about you wandering around creepy churches in the dark—or anywhere in the dark," I amended, catching Aemilia's annoyed expression.

"Look at you, expressing concern for my well being. You're on your way to becoming a normal big sister," she said. "I'm not sure I like it."

"Get used to it. Or be careful what you ask for. Maybe both," I decided.

We left Ilium at the same time, me in a taxi and Aemilia in Adamo's car. It bothered me that however much I glowered, Basilio's handsome servant continued to wave happily at me with a friendly smile whenever we encountered one another. He could have at least pretended to feel threatened to provide me with the illusion that I could protect my 16-year-old sister in a strange country—though I could not in good conscience call Italy foreign, not when it felt dearer to my lungs and closer to my skin than New Jersey ever had. Aemilia merrily called out that she would never relinquish her leggings to me, and they pulled away at what I had to acknowledge was an entirely reasonable speed.

"Monte Palatino," I told the taxi driver, ignoring his look of surprise.

Ilium looked even more foreboding by dark, and as we pulled away, I thought I saw a light flare somewhere within the cavern of a house.

The driver seemed reluctant to leave me on Via di San Gregorio, which was utterly abandoned at that hour. Or so I hoped. But I was determined, and he had no desire to be accused of kidnapping an American tourist. I approached the gate, where a single groundskeeper was sweeping. He had rather nicer pants than I'd have expected of a profession that involved constant exposure to tourists and dirt, and he was whistling the arc of an aria from *Così fan tutte*.

I considered walking right past him into the ruins, but he saw me—looked directly at me and shuddered, as if confronted by a great and terrible ghoul. Wordlessly, he gestured me in and resumed his task without looking back. Clearly, he meant me to vanish into what little remained of the baths and palaces of my first life. I obliged him because it was kind.

I recognized it, in the revelatory hush of pre-predawn, when nothing stirred, and even the wind could not be bothered to casually brush the tips of the pines watching over the city's relics. But if I had expected to be welcome, to walk through the archway of Domus Augustana and be swept into an alternate dimension in which none of my ghosts, past or present, could find me, I knew as soon as I set foot there that wouldn't happen.

Mostly, I felt safe there.

"I know you," I murmured to the trees, with my hands flat on the distressed walls, listening for voices from my past, hoping to imbibe some of the courage it had taken to stand for thousands of years. The Stadium of Domitian, where we'd gathered by the thousands to watch footraces, was purple with flowers. The name was on the tip of my tongue, attempting to fade beyond remembrance, but I wrestled it back.

Petunias. Purple petunias. Purple petunias on Palatine

Hill.

I will say one thing for Palatine Hill 2,000 years past its prime: It was an ideal place to recline and allow yourself to be lost. I began to do the things I'd never tried, because there wasn't time or privacy. I rolled down a gentle green slope, arms flung well above my head, feet twirling over and under one another quickly enough to make a ballerina jealous, even one of the sublime, otherworldly creatures at the Teatro dell'Opera di Roma.

Then, I made myself into the best wheel I possibly could, being neither perfectly round nor particularly sturdy, and cartwheeled until the ground and sky jumbled together. In the stadium, I skipped from one truncated pillar to another, posing as Vesta, as Hercules, as Aemilia delivering a lecture on the 5,001 reasons I should lose the privilege of dressing myself, as an American politician proclaiming mea culpa for being found out in some wrongdoing, despite not knowing the meaning of the term. As my hunter, eager and admired and bright on the night of Bona Dea before I could claim her. I vogued—or did my very best interpretation, anyway, which would not have been recognizable as an established form of expression or dance to any audience, so it was good that I had none.

Then, sleep, deep and more restful than anything I had enjoyed since graduating and being spirited to my homeland. My family had never gone camping while I was growing up, never even pitched a tent in the backyard and pretended it was a great and vast wilderness, and it occurred to me, for the first time, as an invisible blade of grass tickled my cheek, that I had perhaps been robbed of something I might have found pleasurable. Minutes or hours later, in the crucial moment between waking and sleeping, when the eyes are sealed determinedly closed but the mind is wide open to stray impressions and suggestions, I saw Valens' face.

The groundskeeper woke me at 8, before the first eager tourists could trample me into the ground where I could lie peacefully and permanently with the other relics of my era.

He rapped the soles of my shoes timidly with a stick, and must have enjoyed the sound it produced because he continued rapping even after I was clearly awake and looking at him with confusion.

"Awake!" I chastised in exasperation.

"Awake?" His expression was doubtful. Either he didn't fully comprehend the word or wanted to further abuse my shoes.

"*Delirianti isti Romani*," I muttered, shaking out my much-abused dress, which surprisingly showed no evidence of having been dragged ignobly and repeatedly through grass. They are mad, those Romans!

He chuckled, and fear thundered through my blood. I had spoke quietly, but in a dead language nonetheless. It was not wise to be alone with a groundskeeper who spoke Latin on Palatine Hill.

"*Foro Romano.*" He pointed north.

"That way?" I queried, to which he responded "*sì, sì*" and gestured all the more emphatically.

The sun had risen, and though I walked briskly and attempted to replicate my meditative trance from earlier when I cavorted and slept in the dark, it seemed it had been banished along with my solitude. The tourists were already stirring, and a young couple, hands clasped, asked through expectant smiles if I could direct them to Palatine Hill. His shirt was olive colored, like much of the vegetation, and creased, and her clothes were too new, and they were in love—desperately so, as is ever the case on the first go-around. They were at once fiercely trusting of the world around them and fiercely protective of one another. I knew them. I had been them—or half, anyway.

"*Vāde rēctā. Tunc verte ā sinistrā.*" I made an arrow of my arm, sheathed by my side, then darted it forward and veered it to the left to indicate the direction they were to take. She smiled her thanks over her shoulder as they proceeded on their way.

They didn't even notice that I had spoken Latin, probably didn't even know the difference.

"It's almost like you want to be found out and dragged back to the tomb." Aemilia's voice in my head, her reproach at the Vatican, served as a reminder that it did not do to be needlessly reckless. But it was harder and harder to care. Maybe it was the medication, the small blue pills that were supposed to bleed me of anxiety and delusional thinking. But I'd rather believe it was my powers coming back to me after a very long hiatus.

The forum somehow retained its splendor. Perhaps it was because the parade of ruins that preceded it had prepared me, and I knew not to expect a graveyard of freshly fallen noblemen, just bits and pieces—and not terribly important ones at that. It's no coincidence that whatever's least important is always left behind. So it was flattering, really, that someone had found me important enough to revive.

But mostly I was in awe because no one can return home after such a long absence and sneer on the doorstep of things that once were, especially when there was no hope of recalling them to life. There were other people there, and I was distantly aware of them. As the forum became more and more real to me, my contemporaries vanished. And I didn't miss them one whit.

It was a show of very bad form, but I bypassed all the terribly important places: Saturn's temple; Castor and Pollux's temple of worship; the temple of Caesar, where Rome's most famous emperor was cremated and mourned by the men who assassinated him. And because I had a Roman soul, I knew that they meant both—the killing and the memorializing— passionately and wholeheartedly. They could kill a man (or vestal) and venerate him (or her) with complete sincerity.

The last couple of feet were a dream, but there was no harsh jolt back to an even harsher world. I saw the broken circle. There wasn't enough of it to maintain a hearth and fire. And what was there—a handful of pillars—was merely a placeholder for what had been. My home—Vesta's temple— was demolished in 1549, its marble cannibalized to help build papal palaces and churches, perhaps even the sacred places

Aemilia now visited. To the conqueror go the spoils. It was fair. More than fair, really. It was the law I had once abided by.

Strangest of all, it was Benito Mussolini who reconstructed my beloved temple. He hadn't done a very thorough job of it, with barely enough present to indicate that its original shape had been circular, but it was owing to him that Vesta's temple had any kind of presence at all. Who knew what connection a 20th-century fascist dictator had felt to Vesta to inspire such a gesture? Of course I had never participated in the American mating ritual of giving and receiving cards scribbled with poems and other niceties; nothing but reconstructing an ancient temple could impress me, and few teenagers would find it within their means to concoct such a mad, ambitious Valentine.

And there were the statues commemorating the priestesses of note—the chief vestals who had demonstrated such thorough knowledge of religious practices and so keen a desire and commitment to serve Vesta that they now lived forever among the ruins of the Roman forum, enshrined in marble.

I clutched the knees of the nearest figure, washing away the creases in her fine high priestess attire in happy, freshly made tears.

"You don't look a day over 200," I proclaimed with great admiration, clutching her to my chest. If it sounds blasphemous, or possibly ironic, I assure you that it wasn't. I may have dabbled in sacrilegious humor when I wore virgin white, but since betraying my order and violating my oath, I'd been much more successful at suppressing my instincts. It's amazing what guilt can accomplish where willpower fails in your efforts to become a different person entirely.

I made my way down the line like a hostess at an upscale party—the kind they don't invite teenagers from New Jersey to attend—or perhaps, more aptly, like a diner at a buffet—the kind everyone's welcome to partake in. There weren't many hands, but when I encountered them, I offered a gracious, penitent kiss. But what were hands in the grander scheme of things? What priestess required knuckles and fingernails when she had a willing heart and capable mind?

It was true that if these stunted and truncated figures had lurched themselves before the Pontifex Maximus, they would have been met with laughter and horror. Unblemished, the figures were not. But they had survived long and unfriendly centuries, when scavengers and battles and conversions—voluntary and forced—had laid waste to everything and everyone around them. And they did it without Botox or lap bands, teeth whitening or collagen. They neither defied age nor were devoured by it, and there was more of home in those faces peering down at me than there ever had been in any family portrait.

Some pedestals were empty, as though their occupants had tired of being the background figures in an endless litany of selfies, or perhaps abandoned their posts for a smoke break. They hadn't, of course. They wouldn't, even if they could. But it was easier to think that way sometimes.

There were Post-it notes in my purse, which Aemilia liked to give me a hard time about, but which seemed like a better alternative to leaving notes on stray napkins and the crook of my hand where thumb met index finger.

There was a mottled patch of grass near the statues. No one would have called the vegetation healthy or impressive, but you work with what you've got. There, on a dispirited tuft of mostly green grass, I searched for inspiration. I thought about the women I'd known, the powerful camaraderie that came with our shared sense of purpose, a sense of fellowship I'd taken for granted until I was reborn utterly alone. I tried to picture the day the Christian emperor Theodosius I ordered them to extinguish the fire, issuing a death sentence to an order older than the country I now called home.

What did it mean to watch the thing you'd loved, nourished, protected throughout your entire life flicker into nonexistence? They must have doubted whether the world had any place for them, much as I did now.

It was much harder than writing impersonal missives

in a yearbook. I could not tell a Virgo Vestalis Maxima to have a good summer and that I would see her next fall.

The summer day simmered and sweltered, and pockets of heat gathered and mutated into angry touts that chased tourists. And the tourists stewed themselves into a jambalaya only the gargoyles trapped in the Pantheon fountain would be able to digest. The heat didn't touch me. It couldn't, while I was employed in Vesta's service. But that didn't matter, because 20 minutes after I had finished writing notes, I would black out as a reaction to the pharmaceuticals my uncle, who still reeked of licorice, had imposed upon me. I saw it all in a moment of clarity: my uncle holding the tube, an endless river of pills the color of bright corn, my head striking the corner of the pedestal now farthest from me, Aemilia finding me there. I also knew what I wanted to write.

The first Post-it, placed on the shoulder of the first vestal, said, "There is ambition in restraint, and courage also."

On the second, which required both sides of the paper and barely fit even when I used my final exam essay handwriting, I translated the dedication to one of the vestals: "In recognition of her chastity, purity, and her outstanding knowledge in ritual and religious matters, the pontiffs, under the illustratious Pontifex Maximus, Macrinius Sossianus, dedicate this to C——, head priestess of the Vestal Virgins."

The third, just left of a vestal's navel: "We were Rome's hearthfire."

The fourth, on an exposed ankle: "We served Vesta, who served all women."

Then I stood in front of *the* statue, *her* statue, my hand following the trail blazed by her curious palm all those long centuries ago. The blood drained giddily from my head, rushing everywhere it had no place, not with my hand grazing the thigh of a vestal virgin—even a copy, albeit a well-executed one—not when I was married to a jealous empire.

"Nesreen was here," read the Post-it. Just above the knee. As if anyone would have the audacity to forget.

On the final note on the final silhouette, though she

had no head: "Who will keep the fire burning now?" I truly wanted to know. I wanted to write, "We're gonna be OK." There was a place for such reassurances. The world abounded with inspirational and uplifting words and phrases—whole seminars full of them.

Many of the people responsible for releasing such sentiments into the wilds of people's minds didn't even need to know you or your circumstances to assure you that everything was gonna be A-OK. Whatever that meant. If such people had been allowed to exist in my Rome, they probably would have insisted everything was going to turn out fine even as they carried out my death sentence. The night is darkest before the dawn, they would have said. And I'd have tumbled down the ladder and into the dark before the next day broke just the same.

I tell you truthfully: There is blackness darker than the night, and the dawn does not excise it. I've seen it, and it briefly sustained me, filling my lungs when there was nothing else to inflate them. Until it wouldn't anymore.

Nesreen saved me then. The blackness could claim many things, including my life, but not the memories of her, and it was hard to regret those luminous prisms of energy and light that fluttered where not even the emperor could touch them, even from my present vantage hanging around awkwardly at the tail of the story, knowing how it ended.

So there I was, invisible to the other tourists drifting with mediocre interest through the ruins of my former home, tangled in a snare part memory, part reverie, when the world decided to pitch. I tumbled forward, my hands catching at the solid marble pedestal, but it was my clever head that caught the statue first. There was a sharp crack somewhere, and then I greeted the blackness with the restrained civility due any unpleasant acquaintance.

I was there awhile, and for a place I had not wanted to visit, it really wasn't half bad. There were no tourists fastening gum to the nonexistent walls, no past and therefore no ruins, no present and therefore no pain, and no future and therefore no anxiety.

"Seriously, Rhea?" The voice trying to unwind my really rather comfortable cocoon was both irritated and irritating.

"Come on. … Come back to me! … Rhea! … Come back … ."

I wanted to ignore it. The words had a frantic quality that banished the peace I had been so close to claiming, and the closer it came, the more aware I became of an intense pain that washed over me in long, nauseating waves.

No. I would stay here. The voice didn't know what it was talking about, didn't understand what it was asking.

"I wouldn't go making a habit of this," it chastised. "It isn't very dignified." But it wasn't alone. It had an accomplice that shook and pinched my arm. Voices shouldn't be able to twist the delicate flesh of your inner arm.

"Worse, it's really uncool." That's when I recognized the voice. It was still too loud, and distant, as if it were coming from a phone with bad service, but there was one person I knew whose priorities and interests—pinching and rebuking me for my social shortcomings—meshed perfectly with those of the voice. Except that she was supposed to be gallivanting around churches with Valens. No. Adamo.

"Abire," I muttered. Now that I had identified the voice as my sister, I knew that it would not go away, however many times and in however many languages I demanded it. But I had to take a stand somewhere, even if I was technically lying prone when I made it.

"*Cosa c'è?*" Great. Another voice. Speaking another language.

"Nothing!" Aemilia's voice was sharp. "Rhea fell, I think. And now she's speaking nonsense." The last sentence was delivered with another pinch to my arm. Aemilia didn't want me speaking Latin in front of the other voice, which I knew was Adamo, but his relationship with my sister annoyed me, so I pretended otherwise.

Unfortunately, the more I understood, the more I felt

the full impact of my fall. My teeth ached. I didn't know it was possible for them to pound like a branch about to give way in a storm. But that was mere child's play compared to the tempest in my head, which felt oddly flat, like a veil that had settled and refused to be displaced. I had only one recourse.

There was nothing in my stomach, so I spat vile orange bile onto the ground beside me. It didn't relieve my head, but sometimes it helps to sink as deeply into the mire as gravity will take you before attempting to thrash your way out.

Aemilia was regarding me with concern and horror. I noticed for the first time that her disco dress had grass stains around the hem. There was something else as well—a splash of red. Adamo saw it too, and knelt beside me.

"*Porca vacca*!"

He had his jacket off and bundled into a pillow before either Aemilia or I understood what was happening. She just stood above me mouthing the phrase "porca vacca" and looking baffled.

"Please." Adamo was pushing me back onto the pillow, and when Aemilia made no effort to stop him, I figured it was best to cooperate. Besides, he had placed one of his knees directly in the little patch of orange vomit, and I just couldn't square such disregard for his clothing with anything villainous or cruel.

His green eyes were scanning my face, as if intent on solving a puzzle. Gently, carefully, he brushed aside my hair and examined my forehead. Behind him, Aemilia gasped, but Adamo said nothing.

"Ilium," he said grimly. "We take her now."

"Please," he repeated, and began to lift me, but this time I objected.

"I'm perfectly capable of walking." It may have been true. It probably was not. But I could not bear the notion that my fellow vestals would watch me carried away from Vesta's temple in a man's arms. I knew they were just representations, but they were the closest I had ever come to my departed sisters, and I could not heap additional fodder onto the scandal already associated with my name. I'd thought I could fall no further as a disgraced vestal, but it turned out there were always new gutters. They'd probably been there all along, but I'd climbed too high to notice.

Isn't it funny, the things you forget when you finally get wherever it was you were so desperate to go? Not funny like the first time you see a hot dog after you've read *A Confederacy of Dunces* or funny like watching a couple of guys in jerseys go absolutely batty over what they consider a bad call by a man in a striped shirt. More along the lines of funny like visiting someone's house and realizing they don't have books. Or funny like the couple that's trying desperately to pretend they're in a sitcom so they pick at each other's faults in front of their friends.

"Yes, Rhea, those are all things that are funny. Now please let Adamo carry you to the car."

I didn't realize I was speaking. Was Aemilia in my head? I gave her a good glare in case she was, just so she would know that I knew, and feel guilty and stop reading my mind.

"I'm not reading your mind, Rhea. You're muttering. I can hear you. And so can Adamo." She spoke the last line as if she wanted to pinch me again to remind me of something. She'd pinch me later. When the world wasn't balancing on my skull.

Funny like the empire you'd sworn to protect burying you alive and your uncle drugging you and hitting your head on a statue and your sister getting mad at you and threatening to pinch you. Not funny.

"Just pick her up." Aemilia was instructing Adamo. "What's she going to do? She's too weak to fight, and she doesn't even understand what's going on. Plus, she needs help. So unless you're secretly a trained physician, which I very much doubt, the only way you can help is by picking her up and moving her." Aemilia's tone could have chastised Adamo without any words at all. She could have entered the Coliseum with that tone and thrashed almost any opponent. It didn't matter what she said when she used that voice. All that mattered was that she got exactly what she wanted.

"No. Not unless she says it's good."

Adamo was mostly supporting me while we argued. Or they argued and Aemilia secretly read my mind. It was a good thing I'd never bothered to keep a diary. She'd probably have gone through that, too. Still, it was good to know that Adamo had some backbone. It wasn't easy standing up to Aemilia, and even in my state of confusion, I understood that she was trying to take charge because she was worried about me. Marble pedestal: 1. Rhea's head: 0. Ugh. It felt weird referring to myself in the third person. Rhea said this … Rhea did that … Rhea pinched Aemilia for the first time, and it felt amazing. Rhea lost her mind amid the ruins. Rhea lost her mind amid the romantic ruins. Rhea rued losing her mind amid the romantic ruins.

Aemilia cracked. She was leaning back, laughing as heartily as I'd ever seen. It came in peals—loud and low and unrestrained. After a moment of confusion, Adamo smiled as well, but I could tell that he was merely relieved rather than amused by whatever had set her off.

She was saying something as well, but I was too far away to hear and in no condition to shimmy within range.

"All right, here's what we're gonna do!" Aemilia recovered from her amused stupor so quickly that I jerked and would have fallen to the ground if Adamo hadn't caught me. He looked startled as well, but steady.

"Rhea, it's OK that you don't want them to see Adamo carry you." She gestured to the statues. "But you can't walk by yourself. We're going to prop you up together until we're outside the forum. Then Adamo will carry you. But it's not that far to the car, and there's not too many people about, so there's a good chance no one will even notice."

Quickly, because she was worried that I would argue or someone would get distracted, Aemilia wrapped my left arm over her shoulders and tucked my right arm around Adamo. Together, we hobbled to the exit. And I didn't really mind all that much, not even when I looked back and saw one of the statues with eloquent stubs where her arms ought to have been staring after us.

"Don't worry about them," Aemilia whispered into my ear, tickling my forehead with her long hair. "They'd understand. You're injured. You can't serve Vesta or yourself or anybody with a gash in your head. Basilio will pay for this."

Then, more loudly, "Did you really say 'pig cow' back there? I could study Italian an entire lifetime and still not fully understand how swearing works."

"For that, you have to study the people," Adamo said slyly, and I heard, rather than saw, his smile.

Aemilia laughed as if she hadn't a care.

XI

Nesreen chuckled, the richest sound I ever heard. "*Bella gerant alii. Nesreen amet!*" I pleaded playfully. Let others wage wars. Nerseen must love. It was the closest I had ever come to declaring myself, but she did not seem to notice.

"I could stay," she said teasingly, and I could not take my eyes off the happy sheen of her face, the crease where her cheeks met the corner of her lips. "But only if you finally take this off."

She gave my infula a tug, and my hands anxiously set about adjusting the headpiece, making sure it was properly in place. Or properly enough, anyway. Even when I wore nothing else—and I had worn nothing else—I refused to allow Nesreen to remove my veil. I could not get the image of those four hands plaiting my hair each morning. Those four hands were connected to two servants, and those two servants would race one another to Fulvia in order to have the honor of denouncing me for incest.

"You know I cannot, and you know why I cannot." Denying her anything filled me with the deepest dread. It felt desperately unfair to live in a world in which I had to tell Nesreen no.

"And you know why I cannot stay."

She was right, of course. They would kill her, too, if they found her. They would lash her until she bled to death in front of a jeering mob at the Comitium. It would make my own death—buried in a tomb beneath the ground—seem almost decorous by comparison, although there was something barbaric about prolonging it. No one knew how long the vestals lived once they'd been lowered into the chamber. Hours? Days? A week?

"You are right," I sighed. "You cannot stay ... too much longer. Tell me about your family." I pulled her hand from where it rested beside her and began absently to write missives with my finger, hoping to distract her.

"I already did," she laughed. "It is your turn. You have five sisters. Hortensia ... Liviana ... Junia, who almost took your place here ... Aemilia, who is your shadow when you are together, and—"

"Decima," I supplied when it was obvious that she had forgotten. "The youngest of all."

"Decima," she repeated seriously, and I knew that she would remember. "And which is it that sleeps with the emperor?"

Suddenly, it no longer seemed like a good idea to talk about our families, even if it had been my idea.

"Liviana is the emperor's mistress." It was a very great honor, of course. It was also terrifying, especially with rumors of Marcia's penchant for plotting against her rivals. And here's another mistress—one that Commodus seems to like quite well though not so well as Marcia—and this mistress also happens to be a sister of a vestal virgin; Marcia's a Christian and makes no secret of her disdain for what she calls the pagan gods and those who serve them. Fortunately, Commodus appreciated pagan pomp, but it did not matter what Commodus liked. Marcia would hardly ask his permission before poisoning one of his mistresses.

The subject of the emperor was a dangerous one for us. Nesreen disliked Commodus. She had never said so, and I suspected she never would out of respect for my position, but it was there nonetheless, in the gleam of her eye whenever his name was spoken, and the quick spasm of her hand around my own. If we were in public, where I could not take her hand in mine, she would reach for something, anything, and twist it about in her hands as though it preoccupied her. But Nesreen was not the sort of person to go around picking things up on a whim. I never saw her make a nervous gesture, and falling in love is the sort of pastime that demands a veritable buffet of awkward exchanges and ticks that do not represent you at your very best. Not to mention that I had seen her fighting for her life against two leopards. Mostly I think she wanted a distraction that would help her focus on something besides the thoughts that already preoccupied her, but I had already decided to wait awhile before confirming my theory by asking her.

I kissed her to stop her from having to pick anything up. And because I wanted to. As much as I loved my sisters, counting them was not a satisfying use of the precious hours before dawn when Septima would arrive and assume her watch over the flame. Nesreen and I originally agreed that she would not stay past halfway through my watch, but the very first time she snuck into the temple, we broke our decree by nearly an hour. And we had only gotten worse.

It was a riddle with no solution. We both lived indentured to oaths and institutions with rigid codes of conduct. We abided by everyone else's rules—except, in my case, the most important rule dictating that I remain chaste. I tried to both forget about that and make up for it by strictly adhering to all the other rules. But Nesreen and I could not bring ourselves to abide by our own ordinance about how long she was allowed to stay, without which we would probably be found and killed.

It was now two hours until Septima would arrive. I watched over the flame and my slumbering Nesreen, but the minutes fled, and her still form became a greater liability. *Carpe diem* belongs to sanctioned lovers. *Carpe noctem* was my creed. This was only the second time I had seen her sleep, and I looked for patterns, habits, anything that might afford some insight into who she was and what mattered to her. It was vitally important that I understand her.

She slept on her right side, with her face resting against my thigh and a hand curled solidly around my leg, just below the kneecap. She neither muttered nor stirred, and I was surprised at how quickly I became accustomed to the regularity of her breathing. I was propped against the altar, with one cushion beneath me and another just below the small of my back. The temple was not made for comfortable sleeping. Its only purpose—and our only purpose while there—was protecting the fire.

But my venatore did not seem to mind. She had probably endured worse. Ships were not known for their hospitality to slaves when they carried them to Rome. Nesreen assured me that, with the exception of what happened inside the amphitheatre, gladiators were treated well. They were well fed, at least, and she had even made mention of specialized massages. I must have looked doubtful.

"Your father would not abuse a prized horse, would he?" she insisted. "It would be a waste of his investment. I am worth even more."

Still, there was something heartbreaking in how easily she slept on the marble floor. What was worse, she would soon be found there if I did not wake her. I had delayed our parting almost to the point of certain danger.

"*Est mondo in rebus*," I whispered. *There is measure in things*, my mother liked to say. But if there is, I never saw it. There is measure in some people, an inclination to yield, to give. But there is no measure in the law, there is no measure in Rome, and there was no measure in me, no inclination to sacrifice my pleasure, my love, for Rome.

"Venatore," I whispered softly. Servants sometimes lingered just beyond the door, waiting, listening. Nesreen did not budge.

"Hunter, it is past time for you to go." Reluctantly, I shifted my legs so that I was no longer a comfortable pillow.

Still, she did not stir.

The temple door, however, quaked. I stood, as casually as my nerves permitted, nearer the hearth. Whoever opened the door was not trying to catch me sleeping or worse; whenever a servant truly believed she had a chance at snaring a vestal virgin, the door flew as though propelled by the Venti themselves. It was likely just Septima offering to share the final dregs of my overnight watch. Which happened often enough, especially with the long, lonely late watch—though usually only when Nona was the appointed guard, and we knew she would not make it through the night.

The door opened, only it was Cloelia rather than Septima who stepped through.

"Cloelia!" I weighed the amount of surprise my tone ought to carry before speaking. "I thought you might be Septima, come to relieve me."

"I came to ask if you would like her to come to the temple so you can sleep. It may be Martius, but the nights still feel long," she observed with a friendly smile.

I did not dare look down, where Nesreen slept on the floor.

"I will wait for her to assume her watch. It is not that long now." The words had been meant to sound reassuring, but they sounded wooden. Cloelia nodded, but she did not make any move to leave.

"Actually, I am rather tired. Would you mind fetching Septima?"

The servant nodded once more, though this time she turned to leave. I had just one more arrow in my arsenal, one final opportunity to squash any slender vestige of suspicion lurking in her mind.

"Do you think Fulvia will disapprove?" I asked, and I allowed a small quaver to work its way into my voice. "I have tried so hard to please her. I ... I would not want to leave early if it is not the right thing to do." I tried to look conflicted. It was not all that difficult to do with a gladiator asleep at my feet.

Cloelia hesitated. It was not common for a vestal virgin to ask a servant for her opinion, but I had encouraged familiarity more than the other vestals. Perhaps that was the source of my downfall.

"Better to ask for help than endanger the fire," Cloelia counseled. "There is a reason Numa Pompilius, in his wisdom, prescribed that there should be more than one priestess attending Vesta."

"He only intended for there to be two," I countered, but Cloelia was already gone, and I had only minutes to remove Nesreen, and all evidence of her, from the temple.

"Nesreen! This is not the time for sleep!" I shook her, and not very gently, and I did not stop even after her eyes opened and she gripped my shoulders in alarm.

"A servant was here. She is sending another vestal who will be here at any moment." I lifted her as I spoke, my hands darting into the temple's shadows to ensure they sheltered no garment or relic from the venatore. We hastened to the door—Nesreen silent and moving as though in a trance, and I directing her incoherently, with no trace of the jocund girl who had seduced her into staying. Terror had banished all gentleness and reason, and I could not even say whose fate concerned me more: hers or mine.

Nesreen only seemed to truly awaken as I attempted to simultaneously open the heavy temple door and push her through it. The task was impossible given that the door was, as I already mentioned, quite substantial, as you might expect of a barrier intended to protect many of Rome's dearest documents and treasures. But the hunter could not be given credit for helping the situation, for though I was taller, I possessed a slight frame, in the same manner as a bird, whose bones, I am told, are hollow, to enable them to fly. If Septima discovered Nesreen in the temple, we would both have need of hollow bones, as well as a pair of wings apiece. Nesreen was more substantial, and her training at the Ludus Matutinus had taught her to make use of each inch and tendon.

When she balked at the entrance, all I could do was

tear at her arms in an effort to pry them from the door. She released her grip—finally!—and brushed my cheek.

"Death does not concern us, since when we are, death has not come," she reminded me. "And when death has come, we are not."

"You said that already! And I know your beloved Epicurus spoke it long before you, but that does not mean you should run about courting death!"

Why was there always this frantic annoyance hovering just beyond euphoria when I was with Nesreen?

"I will come back to you," she assured me, with a smile so radiant that my heart cracked, and I knew I would kill Septima to protect Nesreen.

"Please," I pleaded. "Be well."

I sent her out into a world that had enslaved her and given her the choice to extinguish or be extinguished, a world that had exalted me to the status of high priestess and linked my fate to that of a flame that would not be extinguished. Because it was the only thing I could do.

XII

The upshot of my tumble at the forum was that Aemilia forced Basilio to reduce my medication. He would not stop it, but she successfully argued that an American tourist falling down among the great Roman ruins was bound to draw attention. Unless he planned on locking me up in Ilium for the duration of my stay in Italy, he would have to let up a little in order to ensure that I was safe.

I would love to report that he vehemently denied any intention of incarcerating me, that he expressed sufficient horror at the mere idea that I felt safe closing my eyes at night, but he didn't say anything at all when Aemilia floated the possibility of his kidnapping me. His eyes were on his glass—half full of the pink lemonade he made whenever he had houseguests—and he didn't flinch or twitch or react at all.

It unnerved me more than it would have if he had boldly stated his intention of imprisoning me. Basilio was dangerous because he believed, unequivocally, in the existence of right and wrong. And the next, natural step, after sweeping everything and everyone into two tidy categories—good and bad—is to treat them accordingly. Basilio had decided that I was bad, or that my brain was, anyway, and that trumped all the regular rules about how people are supposed to treat each other. Like not kidnapping one another or blackmailing someone into taking prescription medication to treat their "psychosis."

Plus, he still smelled like black licorice, which disturbed me sufficiently that on a rare night when Basilio left the house to meet someone for dinner, and Aemilia was off somewhere with Adamo, I searched the kitchen. Thoroughly. I went through every drawer, every cupboard, every spare bowl. I even emptied the dishwasher on the off chance that a spare stick had gotten trapped in a corner crevice, and my meticulous uncle had somehow missed it.

But I didn't find any licorice. There wasn't even a stray can of expired beans behind the breakfast cereal. In fact, there wasn't breakfast cereal. Everything was organized and fresh and organic. It was as if Basilio expected someone to search his kitchen. Fortunately, I'd borrowed Emeline's camera—I couldn't square the idea of Aemilia and 19th-century technology coexisting, so when it came to luxuries like cameras and cell phones and computers, she was Emeline once more— and meticulously documented the arrangement of the cupboards before I set about ransacking them. By the time Basilio, Emeline, and Adamo returned home, it was as if nothing had happened.

The following morning, I awoke to find Emeline regarding me warily. My sleep-fogged brain panicked and began searching for excuses to justify raiding the kitchen. Sadly, there weren't any that didn't make me sound crazy. The only thing I could think of was that I really wanted Frosted Flakes, which sounded sort of plausible unless she somehow knew that I had gone through the dishwasher as well. I could have argued that I was high, but Emeline knew quite well that I'd never gone in for that sort of recreational pastime. When you were busy juggling two lives in your head all day, you needed all the clarity you could get your reincarnated hands on.

"I thought I'd go to the catacombs," she said quite quickly.

"I want Frosted Flakes!" I announced. Even on a reduced dosage, my brain was foggier than I would have liked, resulting in conversational delays that I worried supported the idea that I was crazy. Then my brain registered what she had said, and I could actually feel the blood drain from my face.

"I knew better than to ask you," she said quickly. "I should be back by 3."

"I'm sure I won't be here. I have places to go, too, you know," I replied, knowing I was being childish and hating myself for it. "Just not the catacombs."

Underground burial chambers. Underground. Dark—an eternity of moonless, starless night. Air so thick you really could choke on it, and there was only room in your throat for the oppressive air or your cries for help. Never aid. Aid was something only spoken of by people who didn't require it. When you really needed something, buried-in-an-underground-tomb-and-slowly-suffocating needed something, it was help you asked for. If you knew where to ask. After awhile, up and down and left and right lost all meaning. There was the bed and the lamp and the water, no other reference required. I could feel the air from the tomb in the back of my throat and knew that something terrible was going to happen.

"Rhea, you're shaking. Rhea! Sit down. I'm not asking you to go with me. I wouldn't do that." She walked me over to the bed and placed me in a sitting position the way you would a doll, which confused me because I realized as the thought scuttled across my poor, duressed brain, that I'd never seen Emeline with dolls.

"You never played with dolls," I accused her. "And here I was thinking you were completely normal!"

"No, I didn't," she agreed. She had her index and middle finger on my wrist, and her lips were pursed in concentration. I thought, for a second, that she hadn't really heard me.

"Porca vacca! I don't know why I bother! I have no idea how to do this, and I don't even really know what a normal pulse is supposed to be anyway," she admitted. "What am I, a doctor?"

"No, not yet anyway. I think Dad might harbor some

career expectations along those lines for you, though," I replied. Some people might have been surprised or put off by her sudden display of temper, but it wasn't really all that out of character.

"They reminded me too much of my children," Emeline said softly, busying herself with her purse. "It was disconcerting, and it made me sad."

"I guess I kinda missed all that somehow." Without ever noticing how or when, I had regained the ability to breathe.

"You were preoccupied." It almost didn't sound bitter.

"I really didn't mean to flip out just now," I said by way of apology. "I suppose I felt a little like you were betraying me, almost like you were visiting my own grave ... as a tourist. I'm sorry. I know there isn't any truth to that. I know it's crazy." There was that word again, dogging me in this life the way Valens had shadowed me through the last.

"It is and it isn't," Emeline laughed. "I actually felt guilty, like I was sneaking around behind your back, which is why I wanted to tell you before I left."

"So we're both a little messed up in the head." I laughed. "Go. Have fun. Try not to get lost down there." I tried to keep my voice as light as possible. Tones are like animals; they respond to the feeling behind the words rather than the words themselves.

Emeline finally left, but not before reminding me that she'd be back early in the afternoon.

"There's something I want to talk to you about," she said, except that when Emeline said she wanted to talk to you, it was really an order. She'd been wasted on running an estate in her former life. Commodus should have given her an entire legion and sat back to watch as she conquered the world.

I grabbed my copy of *American Gods*, which Emeline had claimed for herself on the plane and only returned the previous evening, and headed for Palatine Hill. No way was I sticking around Ilium with just Basilio for company.

He was reading in the living room just beyond the

entryway. And he was wearing charcoal dress trousers and a button-down shirt. There was a jacket folded over the couch nearby. All of it irritated me—even the fact that he was reading, for some reason.

"Do you always wear a suit?" I asked in my snarkiest tone, and then left before he could reply.

Despite the fact that it was mid July, Palatine Hill was lush and felt about 10 degrees cooler than the rest of Rome. It may have merely been a placebo effect; I felt calm, therefore Palatine Hill was refreshing and cool. The tourists were less annoying there, too, which I attributed to the fact that it was at the top of a hill, which filtered out most of the lazy and idly curious. Plus, it was a sprawling territory, rich with meandering potential, while the Coliseum was more and more beginning to assume the shape and form of a sardine can in my memory. Sardines, I am fairly confident, don't have the luxury of pausing to scratch an elbow or fin without being trampled, and neither had I during those very stressful hours when Emeline and I circled the amphitheatre.

The Roman forum fell somewhere between the two. It in no way resembled a sardine can, but neither was it a vast ocean of space. Anyway, I couldn't relax there, with the broken temple and all those invisible eyes on me.

So I returned to Palatine Hill pretty much every day after my first very nearly nocturnal visit. The same groundskeeper waved me in each time, no matter the hour, and I was coming to regard tickets as archaic scraps of paper.

There was never any question of bringing anyone along; Emeline had developed the habit of orbiting around me as though I were a doddering old woman or very large planet, and it would be a cool day in Hades before I ever invited Basilio anywhere. The closest I'd come to issuing an invitation was when Emeline announced that she needed "some me time" and left the house with her war notebook and a giant stack of magazines. I found Adamo hovering outside the room I shared with my sister.

My first instinct was to scold him, but he looked so

vulnerable that I instead found myself talking to him, sharing my appreciation for Rome. I don't know if you've traveled much, but there's generally a rule that when you're in someone's homeland and they ask how you like it, it's in everyone's best interest for you to say as many nice things as you can.

I'm not suggesting you lie or anything—merely that you be selective in what you choose to comment upon. And the only things I really liked about Italy—besides the gelato, which is so obviously worthy of praise that complimenting it is almost too simple—were Bracciano and Palatine Hill. I did make a point of stating that I thought I might better enjoy Rome's charms in an alternate season, when the ratio of people to city was a little lower.

Adamo nodded and smiled. He was a good listener, and I was beginning to see why Emeline spent so much time in his company. I remembered his concerned green eyes staring down at me when I hit my head in the forum, and the fact that he listened when I insisted I did not want him to carry me. Too many people would have done it anyway. I was remembering all this, and maybe thinking a little bit about Valens, who was always so eager to please me, and I almost invited him to visit Palatine Hill with me. But just before I could, something shifted, and I glanced behind me and realized Basilio was lurking in the kitchen doorway, listening. And I remembered who had taken my passport.

"Have a nice day, then," I said abruptly, and left. I made a point of avoiding any conversation with him after that. There was no point in giving him the idea that I actually thought he was a halfway decent human being.

So that's how I wound up at Palatine Hill all alone. Or almost alone, anyway, as I'd given a great deal of consideration to the ideal setting for my first round with *American Gods*. You have to be careful where you bring a book on a first date. There are some books I could not have brought to Rome, much less Palatine Hill. They wouldn't have understood one another. But a tale of gods carried unwillingly to a new land,

and then forgotten there? A hero named Shadow? It was practically written for me, and for this hill. The ancient ruins deserved that story even more than I did, and I was thrilled and a little nervous to once again assume my role as vassal to the great, almost-forgotten Roman gods. I could be their shadow. I already felt like one most of the time, anyway.

The thing I like best about Palatine Hill is that there aren't any clocks, and since most people, myself included, tend to conflate clocks and time, I could pretend there was no such thing as a past, present, or future while I was there. It tended to simplify things.

I was about 300 pages in when I heard a familiar voice calling my name. The voice would get closer for a while and then suddenly sound off from another direction entirely, leading me to conclude that the voice's legs were walking it in a loop. I was tucked comfortably against a wall of stone, but on the side that wasn't visible—or accessible, technically—from the tourist path. It was a truly wonderful place to read, and I considered staying where I was and consigning Aemilia to wander the ruins, looking for me. But there was a good chance, knowing her, that she'd enlist someone's help, and then there would be a grand ruckus with fireworks and kazoos and awkward questions about why I was sitting on the other side of the wall when they eventually found me. So, I clambered over the wall and onto the tourist path, where I allowed myself to be found.

"There you are! I've been wandering all over looking for you for the past hour!"

Twenty minutes at most.

"Huh. That's weird. I've been right here." I shook my head, as though truly baffled by the fact that we hadn't seen one another sooner.

"I assume I have Adamo to thank for the fact that you knew where to look for me?" Since Aemilia seemed almost pleased that I found Adamo annoying, I liked to play up the fact that I disliked him. Some day we would probably have to work through the uncomfortable tangle of emotions that had thus far prevented us from talking about Valens, and I didn't want some good-looking Italian kid to become a bone of contention between us as well, especially when I didn't want him.

"He had a hunch you might be here. You can explain why that is some other time." She sat on the grass, carefully arranged her skirt around her legs, and reached for the book in my hand. I held it beyond her reach and sat down beside her, close enough for us to talk, but with enough distance that she couldn't suddenly lunge for it. She'd already read it, but her kid sister instincts seemed to have kicked in, and she decided she didn't want me to have it despite it being mine.

"How'd you like the catacombs?" I didn't feel like fighting over the book, so I decided to distract her.

"I didn't. I think I spent a total of two minutes in them and decided they weren't for me."

"Guess they'll have to find some way of burying you above ground."

"I've already decided I want a taxidermist to do all that stuffing and mounting stuff to me so I can be posed like a bear by the fireplace of my nearest surviving family member—probably my kids." She said this nonchalantly. "It probably doesn't matter anyway, since the gods will just spit me right back out again. Who knows what the world will be like then? We'd better hope the circumstances are favorable, and we don't land smack in the middle of some kind of bell-bottom revival. Or worse." Her blue eyes were wide with alarm, making it difficult to determine how much of what she said was meant to be serious.

"*We'd* better hope?"

"Well, so far everywhere I've turned up, you've turned up, too. It's like you're following me or something." Now she was smiling, but she still looked worried, and I doubted it could all be chalked up to an aversion to a decades-old fashion fad.

"More like everywhere I've turned up, you've turned up. Congratulations. You've successfully stalked me across more than 18 centuries, which makes the creepers back at high school look like total amateurs."

"Yeah, I doubt most of them could make it through a year with you," she laughed. "Can you picture Alain and his dopey baseball cap in the forum back home?" The idea seemed to appeal to her, because she'd gone from laughing before and after she spoke as a kind of complement to her words, to struggling to fit her words in between the hearty guffaws that I always found so unlikely and endearing.

I groaned loudly, trying to picture any one of our classmates in ancient Rome, wearing a toga and preparing for a career in the military or learning how to run a large estate. None of them fit. Aemilia did, though. She was just so comfortable with herself that you could put her anywhere, and she would make a life for herself.

"You know, something tells me you'll do just fine wherever the gods decide to plop you. And if you did find yourself surrounded by bell-bottom bimbos, you'd just throw on a skirt and lead them out of Egypt and into the holy land." I wasn't looking at Aemilia when I said it, in part because the path that disappeared in the distance was a much more satisfactory backdrop for my fantasy, and in part because I despised emotional conversations, and I could see that our talk was heading that way.

"I don't know if I'd necessarily choose a skirt for my big moment leading the lost children out of the fashion wasteland, and there are a few other fashion icons I can think of that might be a better comparison than Moses, but I see what you were saying there. Thanks."

"You wanna head back to Ilium?" I knew she didn't, but I started to get up anyway.

"No. I wanted to talk to you. Remember?"

"Oh yeah. Sorry. I guess I forgot." I sat back down. Reluctantly.

"No, you didn't. You never forget anything. You just hate talks." She looked grim.

"No, I ... ."

"Don't say you don't, Rhea. Don't lie. You know you do. I'm not mad about it or anything. I just don't want you to lie to me. And I really do need to talk to you, so you'll have to just set your discomfort aside."

"Fine," I pouted. "But I would like to point out, before you begin, that you've been asking me to set aside my discomfort a lot lately. And I've been a pretty good sport about it, but there's going to come a time when you're going to have to stop telling me that you know what's best for me better than I do."

"I agree," she replied, completely shocking me. "I'm not going to say that I'll never try to lure you out of yourself or do something that I think will make life easier for you again, but it's your choice. It is your life, and I know that. But I asked for Rome, for you to trust me for one summer so we can just deal with our pasts and go back home and make the decisions that need to be made without fear. Or at least with just the normal amount of fear. You know, what if I major in the wrong thing and then wind up in a career that I don't find fulfilling and spend the rest of my life stuck at a job that holds no meaning until I retire and die, having accomplished nothing of value? Those types of problems."

"Holy gargoyle spit, Aemilia, what's wrong with you?" I was genuinely distressed by what she'd just said. "I haven't even thought about that stuff yet. I can't think about it. There isn't enough room in my head."

"Then maybe it's better if you don't leave Rome until you are ready to think about it. You know, I'm not saying you have to go to college. Mom and Dad wouldn't even make that argument, and you know how badly they want us to go. Just allow yourself to start thinking about what you'd like to do, what would make you happy, what you would like to see. There was this kid in my chemistry class, and he kept talking about how he was going to skip across a bridge in every country, and you know, good for him."

I rolled my eyes. I knew it was a silly thing to do, but any time someone is talking earnestly to me about what I want to do with my life—whether it's my parents or a guidance counselor or my little sister—I can't take them seriously. Because it always sounds like they're reading from some script handed down to them from previous guidance counselors and parents, which means that a lot of what they're saying probably isn't even true. They're sitting there saying all this stuff about how I can be and do anything, but in their head, they know it isn't true.

Because when they were my age, they probably never saw themselves as high school guidance counselors and human resources specialists, but here they are. The world was a lot harder and more complicated than they gave it credit for being. Stuff happened, and some of it was within their control and some of it wasn't. And maybe they really were among the kids who were going somewhere when they were my age, the students the teachers would slip extra books to after class and talk to during lunch, but here they were nonetheless. No one had ever bothered to slip me an extra book, and I knew that they didn't look at me and think that I was going places. I just wasn't that student. Emeline, maybe. But not me. And now my little sister was telling me to take a vow to skip across a bridge in every single country. She had the best of intentions, but it was just too demeaning.

"Stop it, Rhea! God, do you really think rolling your eyes at everything masks the fact that you're just as scared as the rest of us? Eventually, everyone's going to get tired of having these talks with you, and we're all just going to give up. And you know what I think? I think you'll be mad when that day comes. So just, just stop it, OK? Try to meet me halfway."

"Sorry, sorry. I'm a jerk. I know."

"No! I mean, yeah, you are. But don't say so because you think that gives you license to keep being a jerk. Don't apologize for being a jerk, which you absolutely are, and much worse besides. Just stop being a jerk."

I couldn't help but smile. Aemilia was annoying as hell, but she was also an amazing person.

"Alright. I'm sorry. And if you want me to hop across

one bridge in each country to prove it to you, I'm willing to do it. But I'm going to need my passport back first."

"I want you to prove it by figuring out what your dream is and pursuing it the way you pursued that gladiator you seduced in Vesta's temple," she replied smartly. "Here, I've been carrying this around with me for several weeks, and I'm sick of seeing them."

She handed me a saffron-colored suede pouch with a drawstring. It was small enough to fit in my hand, but the brown, knotted cord was long enough that I could wear the pouch as a necklace.

"Open it," Aemilia insisted.

I flipped the pouch upside down and shook until four bone-colored lumps roughly the size of quarters fell into my palm. Aemilia was watching me intently. I couldn't see her, since my eyes were still trained on the as-yet unidentified objects that had fallen from the pouch, but I could feel her intense interest.

It was my fingers that remembered what I was holding.

"Knucklebones!" I marveled, as I explored the dents and curves of the tiny game pieces with my index finger and thumb.

"I must have thrown these, how many times? Hundreds? Thousands?"

It wasn't an exaggeration. There had been one day when the tutor was sick and *Mater* too busy to replace him, and Aemilia and I hid in the atrium—or thought we were hidden, anyway—and we tossed knucklebones until our hands ached, probably 100 tosses apiece. Junia refused to play with us, despite being a year older than me and three years older than Aemilia, and though Liviana would sometimes play, she often got bored or frustrated and would quit well before we were through.

They really were knucklebones—at least the ones we played with back home were. I was pretty sure these were not authentic knucklebones from sheep. In fact, I found myself hoping they weren't. The texture wasn't quite right, but the shape was exactly as I remembered.

Each bone was roughly rectangular with two broad sides and two narrow sides, capped off by two rounded ends. Two sides—one narrow, one broad—were concave, while the other two were convex. They're difficult to describe in that they don't look like anything else. The corner that's convex and narrow is called *chios*, the dog, and counts for only one point.

Anyone who throws four ones was required to add a denarius to the pot. The broad convex side counts for three, the broad concave side earns four points, and the narrow concave side is the real jackpot at six points. The highest toss is Venus—each of the bones landing on a different side—but there were 35 possible throws, and you were much more likely to land a King or Vulture. My fingers were starting to itch just thinking about it.

"Where did you get these?" I asked gently, to convey how precious they were.

"Soren made 'em in shop class." She grinned, but there was a wicked hint to it. "They're clay with a porcelain finish. It took him ages to get them exactly right."

"But what are these for? I thought the incredibly gorgeous shoes were my graduation gift."

"Where did you get that idea? This is your graduation gift, and the incredibly expensive shoes are your next 50 birthday gifts. Also, they're mine in the event that you decide to go and get yourself buried again."

"That sounds fair," I announced. I was still too surprised by the sudden appearance of the knucklebones to maintain my end of the banter, but Aemilia wouldn't mind. She liked getting the final word in. Still, she was surprisingly quiet as I turned them over and over in my fingers, experimentally flipped one from my palm onto the back of my hand, then back to my palm, then began the process again with an additional knucklebone. They fell a lot more often than I remembered ever happening in those carefree days in the atrium, and I found myself wondering if muscle memory could cross hundreds of years and different bodies. It seemed unlikely.

"When did you think of this?" I asked, realizing that Aemilia must have asked Soren to make the knucklebones well before she outed me on my graduation day.

"On your birthday. I bought you that stupid shirt that I knew you would never wear, and I was kind of mad at you because I knew you would never wear it even though it was a perfectly fine shirt, and I was kind of mad at myself for buying something I knew you wouldn't even like. And I just really, really wanted to give you something that would make you happy. Deliriously happy. And for some reason, I flashed back to those games. I dunno. It was silly." Aemilia looked down as though intensely absorbed in the silent, minute growth of her cuticles, overwhelmed by a rare bout of embarrassment.

"No. It's the best present I've ever gotten. Truly, even better than those shoes, and you and I both know I will never own anything half so cool as those." I thought about hugging her, but pulled back at the last second, and I was grateful I did, because we were both feeling awkward enough without throwing physical contact into the equation.

"Wait a minute … seven months ago? You weren't dating Soren seven months ago."

"Yeah, we started dating soon after that. And he just happened to be the best shop student in the school, which worked out perfectly." She sounded smug, and just the slightest bit guilty.

"He just happened to be? And when did he happen to finish the knucklebones for you?" I knew it wasn't nice to interrogate someone directly after they've given you the best gift you've ever received, but I liked to make sure everything I owned was ethically sourced, and beginning to get the impression that Soren might have been a casualty of my sister's drive to obtain the perfect present.

"How am I supposed to remember when he finished them?"

"Aemilia Prudence—"

"Alright, alright. Geez. Where do you think Mom came up with that name, anyway? Prudence?" She puckered her face. "Soren gave me the knucklebones two weeks before your graduation. It was like he wanted to cut it as close as possible."

"And you never did tell me: When did the two of you break up?"

"Oh, gosh, a week and a half or so before your graduation." Aemilia knew she was busted, but she didn't look all that guilty, the way someone is supposed to when it's discovered that they used another person for their own ends.

"Rhea, don't make that face—and don't you dare put down those knucklebones. Don't worry about Soren. He was using me, too."

No big sister wants to hear her sister say she was being used by a senior who makes Wolverine look domesticated.

"Aemilia … ."

"No, not like that. Calm down, Rhea. This isn't an afterschool special. Soren just liked having a girlfriend who was popular. He was going to break up with me anyway, either as soon as he graduated or before he went away to college. We never pretended we were going to be together forever or any of that make believe."

I really didn't understand high school. "Wow. And people think I'm the weird one."

"Please, if I went around spouting off about how he was my soul mate and no one understood our love and I'd do anything to stay with him, you'd call me a naive fool and act all worldly. You, of all people, should know better than to apply double standards to people, especially someone who's the exact age you were when it happened."

"You've joked about it, like, 50 times, but now you can't say it?"

"Just the twice, and it didn't feel great either time, to tell you the truth." Her voice had a tinge of melancholy to it. "Look, do you want the knucklebones or not? Because if you don't, I'm not really sure what to do with them. Mom might try to wear them as a necklace or something out of kindness, but I'm not sure I want her wearing faux bones I conned my ex-boyfriend into making in shop class. They're meant for you."

"Good, 'cause I wasn't planning on giving them up. I just wanted to go on the record as having protested the way you obtained them."

Without any visible hesitation—despite my brain shrieking that the entire gesture was so very, terribly uncomfortable—I hugged my sister. I didn't try to count the days, weeks, months, and years that had elapsed since we last hugged; I didn't bother to regret the great chasm between us, which at the time of my graduation was so vast that the world's entire supply of Jell-O could not have filled it; but I did breathe a silent prayer thanking Jupiter, Vesta, Juno, and Pluto for their wisdom and restraint in not dumping me into an unfamiliar century all alone.

With the knucklebone pouch in my hand and Aemilia hugging me right back despite the fact that we were in public and I was being profoundly demonstrative, I was even a little grateful for Rome and second chances; without them, I wouldn't even know that Aemilia's favorite flavor of Jell-O was raspberry—useful information in my battle to conquer the chasm.

XIII

Plebeians can never comprehend how difficult it is to throw a party with the intent of impressing an emperor and intimidating one's rivals while the better part of the city riots over food shortages, and any ostentatious display is likely to set them off like wildfire. Still, my parents were doing their best, and when Aetius and Quinta Equitia set their will to something, there was no force short of an emperor or god that could stop them.

No Roman, however hungry or bloodthirsty, would lay so much as a finger on a vestal virgin. So my parents recruited Caecilia and me to preside over their fete: two teenage priestesses clad in white against a legion of hundreds, if not thousands, with a pretty substantial quarrel against the empire. It should not have worked, but it never failed. That is the power of faith.

Liviana was pregnant, and my parents were triumphant. At least, they were supposed to be. Maybe it really was their fear of inciting the starving hordes, but they were showing hints that a degree of their joy, at least, was feigned. Father never stopped using what I called his senator voice, which made everything he said come out as though it were a rehearsed speech. When you are a senator, that is how everything is supposed to sound. When you are excited because your daughter who has been the emperor's mistress for two years is pregnant, you should not have to worry about how things sound. But he was.

I watched my mother—the woman who educated and trained my sisters and me to ensure that we would not merely be passive tools, acted upon by forces greater than ourselves, in the political arena—for an indication as to how I was to behave and what they required of me. She was much more astute than my father at concealing her emotions, and it would have required someone who both knew her very well and watched her very closely, but she had a tell. It wasn't a tic or habit or gesture, but a hint of rigid posture when something bothered her. It was there that evening, the slightest tilt of her noble slate head.

My parents were worried. That was my cue to be worried.

"Liviana." I greeted my sister with a kiss on the cheek. A very pale cheek, I noticed when I pulled away from her, but I said nothing.

"Appius Claudius." I had a smile for Liviana's husband, whom I genuinely liked and who had, I felt, befallen a rather unfortunate circumstance. He loved my sister and was now receiving congratulations on her condition as though we did not all know that he played no role in it. There was nothing to be done besides accepting tokens of friendship from Commodus.

Curiously, the emperor did not seem particularly pleased with the arrangement—at least not from what I witnessed that night. He sulked over his wine, which I knew would concern my father, who had likely hunted all over the empire for the very best drink. He refused to touch the food, which everyone knew was owing to his fear of being poisoned, but still it was difficult to eat while he stared at your plate as though he expected its contents to suddenly leap up and attack him.

In fact, the more I watched people circulating through my parent's estate, the less it resembled a party than a show. It was my responsibility to speak with them all, to put them at ease, to unburden them of some of their worry, and I did my best in this, but I found myself beleaguered by a hardship of my own.

Valens followed me through the house, but had not made any effort to converse with me. He did not touch the wine, and my instinct told me that he was waiting until everyone else had imbibed before approaching me. Cloelia had already confirmed that she had pulled him aside and warned him of the dangers of appearing familiar with a vestal virgin after he monopolized my attention the day of Vestalia. His solution, apparently, was to wait until they were drunk or dispersed and Cloelia, unfortunately, was back at the temple. I knew my mother could be counted on to head him off, if the situation required it, but she was channeling all of her attention and charm into her guests, and I did not want to distract her. I was here to protect my family, not the other way around.

Caecilia detached herself from Decima, who appeared to have developed a preference for her, and practically floated toward me. Truly, it was as though her feet never touched the ground. It would have driven me mad if she were not such a qualified confidante.

"He is going to be a problem soon," she said with certainty, tilting her head gently in Valens' direction.

"I know it," I agreed, resigned as always to the inconvenience of Valens' existence. "Father always thought it was sweet, his stumbling around after me. I guess it did not occur to him that I might become a vestal virgin, and the childhood infatuation might one day prove a problem."

"Your father likely planned to simply marry you off," Caecilia said thoughtfully. She was the only vestal virgin who would dare mention the idea that one of us would be married, even in another life in which we had not sworn oaths of chastity. It was one of the reasons I enjoyed her company. "You would probably be married now if you had not been chosen by the emperor. Sworn to each other, at the very least."

"No." She may have been correct. If I paused to

evaluate what she said, I would probably find more than a small measure of truth to it. Caecilia was sharp. She saw things, and sometimes she saw through them, but she had apparently not yet seen through me. And I would not have that fate foisted on me, not even through a fanciful scenario in Caecilia's head.

She did not press the point, as anyone incapable of seeing the big picture and determined to score a point over me would have. Valens was still out there, lurking around my parents' estate inasmuch as a wealthy and relatively handsome young man can lurk around a house where he was invited and all but one person welcomed his company.

"Did you always find his company so distasteful?" Caecilia inquired.

"No," I replied, after a little thought. "When we were very young, he was intelligent, gentle, eager to please. We would all play together—Junia and Valens and I, and later Aemilia as well. He was never cruel, as some young boys are, and Mother and Father found his company sufficiently agreeable that he was sometimes tutored with us."

"And yet you appear to despise him."

"Maybe I do now. Suddenly he was just always there. Not just here at our house, but by my side. I felt crowded and did not know how to articulate any of this, so instead I would insist on playing games I knew he did not like, or making up rules that would make it impossible for him to win, trying to drive him away. He would not go. Liviana used to tease me about it, but she would also say that it was sweet that he would pay me so much attention when I did everything in my power to make myself undeserving of that attention."

"But it was not sweet," Caecilia stated, calmly and clearly. "It was not right for him to impose his attention on you if it was unwanted, and it was not right for your family to encourage it. He may have only been a young boy, but now he is older, and because no one has taught him the difference, he mistakes harassment for romance."

"You do not think he actually nourishes those sorts of

feelings, do you?" I asked. "I was taken away when I was 6. He has had an entire decade to form an alternate attachment."

"Well, perhaps his strategy is to ignore the real subject of his affection while pestering you sufficiently to get you charged with incest and condemned to death." Caecilia spoke dryly. "Then, when you have been buried alive, he can dramatically pronounce himself to his real love, we will all have a good laugh about how cleverly he fooled us, and they can name their first daughter Rhea in honor of the now long-deceased vestal virgin."

"I know you speak in jest. Rather, I am certain you are serious, but should not something be humorous in order to qualify as a jest?" I smiled and began counting down the seconds to her retort. I never heard it, though, because we were interrupted.

"Ah, the impossible question! Many a philosopher has cracked his head over a grindstone trying to develop an equation for humor."

"There is much humor in the company of men," Caecilia said sweetly. "You are Aetius Equitius' neighbor."

"And Rhea's." Valens always had the air of someone who wanted to please, but he had an underlying stubbornness that would always triumph over his desire to impress.

"You have a home near the temple?" Caecilia inquired politely, knowing he did not.

"No, my father's estate borders this one."

"Rhea lives at the house of Vesta. She has lived the greater part of her life there."

She was right, and more importantly, her words felt right, but it was still a shock to hear and realize that it was true.

"As long as her family lives here, a part of Rhea will always be here as well," Valens countered.

"When her sister, who is the emperor's mistress, is once again with child, Rhea will likely visit again for several hours before returning home to the temple." Caecilia was smooth. "She will visit, much as a guest does. But she belongs to the temple and to the people of Rome. She does not belong to one family … and certainly not to a single person."

Valens stared intensely at Caecilia, and there was violence written in his expression. But the boldest of the vestals met his gaze, and both her posture and face declared that she was utterly undaunted by his threatening looks and stance.

"Strike me, if you dare," she seemed to say, "and it is you, rather than I, who will become one with the earth before the day is over." I had been witness to several standoffs, but never in a capacity as the subject of contention. There was no one close enough to intervene should my childhood shadow decide to vent his frustrations physically.

But worst of all, I opened my mouth and found myself wanting to argue with Caecilia. Initially, I had been relieved when she took up my cause, determined to rout Valens and send the eager puppy back to his own estate, where he belonged. But she was not simply banishing Valens. This golden-haired vestal, my partner in service to Vesta, would banish anyone who sought to claim me. And if I could belong to no one, then how could Nesreen belong to me?

Valens saw the mad scrum of emotion that wreaked havoc with my expression—clouding the certainty from my eyes, furrowing my brow with confusion, heating my cheeks with guilt and shame, drawing and compressing my lips to prevent my giving vent to the hot, unhappy words Caecilia's own cool speech had inspired. And he thought the heightened emotion was for him.

"Caecilia … It is Caecilia?" Valens spoke gently now, as I remembered from when we were children. "I apologize for my behavior. You were merely protecting Rhea, and I hope I never behave ungratefully toward a friend of Rhea's, whose goals are very much my own." He offered me a glowing smile, full of meaning, and walked away in the direction of his estate.

Caecilia looked speechless. Unfortunately, her appearance did not match the potent reserve of words behind her tongue.

"Did you mean to encourage him?" Caecilia stood so

close that I could feel her breath on my neck. Had she been just two inches taller, her nose would have grazed my cheek. "Have you been secretly teasing him, while feigning annoyance all along? If you harbor some feeling toward him, you must let it die. There is no hope of anything for 20 years more, and no man is going to wait that long for you ... not quietly at least."

"You know me better than that," I insisted bitterly, torn between pushing her away and keeping her close—and our conversation discreet. "I do not speak out of both sides of my mouth. And even if I were to falter, I certainly would not choose Valens!"

"You have no place choosing anyone at all." Caecilia's eyes were wide and wary, but she sounded confident and commanding. "You know I am not like the others, outraged by instincts and longings that are perfectly natural. I do not pretend that everything about this life is easy and idyllic, but it is our life. And Rhea, this Valens will see to it that you are buried alive beneath the ground, never again to see the light or home. I feel it, Rhea, and this dread in my bones is a gift from Vesta, a warning that Valens' desire will be the end of you, if left unchecked."

She was right. About Valens, at least.

"I will speak to my mother. She will know how to curb this. Unless you do not trust me, and would like to speak to her yourself."

"If I did not trust you, it is not your mother I would speak to, but the Virgo Vestalis Maxima. It is because I trust you that I speak so candidly with you, with the expectation that you will embark on the path of wisdom." Caecilia spoke in a sober voice and had begun to distance herself from me after mentioning Fulvia.

"I have no use for Valens," I said through gritted teeth. "Speak with whomever you wish. I will not be buried for incest I did not commit." I stared coldly down at her, grateful for every sliver of height with which to accentuate my disdain.

If I was going to be executed, it would be for the crime I had committed, not the one that did not even enter my mind, but was placed there by someone else.

"You are right," Caecilia conceded. "Quinta Equitia will know what to do. I should not have mentioned Fulvia. I do not believe you are guilty of anything, and it would not be right to cast a pall of suspicion over you. We cannot help those who are struck by our beauty and throw themselves across our path."

The last sentence was delivered laughingly, so that I would forgive her with more than just my words. And I smiled back at her because I needed a friend in the house if I was to survive there. But if the right corner of my lip didn't lift quite as buoyantly as my left, it was because I remembered her threat to speak with the Virgo Vestalis Maxima, and I believed her.

*   *   *

It was July 20, the first day of Ludi Victoriae Caesaris, an eight-day pageant of games and merriment to celebrate Julius Caesar's military conquests. There was a sudden, crushing weight on my sandaled left foot, and I looked down to find a man casually standing on it. It was true that the Pantheon was crowded, more so even than the Coliseum—if that was possible—but I found it difficult to believe that he didn't notice the slight shift in elevation. Then again, he was wearing a pair of really nice Italian shoes, the kind that make you feel like you're walking on a cloud. So maybe he just assumed the cloud he was walking on had a slight bump.

I waited for him to realize his error and apologize for standing on me, morbidly curious as to how long it would take.

"*Spostare!*" A pair of hands reached forward and shoved the man off my foot, and he shuffled through the thick fog of tourists without a word of apology. His wife looked backward and unleashed a string of angry-sounding Italian I was glad I only partially understood.

The Pantheon was easily the most interesting structure in all of Rome, but I wanted to leave. I didn't believe there were any gods left here.

"I don't believe there are any gods left here," Aemilia announced. She had a combative expression, reminding me that I hadn't thanked her for intervening.

"*Sopostre?*"

"Spostare," she corrected gruffly. "Move."

"That would've been a useful word to know several weeks ago. Wanna get coffee?"

"Oh yeah."

I made sure to walk through the beam of light streaming from the oculus at the top of the circular dome—not as any kind of superstitious fulfillment, but because it used to be my favorite thing to do. Standing in that circle of light made me feel as though I was at the center of everything, deeply and importantly part of it all. I'd believed that the gods could really see me there. Vesta's temple was my home, but the Pantheon belonged to all the gods, and there was something undeniably special about it, an inclusiveness I'd not found at other religious institutions and temples.

Now, though, the oculus held no special wonder or epiphany for me. It was as beautiful as ever, but without any sacred deities at the other end, without a tribe and homeland I loved more dearly than my own life, it was just a hole in the ceiling, more like an accident than any grand architectural design.

We found a café with a host who promised not to charge table service, and we sat down.

"You know there's going to be a table service charge on the bill, whatever he promised," I warned Aemilia. "And then I'm going to be mad because he said otherwise. I'd rather we just sat down knowing there would be a table charge than be lied to. Besides, we're too close to the Pantheon for them not to charge for the table."

"You and your injustices." Aemilia gave a long-suffering sigh. "It's almost as though someone forgot to tell you that the world is not fair."

"That's rich coming from the girl who tried to light Ab—Mom's hair on fire because she didn't get you a pony for your birthday."

"I was 6! And that's enough banter. Let's see 'em!" She thumped the table impatiently and fluently tossed a couple sentences of Italian at the waiter who had arrived to take our order. He hurried away, but not before I caught his surprised expression over the young American speaking nearly fluent Italian.

"I told him to keep the cappuccinos and gnocchi coming. It's going to be a long night," Aemilia explained, casually cracking her knuckles.

I quickly untangled the drawstring I'd looped around my belt buckle and withdrew the pouch Aemilia had given me on Palatine Hill. Five knucklebones clattered to the table, and the waiter responsible for bringing our cappuccinos raised a single, scandalized eyebrow and hastened off to serve his more respectable patrons.

Aemilia didn't notice. Her eyes were locked greedily on the knucklebones that lay basking in the sun like pale tourists on holiday.

The knucklebones had been confined to the drawstring pouch, which had, in turn, been fastened to my belt buckle since Aemilia gave it to me two days earlier. I was treating Aemilia's present the way I wished I'd cared for my passport. If I'd physically strapped it to my person, the way Abri had told me to, I wouldn't be forced to start off each morning with a round risperidone tablet, which Basilio stared at until it disappeared behind my lips, at which point he transferred his attention to my throat as though he was miraculously possessed of x-ray vision and could watch as it made its way into my system, dulling the parts of me he deemed objectionable … perhaps even killing my memories of Nesreen … .

"Don't think about him, Rhea." Aemilia's words startled me. I'd thought she was still staring at the knucklebones on the table. "You always get that particular frown when you're thinking about him. Your forehead looks like a thunderstorm, but your eyes get that sad, desperate expression. You used to be better at hiding this stuff."

"I didn't use to have someone fumbling around in my brain via chemical proxy," I grumbled, too depressed to argue. "Who knows how much of me will be left when all this is over? I might not even be myself anymore. I certainly won't be if Basilio has his way."

Just thinking about him clogged my senses with the putrid stench of black licorice.

"Does it affect you that much?" Aemilia sounded curious. "Like, do you feel it right now?"

I racked my memory, but struggled to separate my natural discomfort with large crowds from feelings or sensations that could be attributed to the unwanted chemicals circulating through my brain.

"I don't know," I answered honestly. "I definitely felt it at first. I was dizzy and couldn't handle the heat. Speaking felt like trying to assemble a puzzle. I haven't felt that way in a while, but I guess I've just gotten used to the medication, and it feels normal now. The new normal."

"Maybe," Aemilia agreed, flipping a pair of knucklebones from her palm to her wrist with a slight smile. "Or maybe those pills aren't what they seem." She flipped them again, catching them in her hand.

"I know what they do. I looked them up online. Basilio might be a big bully, but he knows what he's about."

"Oh, I'm certain he knows what he intended to give you. But are you certain you've been taking what he intended to give you?"

She had a maddening smile—the one she wore when absolutely certain she knew something important that I did not.

"He watches me take it," I argued, now frustrated and regretting that I'd brought any of it up. "The sooner you get to your point, the sooner we can play." I swept the knucklebones from the table and held them over the pouch as though I intended to pocket them.

"Yeah, right. You want to play as badly as I do.

Anyway, you've been eating sugar pills," Aemilia said flatly. "Remember when you spit out the first pill, and Basilio caught you and made you take another one? I grabbed the pill out of the trash, took it to a bakery the next day, and told the woman I needed 200 pills just like that one for a birthday cake for a friend of mine with weird taste. I got the key to Basilio's desk from Adamo, went in when Basilio was at the symphony, and switched the pills."

She caught my expression: open-mouthed, gaping as awkwardly as I had the first time I saw a group of yuppies outside a yoga studio doing a rain dance one dry winter.

"It was really easy, actually, once I decided to do something," Aemilia said with a shrug.

"You mean to tell me, I'm normal?" I was shaking with excitement and reached across the table to try to hug her. I was also congratulating myself for not bringing up the subject of the Ludi Victoriae Caesaris. The last thing I needed was my best and only ally deciding I was unnaturally fixated on my old life and siding with my uncle to help purge me of it.

"You know I'd never call you that," Aemilia quipped.

"Why didn't you tell me?"

"I figured if you knew you'd behave differently, and then Uncle would know. And, I don't know, I guess I was hoping for some kind of placebo effect. I figured if you thought you were supposed to feel like everybody else, maybe that would take some of the pressure off you to feel alienated from everyone. Maybe that would be your excuse to start living."

"I worried there was a chance I might forget … ."

"I know," Aemilia said. "That's why I did it."

"So what did you do with the real pills? Did you flush them? Or grind them into Basilio's morning oatmeal?" I couldn't keep my voice from becoming hopeful.

Aemilia chuckled. "I got a locker at the train station and left the pills there, for evidence, or in case Basilio got suspicious. I couldn't risk leaving them in my luggage, because I figure there's a good chance Uncle searches through it."

"Wow, you really are incredible. You know, I'm lucky you weren't old enough to be a candidate for vestal virgin. They'd have chosen you." For once, my words and tone were in complete agreement. I meant exactly what I said.

"Yeah, probably. But I wouldn't have wanted the gig anyway," Aemilia said with a lopsided smile that looked more like mine.

I dropped the knucklebones back onto the table. The cappuccino was cold, but it was so warm outside that I didn't care.

"Modern rules?" I joked.

Aemilia made a noise halfway between spitting and guffawing.

"Old school," she commanded. "I'm not even sure I know what the modern rules are. And I don't wanna know. There's no room for improvement where knucklebones are concerned."

We played until Aemilia didn't have any change left to bet, and I had a small pile of coins blocking my access to the plate of gnocchi. The Coliseum was immediately recognizable on the five-cent coin, and I spotted Venus on the 10-cent piece. Aemilia had lost badly enough that I even had a few one-Euro Vitruvian men staring up at me.

"Well, looks like I have all your money. Game's over, unless you want to fork over Fedele's credit card."

Aemilia had been mostly quiet while we played. Junia, Hortensia, and Liviana used to joke that the only way to shut her up was to put a set of knucklebones in front of her, and I was tickled that their strategy still held true today.

"Why not bet for something else?" she asked suddenly.

"Like what?" I was a little wary. In ancient Rome, there had been rumors of Romans of all ages and castes setting stakes decidedly more titillating and erotic than a few denarii. But knowing Aemilia, she was looking to humiliate me: make me go dancing with her or visit the catacombs or something equally distressing.

"Truths. Loser has to give up a secret in lieu of Euros."

"I'd rather play for coins," I insisted. "I'll give you half of mine, since I'd rather keep playing than keep your Euros. You already know my secret anyway."

"That's not fair," Aemilia objected. "You won those coins fairly, and I'm not going to take them from you as charity. How about you keep playing with coins, and I'll play with secrets. That way, maybe I can win back enough Euros to go back to playing for money."

"Are you sure? That doesn't sound very agreeable for you." It also didn't sound like the little sister I used to catch hoarding Monopoly money by stuffing it up her sleeves and into her pockets before each game.

"It's fair," she said steadily.

I shrugged and took the first throw.

Aemilia managed to win back 50 cents, but she followed her series of modest wins by placing a large bet. After she'd lost the final toss, she faced me with a thoughtful expression.

"Don't worry about it," I assured her. "I was never big on the whole confession idea anyway. I'd rather call it quits."

It was well past dark, and the crowd at the café was triple what it had been when we sat down. Back home, everyone was properly finished with dinner by 10 p.m., but Romans, predictably, had a more cosmopolitan sense of time. The observation made me feel unbearably provincial.

"A deal's a deal," Aemilia insisted, and it occurred to me that perhaps she had something she needed to say, and the knucklebones were just the path she had to travel to get there.

"OK. You're right. Fair is fair. What's your secret?"

"I was scared to come to Rome," she said. "I was afraid they might be looking for me, too ... whoever was hunting you ... or might be hunting you. Whoever's probably hunting you? Where did we wind up on the whole 'someone's hunting you' theory?"

Aemilia was staring at the final lump of gnocchi as

though it contained the answers she was looking for. I found it unlikely that some secret order dedicated to executing fallen vestals had taken the gnocchi into its confidence, but at least Aemilia wasn't one of those people who shredded paper napkins when she was nervous. I hated that. Not only was it an unforgivably obvious tell, but then you had to clean up confetti after you'd dealt with whatever made the person feel awkward in the first place: lack of communication, the fact that you speak Latin fluently, the fact that you call your parents by their actual names—normal type stuff. A 16-year-old being worried about visiting a foreign country wasn't exactly a major scoop.

"I know why I was scared to come here. I don't mean to brag, but I violated a promise I swore to gods not bound by time or place, who are now free to chase me across countless centuries and continents. You ... what did you do?"

"Valens wasn't the only one who got caught trying to dig you out."

But she whispered it, and I so badly wanted to hear what I thought she might be saying that I doubted my ears. The contents of my stomach—way too many cappuccinos, and twice as much gnocchi—rose in the direction of my throat, buoyed by hope and terror.

"What?" I asked lightly. "Were you trying to make that sound muffled?"

"I told you Valens got caught trying to dig you out. I didn't tell you he wasn't alone."

Still, I didn't dare hope my sister was saying what I thought.

"Did you try to rescue me?"

"Of course I tried to rescue you. I adored you, Rhea. Of all of us—Hortensia, Decima, Junia, Liviana—you were the one who believed in something, the only one who knew how to grasp your happiness. The only one who knew you could make your own happiness."

"What did they do to you when you got caught?" I clutched Aemilia's hand, utterly indifferent to the fact that we were making a scene in a perfectly respectable palazzo.

"I convinced them that I came to dig you out and that Valens had to stop me. Father convinced them not to exile me. He painted a picture of a morally upright child rendered senseless by grief. They said that whatever tainted blood had coursed through your veins must also exist in mine. Father had to promise not to arrange a marriage for me without approval from the Senate."

I gasped. Depriving a father of his patria potestas was about the worst thing you could do to a man. Part of me wondered why our father had borne it rather than see Aemilia exiled to some remote territory.

"He'd just lost one daughter," Aemilia whispered. "Even if you were no longer properly ours, you were still his daughter. He still loved you."

"So how did you manage to marry Valens, if it required senate approval?"

"Easily. By the time Valens realized he loved me, Father was eager to see me married. And the Senate remembered Valens as the man who prevented me from digging up the disgraced vestal. They willingly gave their permission on the condition that he watch over me and immediately report any behavior on my part that ran contrary to the interests of the empire."

"Thank you for risking so much for me," I told her, knowing it was inadequate to express how much her gesture meant to me. I knew she never could have dug me out of the ground alive—not when all of Rome wanted me dead—but that just made her all the braver for trying.

"I wish I'd known all along that it was you who tried to dig me out. I think it would have changed a lot of things. Not that I'm blaming you for not saying anything," I hastened to assure her.

"I've been wondering about that: if things would have been easier for you if you'd felt less lonely," Aemilia admitted. "Honestly, I think I was kind of mad at you for not recognizing me, and then we were just so different that I kept doubting myself about you … and I guess I wasn't sure I wanted that kind of bond with you. The truth is, I was worried you might bring me down."

"Loose lips sink ships," I quipped, remembering the World War II idiom from my junior year history class.

Aemilia gave me a weird look. "Yeah, I guess. Something like that, anyway. I think."

She caught my eye and started to cry in earnest.

"Some rescue effort. You know, they wouldn't even let us recover your body to have it placed in the family tomb."

That's what she said, anyway, but there were so many sniffs and gulps between words that it took nearly a minute for her to complete her thought. It's a strange feeling to sit next to someone while they cry about your death.

"We both know how the story ended," I said, comforting her. "The fact that there was an effort, that anybody cared, after what I did … ." You could have dangled a lifetime supply of gelato in front of me, and still I would not have been able to finish my sentence. I flapped my hand in front of my face, hating myself for it, wondering what good it was supposed to do. Best I could figure, it alerted other people to the fact that you were properly ashamed of your tears and wanted to stop crying.

I glanced over my shoulder and noticed our waiter watching us with undisguised interest.

"Wanna go?"

Aemilia nodded, and I gathered the knucklebones and coins into the pouch. We walked along Via del Seminario and Via del Muratte, oddly mellow, exhausted perhaps by the ceaseless onslaught of confessions and apologies.

We strolled idly, stopping to look and chat wherever we liked, but it only took half an hour to reach the Trevi Fountain, which was a feature of Rome I had never before seen, except on postcards from Abri and Fedele. The fountain I'd seen on the small, rectangular piece of paper gleamed solid and pale. It reminded me of the star quarterback in movies about small southern and midwestern towns. I didn't expect to dislike it, exactly, but it had a jaunty, wholesome quality that just didn't ring true with what I remembered of Rome.

By night, however, the fountain was enameled in gold, burnished and decadent. Easier to love, somehow.

"I never really get used to this," Aemilia said with unconcealed awe. "It's even better late at night when you have it to yourself." She propped herself on a bench positioned a few feet in front of the fountain.

"Does he look like anyone to you?" She gestured at the figure of Oceanus at the center of the display, standing watch over the water.

I studied the stern expression and long expanse of beard, the muscular figure that only ever appeared in movies about defiant men with nothing to lose, and shook my head.

"No. Certainly no one I know. Should I recognize him?"

"No," Aemilia said with a heavy sigh, indicating she was deeply disappointed. "I just keep thinking I should know him."

Someone bumped into me, and my hands went automatically to the pouch at my waist to ensure it was secure. When Aemilia witnessed this protective gesture earlier in the day, she mocked me, asking who would want to steal a couple knucklebones. After I reminded her that potential thieves didn't know what was inside the pouch and she'd have to go back to dating Soren to convince him to make me a new set if they were lost, she understood my point and took to looking for them every so often.

We started to leave, but Aemilia stopped with an exclamation in Italian that I didn't understand.

"Toss in a coin, and you're guaranteed to come back," she said teasingly, tugging at my sleeve.

I pulled a 50-cent piece I'd won and handed it to her. "Knock yourself out."

I continued strolling, watching out of the corner of my eye as Aemilia lingered uncertainly around the fountain's edge, trailing her hand in the water, biting her lip indecisively. What was she so afraid of? I had my own reasons for wanting to avoid Rome, but Aemilia was her own person—and fearless in this new life. Surely, she didn't really believe attempting to dig me out of my grave constituted so serious a crime? Not when she'd been forgiven by the Senate and allowed to go on living.

She pocketed the coin and caught up with me, and I pretended not to notice her change of heart.

XIV

All signs pointed to disaster. I had only seen Nesreen twice between Martius and the end of Iunius—one fewer time than she fought in the Coliseum during that period. And the first of these was in the company of the Virgo Vestalis Maxima and half the active vestals.

Swayed by my passionate championing, Fulvia agreed to employ Nesreen as an emissary to the ship's captain who had brought her to Rome. She was charged with purchasing as much silphium as she could legally obtain—illegally, if she thought she could manage without being caught, and on the agreement that the House of Vesta would not be mentioned if she fell into some mishap.

You might reasonably wonder why I not only allowed but encouraged a person I cherished as dearly as Nesreen to undertake potentially rough trade on behalf of my order, but the gesture was a protective one.

By engaging in business with the vestal virgins, Nesreen ascended noticeably higher in the social order. There were now important people who would miss her if she were mauled by a leopard in the arena, and little details like that have a habit of shifting the odds, even in venationes. Perhaps she would be given slightly better armor, or an extra weapon. Maybe she would be spared the deadliest animals, and only be used to pick off the piteous herbivores that loped and gazed in terror at what amounted to large, stone mountains they would never escape.

I had come to genuinely believe that my position could and must be leveraged to some additional purpose. If Atrium Vestae could accelerate the hunt for fresh reserves of silphium and establish a reserve for women in need, we would be directly improving their lives, granting them a degree of agency that was necessary for them to truly be free.

Make no mistake: I would have done it for Nesreen alone. But when I first approached Fulvia to pitch my ambitious project and her eyebrows rose higher and higher— and I matched her doubt with a level of passion that surprised us both, I suspect—it was not until I was making my case that I realized how much I meant it all.

Nesreen was supposed to make regular visits to report her progress on her work, but the trainers at her ludi were frantic and reluctant to let any gladiator beyond their sight.

Each gladiator was only supposed to fight a few times a year. There was no formal rule, but the games were only held on special occasions, to commemorate important victories and anniversaries of importance. It was too expensive to create spectacles of the quality and scale to which we were now accustomed on a daily basis. But Commodus did not seem much preoccupied with the financial realities of running an empire. There still was not enough grain to feed the poor, and the angrier the hungry mobs became, the more certain Commodus seemed to be that he could feed their hunger with gore and violence. Unfortunately, he was not far off.

Liviana told me the *haena*—the sand covering the Coliseum floor—was no longer yellow, but a different color practically every day. They imported the sand from Monte Mario, Rome's highest hill, which lies northwest of the city. But sometimes they would cover the floor in specially colored minerals. The day before Liviana and I talked, she said the Coliseum shimmered like the sea—which she had the opportunity to see firsthand while traveling with Commodus—

and when I asked her to describe it, she shook her head and merely whispered "turquoise, sapphire, green."

I know she meant well. She was tired—no amount of powder could conceal the black half moons beneath her eyes—and bored and seemed to want her pregnancy to be over. What's more, I had never given her any indication that I did not want to hear about the goings on of the Coliseum. Had there been some measure of sisterly understanding between us, she might have inferred it from the fact that I stopped going to the Coliseum and carefully avoided mentioning it in conversation, but Liviana was not the sort of person who searches very deeply into another person's words or actions.

And now, when I fell asleep and dreamed of Nesreen's death in the arena, I could see her head strike the glittering ground, green one night, violet the next. Every morning I awoke hating a new color. Caecilia saw me shudder at Marcia's royal, amethyst robes and mistook my reaction for distaste of Marcia. Fortunately, no one, including Caecilia, liked the emperor's Christian mistress, but I was still fortunate that Caecilia rather than Commodus witnessed my feeble convulsion.

To make matters worse, grain remained in short supply, and politicians, sensing an impending eruption, took to casting blame on whomever happened to be nearest. No one had died thus far, but it was only a matter of time. The praefectus annonea Papirius Dionysius, who was in charge of the city's grain supply, publicly denounced Cleander, Commodus' favored chamberlain. A mob gathered at a horse race at the Circus Maximus, calling for Cleander's death, and the beleaguered emperor's pet ordered the praetorian guard to disperse and punish the mob. City prefect Pertinax countered Cleander's defense by ordering the Vigiles Urbani to defend the mob. Cleander managed to evade the mob long enough to reach Commodus at an estate in Laurentum.

I knew all this because the Virgo Vestalis Maxima dismissed the servants and called us all into the temple to discuss the standoff. There were a few days left of Iunius, and the city was marching steadily toward the unbearable swelter characteristic of our summers. Even priestesses were irritable under these conditions, impatient about being crammed into the small, stifling temple, but curious because it happened so rarely.

I was worried—but then, I had been worried ever since I almost saw a leopard make a meal of Nesreen in the Coliseum. When Fulvia ordered Tuccia to stand guard at the temple door, lest any curious servants or passersby attempt to spy on our conversation, the other vestals looked nervous as well. Tuccia was the youngest girl currently studying to become a vestal, and there was nothing imposing about her besides the white cloak and veil that named her to our order. It was sufficient, though. We needed her eyes, not her brute strength.

"If Cleander is with the emperor, then it is just a matter of them making it safely back to Rome," Saufeia said with youthful simplicity. "The army will come and rescue them."

"There is no question of the emperor not making it back safely," Fulvia said patiently, despite the fact that nearly everyone in the temple already understood that fact. Of course the youngest among the students—Tuccia, Saufeia, Vita, and possibly Nona—did not immediately understand Cleander's danger. But I did not begrudge them their innocence, not when I sensed the limitations of my own understanding. It would be like laughing at someone for falling into a sinkhole while you stood on the tail of a venomous snake.

"Within the day, I expect to hear that Commodus has ordered Cleander's execution." Fulvia spoke slowly and clearly. The younger vestals, and those who had not been trained to keep an ear always to the empire's pulse, gasped.

"But it is not technically Cleander's fault about the grain." Tuccia spoke softly from her post at the door. "And he is the emperor's favorite."

I cast through my memory, searching for the first time I was cognizant of one politician betraying another to save his own skin, or perhaps merely for a greater portion of wealth or power. I wanted to remember that innocence, the shock that jarred your mind and rattled your teeth. I could not remember. It must have happened, though. There must have been a day I realized there were practical considerations that trumped virtue.

"Cleander called a dangerous type of attention to himself, if only by being Commodus' favored confidante for so many years," Fulvia explained. "Even the emperor cannot ignore the will of the people when they have found their voice, whether they have been misled with false information or speak wisely. Cleander's death will rein in the mob. But I do not think the decision will come from Commodus."

A chill prickled the back of my neck and raised the hair on my arms. A rash of whispers and uncomfortable fumbling swept through the temple, and this time it was not just the younger vestals who were baffled. Vibiana, rich in her understanding of the Coliseum and its nuances, had two creases in her forehead that betrayed her lack of understanding. Caecilia's eyes caught mine. She knew what Fulvia meant.

"Marcia." I broke through the whispers, without meaning to, trampling over them with one brash word.

"Yes," Fulvia agreed. "Marcia resents Cleander's influence over the emperor and will insist that he be executed. It is the easiest option for the emperor, and he will probably take it. The mob will be somewhat pacified—until they remember they are still hungry. It may take a while, but empty stomachs have a habit of making themselves known. Then there will be other deaths to distract them from remembering."

Tuccia looked not at the door, but at Fulvia, at the face that barely showed its decades of service to Vesta, a face that was compassionate, stern, and, very rarely, quite ferocious. Over the years, Fulvia had grown into her veil in much the same manner as a buck grows into his antlers. It identified her, but did so in a manner that did not impose upon her agency and power. Fulvia's veil was more deadly than Nesreen's sword.

"We are in danger." Caecilia spoke in her low, bold

voice, but her words did not have their habitual brashness.

"More than I probably realize," Fulvia admitted. Finally, the temple was quiet. The temperature was no cooler, the temple no less crowded than it had been when we shifted restlessly like pupae eager to shed pale linen cocoons. The odd thing about fear is that it collapses one's desire for space and independence. Commodus understood that as well as any other emperor with tens of millions of people to pacify and subdue.

"They are going to be looking for people to blame soon. Once the satisfaction over Cleander's death has waned … if it goes that way. There are … many ways a vestal can fall, and violating your oath is just one of them." Fulvia spoke cautiously, and her eyes flickered to the door more than once.

I could feel Caecilia's eyes on me, could hear them shouting, "Do you see? Do you now understand the dangers? I warned you!" But rather than having its intended effect—compounding shame and fear until I was so overcome with both that I was stripped of all defiance—I was growing angrier with them—Caecilia and, to a lesser extent, Fulvia—for making every moment with Nesreen feel like an act of theft. I gathered my height and rage and dignity about me and stared coolly back at my former confidante and friend. She was the first to turn away, and I counted it a significant victory that her face had an unbecoming florid hue when she did.

"Not many vestals have fallen prey to the Evil Field in the 800 years since our order was founded by Numa Pompilius, but of those who have, not all fell prey to their baser instincts and desires," Fulvia said, circling the point but reluctant to roost there. Even Fulvia did not like to speak of Campus Sceleratus, the underground chambers where vestal virgins deemed impure were buried.

"I do not understand," Septima said despairingly. A wispy black curl had escaped the corner of her veil, but she had such a sense of rightness about her that no one ever chastised her for unruly hair.

Fulvia was suspended between her loyalty to the order and the practical difficulties that would attend agitating an emperor whose spleen was near bursting with rancor. She could not serve Vesta from a tomb beneath the ground. I had even heard speculation among the older vestals that Commodus was not inclined to spare a priestess the humiliation and pain of death in the Coliseum. Despite my personal vow to avoid undue attention and place piety above all other concerns, excepting Nesreen, I decided to speak the words the Virgo Vestalis Maxima could not. Her words had the weight of the entire order behind them, and the effect of proclamations. My own words were important, but they could not be leveraged against Vesta's temple and handmaidens.

"Not every woman who was killed was guilty," I said, feeling both noble and guilty for speaking out of turn.

Fulvia did not look mad, exactly, but she did not look pleased, either. But then, what did she have to look pleased about? We were huddled in the temple like criminals or refugees, whispering fearful nightmares to one another about things that had yet to come to pass. They had to know. We all did. But that did not change how lowering it all felt.

"Then why … ."

Fulvia answered before I had time to distinguish the speaker.

"It was convenient," she said. "Just as Cleander was convenient. Just as the gladiators are convenient. The dearer the sacrifice, the more prolonged the mourning, the greater the people's terror, the more they are in your power. A vestal virgin is the highest sacrifice an emperor can make. Commodus is vulnerable, and we are within reach."

"If we might be killed either way, why bother making us swear an oath?" I winced at how petulant Maximiliana sounded.

"In order to protect yourself and each other, you must look beyond your oath," said Aurelia, who had taught me to make mola salsa. "Not forget it, precisely, but set aside the illusion an oath will protect you. If the emperor is looking for a scapegoat, the appearance of impiety will be enough. Virgins have been condemned for nothing more than seeming to care for their dress and appearance more than they should. It takes only a servant's word, or even a stranger's, and if it happens, there will not be space and time to mount any kind of defense. What would earn you a reprimand or additional attention from one of the servants watching you could now be your death sentence."

A vice gripped my arm, and I looked down to find Vibiana's hand clutching the flesh just below my elbow, clearly unaware of what she was doing. I did not stop her, because she seemed to profit from the contact, and because I found it comforting as well, even if I stood a good chance of finding a bruise there the following morning.

She was probably regretting getting drunk on the so-called milk at Bona Dea, but I remembered her warm, happy eyes and the rich spread of hair the exact color of a fig that has been baked and split apart, all features that rendered her nearly a stranger on that night, as merry and carefree a young woman as any other in Severina's house. Affection coursed through me, hijacking all rational thought and self-interest; I loved my sisters—those bound to me by blood, and those bound by common purpose and belief. It was impossible to wish away Vibiana's brief fling with Bacchus and Caecilia's sharp, perceptive words when I had witnessed the joy it brought them. I fervently hoped they would think the same of me if they ever discovered my affair with the gladiator. Fulvia's warning leveled all transgressions to the same severity, whether the rest of the vestals realized it or not.

By the time Nesreen and I met in the temple two days later, Cleander was dead: beheaded at the emperor's order, though it was being widely reported that it was Marcia who issued the fatal opinion. If Fulvia was correct about Cleander, then she was probably correct in her assessment that we were no different from the caged beasts at the vivarium waiting to be picked off at Marcia's whim.

I had trained my mind not to dwell on fear— imperfectly, of course, because my fears had a habit of finding me in dreams—but it is not an easy thing to sleep in a house filled with fear-crazed virgins. They are afraid to leave their beds, lest someone should suspect them of nocturnal dalliance. They are afraid to remain in their beds, should the emperor seek them out in the likeliest of places.

By night, the halls were filled with ghoulish figures frightened of sleep, frightened of waking. It made the temple safer for my own nocturnal dalliance. Most of the vestals did not want to wander into the night—both for the sake of their reputations and because they seemed to have collectively agreed that Commodus would take the form of some demon lurking in crevices concealed by darkness to snatch them away. They had completely overlooked the fact that precisely what was terrifying about Commodus was that he needn't lurk in the night. He would kill you in the daylight in front of a roaring crowd. That was the mark of a man to be feared.

I did not burden Nesreen with my worries, in part because she had concerns of her own, but also because it would have required revealing the details of the conversation between Fulvia and the vestals in the temple. Having betrayed my oath, it might sound logical that all other moral boundaries would fall as well, that I would hold nothing sacred. But falling in love with Nesreen had the opposite effect; having culled an important ideological pillar that I had begun to suspect was more ornamental than anything else—the oath—the bonds that remained were more precious to me than they had ever been. I was like a surgeon who, having carved away the rotten and corrupted flesh, expected better returns for what remained.

Was I justifying my sin? My crime?

Of course. I could live with a certain degree of hypocrisy, but discarding a central tenet of my service to Vesta while watching over her flame most nights was a level of prevarication worthy of far wealthier and more important people than I. An oath you swear when you are 6 years old is not meant to be challenged or evaluated. And the truth was, until I first saw the venatore at the Coliseum, I never considered whether my oath of chastity was right or wrong. If it was right for Rome, then it was right for me. But what if Rome's best interests weren't mine? What if the purity vow was not in Rome's best interests? These were rules that had existed for centuries—long enough that anyone who questioned them would be charged with heresy.

These were the subjects I ruminated on while alone in Vesta's temple. I knew Nesreen had a meeting with Fulvia to discuss progress on the silphium project. Of course, I always wanted to be present at these meetings, but, by private agreement with Nesreen, I ensured I was on watch in the temple when they took place, which helped me to avoid the appearance of being overly interested in her. Once they had concluded their business, she would sneak back to the temple. If anyone caught her, she would argue that she wanted to update me about the project since I had been on watch and was unable to take part in the discussion. We had even written and rehearsed a script, in which I played the part of the arrogant priestess frustrated by delays in my efforts to increase silphium access in Rome. Nesreen was respectful, though understandably huffy. We did not want to overdo it and risk Fulvia pulling one or both of us off the project, but it would be far worse to be viewed as pushing beyond the reasonable boundaries of friendship.

I was watching the flames, with my back to the door, so I did not see or hear it open so much as notice that the light in the temple had subtly changed. It was night, so there was no brash show of exterior light to come tumbling through the doorframe, but I had spent so many thousands of hours in the sanctuary that I knew it in all of its moods. Though I was confined to the same chaste garb, she changed her vestment hourly, and more often than that, if the sacred fire was in a dancing way.

I did not turn. Nesreen had an audience with Fulvia that evening, but she could not always escape the many prying eyes that fed on the house's comings and goings. And Cloelia frequently interrupted my night watches with offers of food and drink. It was inconvenient for Nesreen and me, but I had seen her so rarely that I appreciated Cloelia's company and was touched by her obvious concern.

"*Salve mea Rhea.*" The voice was the one I wanted to hear above all others.

"You are here! I was beginning to worry you had forgotten the path to the temple." I teased her to make up for the naked joy in my voice.

"The path is the same, though I worry it is more popular of late." She frowned.

"Are you saying?" I stopped myself. I had risked so much already, and so had she.

"No. Not like that," she assured me, as urgently as it was possible for her to speak. "But ... I am not certain. I suspect there are watchers about. More than usual. I sense eyes now, outside the temple. Perhaps I have been spending too much time in the Coliseum. I feel things differently than I did before."

"We have been on heightened alert. There is some concern about the emperor and the city's dark mood. The city always goes a little mad at the onset of summer," I hastened to assure her. I could not bear to see the worry and defeat in her eyes.

She nodded.

My head was a ball of tension; my feet barely brushed the ground. I had begun a game of counting the seconds between when Nesreen entered the room and when she finally touched me. In the interim, I stared, feigned indifference, blushed, tried not to appear indifferent. I balled my hand into a fist and tried to rub the tension from my forehead. But I did not make the first move toward her. Mine was a shy courtship, comprised mostly of waiting and alternately hoping she understood the bent of my feelings for her and hoping she did not. It was not fair that she bore the burden of responsibility for first contact, but she had been the first to touch me when she plied the gladiolus into my wreath. I often dreamed of the petals, so rich in color they dripped red in their wake.

She brushed her lips against my cheek, and my body

exhaled its unhappy tension. Someday I would touch her first. We had time ... I hoped. Of course, she had no sooner kissed me than I wanted more. I was like Vesta's flame: semper ardens. Always burning.

"How long do we have?" she asked.

"All the time that is ours to give," I replied.

"How long do we have until they separate us?"

"*Quis separabit?*" Who will separate us? I asked playfully, lovingly, but also sadly, for someone surely would.

*   *   *

I had hated Ilium on sight, making it impossible to appreciate the ambition and deliberation of the house's design. Perhaps a true student of architecture or art wouldn't have held enmity for the master against his house, but at present I was a student of nothing in particular and free to carry my grudge against Basilio to the house he prized above all else.

It was readily apparent that I had overlooked key features in the house's design while trapped in the foggy haze of Basilio's anti-hallucinogens. I quietly amassed facts about Ilium, uncertain which information I would require in order to escape. Aemilia was still convinced Basilio would simply let me go when the time came, but our scheduled departure was less than a week away and I still hadn't seen my passport.

Ilium's colors were mutable and largely dependent on the time of day. When the sun rose and set, the house was as gold as the Trevi Fountain by night; the better part of the day, it was an aseptic shade of gray befitting a medical institution. Though I never felt comfortable in the house, I was least unhappy there when Basilio was absent and the walls were suffused with natural light.

Once, a caravan of students arrived in the driveway to admire the house, and several gushed to me how lucky I was to live there.

"If one of you is willing to give up your passport, I'll gladly trade places," I said stonily, not feeling up to the role of gracious host or grateful guest. They smiled, confused by my English, and wandered around the structure until Basilio appeared at the door and offered a spontaneous tour. He loved nothing better than sharing Ilium with people who appreciated it properly. It must have been a great disappointment to have one niece who feared it and another whose admiration was limited to the teenaged servant.

I was slow to see it, perhaps because I did not want to, but Ilium bore certain aesthetic similarities to Vesta's temple that were too obvious to deny. Both had unadorned walls that depended on natural light for a warm, sophisticated color palette. And Ilium was the first contemporary structure I'd seen that wasn't a traditional rectangle or square. Its exterior shape was that of a shell or modified ampersand, but the living room was a spacious circle that could have fit two temples within its walls. If it hadn't reminded me so powerfully of my underground tomb, I probably would have been very comfortable there, but that's like saying you'd like the look of someone if only they didn't resemble the person who murdered your family.

Basilio and I had kept an uneasy peace since he first confronted me about speaking Latin and threatened to institutionalize me. I was never alone with him, and I never spoke more than a sentence to him, beyond a direct response to a question.

So when he found me reading in the living room and confidently declared, "I can't consider your reasons for leaving Rome two days before Ferragosto," I was speechless with terror. I had seen him leave Ilium not an hour earlier, and I'd crept quietly from the bedroom, which I kept locked at all times. He must have returned very quietly for me not to have heard the door open.

"We didn't take Ferragosto into account when making our plans," I said coolly, returning my eyes, if not attention, to my book. I refused to feign interest in one of Italy's many public holidays, especially one that the church had co-opted and claimed as a religious day.

"Now that you are here, and know that I want you to go, you can take it into account," he said, sounding reasonable as usual—and issuing a command as usual.

"Emeline can't miss her first day of school. We're cutting it close enough as it is," I replied, proud that I hadn't tripped over her name.

"People travel from around the world to experience Ferragosto," Basilio argued, "and do you know which city has the best festival in all Italy?"

"No." I knew I was meant to say Rome, but I wouldn't give him the satisfaction.

"Rome! Every corner of the city fills with dancing, every type of dancing, every type of music! Everywhere else, just Ferragosto. But in Rome, we call it The Gran Ballo di Ferragosto. You can't miss it."

"Unfortunately, we can, and sadly, we must. America has rules about delinquency, and we don't want Emeline to start off her junior year on the wrong foot." I refused to look away from the book, even if it was obvious I wasn't actually reading.

"I will call your mother. I'm sure she can work something out with the school. She's very charming." Basilio turned in the direction of his study, and I forced myself to consider the prospect of being trapped here at least three more days. The surge of panic and helplessness that followed filled me with rage—the kind that wants to be known and acknowledged, not the kind that simmers quietly, damaging only its keeper.

"I shouldn't have bothered speaking, and you shouldn't haven't wasted my time asking if you'd already made up your mind to speak with Abri." I finally set my book aside.

"Where's the waste in making plans to attend a festival everybody loves?" my uncle asked, sounding believably wounded.

"I told you we can't go. We already have plans. But you don't listen," I said bitterly.

"Plans can change," he reasoned. "Especially when

they were ignorantly made. You couldn't have taken Ferragosto into account when you made your plans because you didn't know of it. If you had, you would have delayed leaving."

"If we had, we might have regretted leaving so early, but it still would have been necessary. Emeline's school—"

"I've heard all about American public schools," Basilio said dismissively. "She'll learn more, and see more, at Ferragosto."

"She won't, because she won't be going to Ferragosto. It's not your decision."

"You're speaking childishly. If I didn't know otherwise, I would believe Emeline was the older sister." Though his words were hostile, he still wore his I'm-being-reasonable-in-the-face-of-near-insurmountable-childishness expression. It made me hate him all the more.

"What do you know of children? You have none, and your only contribution to your sister's children are to bully, meddle, and belittle them. If you think that's all there is to parenting, then the world's a much better place for not being burdened with your offspring."

There. He wasn't smiling that thin, phony smile anymore. His face was red, and his whole body was trembling. Let his face match his words for a change. I knew it was foolish, but he hadn't quite gone over the edge, and I wanted to see what it would take.

"For that matter, you seem to know very little of women if you think anyone would willingly tolerate your patronizing lord-of-the-manor attitude. No wonder you have to practically kidnap your houseguests—even if they are your relatives!"

He stopped trembling. His thick eyebrows had been swallowed entirely in the angry lines and folds of his face.

I waited for him to call me ungrateful, for him to threaten to have me institutionalized, perhaps even for him to hit me. At least then I would have a grievance the civilized world considered logical. The world was rigged to the advantage of a select few emperors, priests, and senators nearly 2,000 years ago, and it was the same today. But it was something to know that I could still draw blood.

"*Flagellum dei!*" Scourge of god.

I recoiled. I'd been called that before. Someone called it out just before they put me in the tomb. Just like that. "Flagellum dei!"

"I guess Latin just runs in our blood," I said smugly. "I wonder if Mom knows you speak a third language. Maybe we should both call her. You can try to bully her into making Emeline and me stay a couple extra days, and I can ask why she never mentioned that her big brother speaks Latin. Seems like the type of thing she would have mentioned, especially after … ."

I had a lot more to say: barbed taunts against the man who lived in an expensive house all alone and secretly spoke a third language. But another part of my brain had begun assembling this new information into an unpleasant theory, and I was so startled and frightened that I stopped speaking.

He lived alone in Rome in a house that resembled a tomb.

He spoke Latin.

He knew that I had been speaking Latin since I was a child and never asked me how I learned.

He'd drugged me and threatened to have me locked away in a mental institution.

He'd stolen my passport.

He'd spoken of making me stay after Emeline went home.

He hated me.

I knew he was watching as I came to a terribly important conclusion, knew that it was important to escape my head and rejoin the argument, but it was difficult. When I finally did look up at him, he was grinning, but unlike his previous expressions, there was nothing polite about it whatsoever.

"So they just sent you to sit here and wait for me, or

something?" I regained my voice. "It's pretty demeaning when your life's work is to capture a teenager for something she did nearly 2,000 years ago."

"*Dura lex sed lex.*" The law is harsh, but it is the law. The grim words were accompanied by a smile that showed too many teeth.

"I have waited longer than you know, and have searched in places your precious American passport can't take you," he continued, and he didn't sound angry at all, which frightened me.

"And I was buried alive in a tomb the size of your walk-in closet," I said disdainfully. "Don't think you can scare me, Uncle!" I spat out the last word as though it were dirt in my mouth. "I broke the law, and I suffered my punishment without complaint or denial. It is done. All I desire is peace."

"*Radix malorum est cupiditas,*" he replied in a lecturing sing-song voice. The root of evil is desire. I began to understand that he was speaking Latin to remind himself, or possibly me, of what I really was, of the world I came from, and of the terrible thing I did there. If we were two distinct people—past Rhea and present Rhea—then it would be difficult, if not impossible, to carry out whatever he had planned. He obviously wanted to draw me into a fight in Latin. A rather large part of me—the part that desperately missed speaking in my native language—was tempted, despite the obvious dangers.

"Don't speak to me about evil, Uncle. My mind may be cluttered with memories of another life, but my conscience is clean on that front. The pursuit of my desires has never led me to kidnap or interrogate someone. For that matter, it has never, for even the briefest of moments, harmed another person."

"What about the flame? The sacred fire you swore to protect? You were given everything: wealth beyond imagination, power, independence that most women could only dream of. Did you complain about the benefits of your station? No. But you abandoned the sacred flame. You took what you wanted from your station, and you left Rome vulnerable. *Sic et non. Sic et non.*" Yes and no. Yes and no. Basilio wasn't smiling anymore. Not the fake friendly smile, nor the more honest predatory one.

"*Roma invicta!*" I spat back at him, stung by the fact that there was some truth to what he said. I had bought into the order, had benefited from and ultimately betrayed my position. Still, I was merely an imperfect part of an imperfect system.

"How dare you imply that a single person could bring the empire to its knees? I was a vestal virgin, committed to the care and keeping of the eternal flame. And I am ashamed of my failure, but it was not Rome that extinguished that day, but my life. I died and Rome went on waxing and waning without me, without any flame at all."

Basilio suddenly looked tired. Maybe arguing in Latin wasn't as thrilling as he thought it would be. Maybe he, too, was simply an imperfect part of an imperfect system.

"I hoped I wouldn't find you," he admitted.

"Can't you pretend you didn't?" I asked, knowing the answer, but also curious about how it all worked.

"No. You should have landed somewhere else—far from me. You never should have come to Rome. I might not have found you. But for you to arrive at my house … I can't ignore that. I have an important job, to protect the Roman empire."

"Even when there's no empire left to protect?"

"Of course there's an empire to protect. It exists mainly in memories, and finds its way into books and movies. Rome is not all the world to many people, but when something like Rome—incomparable, peerless—dims and declines, you love it all the more fiercely. This is when it requires its staunchest defense. If Rome were as strong as it was 2,000 years ago, perhaps it would matter less. Perhaps I could let you go."

The really sick part of all this was that I could see what he meant. If a vestal virgin was important long centuries ago when there were 18 women in the order at any given time, how much more precious were we now when there were so few of us? Perhaps just myself?

Maybe I endlessly regenerated and was punished just to keep the meager flame kindled, because it wasn't fair to punish the vestals who had served faithfully and honorably. It had to be me.

"Did I … did I … know you … then?"

"No. I was a *praetoriani*—a soldier of the imperial palace. I attended your trial, and I was there when they carried out your sentence, but like all guards, I avoided contact with vestal virgins. The emperor never had the same respect for high priestesses as his father." His tone was proud, but also the slightest bit apologetic, as though he were acknowledging that politics had played as much a role in my demise as my own actions. Or perhaps that was wishful thinking on my part.

"What happens now?" I asked the way a fencer salutes an opponent before a match, already knowing the answer.

"No more leaving the house."

It wasn't what I wanted to hear, but if it was a death sentence, it was at least less terrifying the second time around.

XV

"**D**omi ego sum." The words were muffled by Nesreen's shoulder. I am home. The night was thick with urgency. All thoughts, all impulses were reasonable. The only crimes tonight were those of omission, withholding precious sentiments from the person who could make best use of them.

Tomorrow was Iulius 5, the first day of Ludi Apollinares—several days of games held in Apollo's honor. We were preparing for the worst. All the gladiators were; those who did not have wills rushed to have them made. The poorest among them made deals with one another to help cover funeral expenses should they die in the Coliseum.

Nesreen told me that the trainers at the school where she lived issued much the same warning that Fulvia had given the vestals: "You are expendable, and these are unstable times, so you must be prepared to die." There was no training they could provide for odds stacked so high against them. They may as well have been giraffes loping in terrified, useless circles.

There was a certain respect and even fondness between the trainers and warriors at the ludi, so the trainers did whatever they could to prepare the warriors mentally for what was to come. If you have to die, you have to die. People will remember you for how you do it—whether you smile or cry, cling to your sword or piss yourself with fear.

I would not be in the crowd to watch Nesreen do any of these things. I would remember my hunter as she was here and now, in life—warm and brave and generous and happy. I saw to it that she was very happy. And I hoped I would not be forced to remember her at all.

We were stationed, surprisingly comfortably, on the floor in the relic room, which was adjacent to the temple, but opposite the door. I hoped it would afford a few precious seconds of privacy if someone entered the temple—time enough at least for me to assemble my clothes and put on a passable show as virginal priestess.

Nesreen had never seen me without my infula and could not stop herself from running her hands through my hair, which was longer than hers and had an almost leaden blue tint to it, whereas her own black hair was warm and light, as though it wanted to be brown, then changed its mind. She wore an expression I called honey-smiling. But it was difficult to maintain on this particular night.

"I just hope they give me a weapon," she said, twining her fingers through my hair.

I frowned, and there was no honey in my face or lips.

"They said we might not get weapons. Or armor. I can fight without armor, but to send us in without weapons … that is a massacre." She shook her head, the gesture more discouraged than scared.

"You may have plenty of both," I said lightly. "More weapons than you can reasonably carry."

"Sometimes a single weapon is more than I can carry," she said, still dwelling in the world I wanted to shake her from. "It takes a lot of training to learn to carry a gladius you cannot lift above your waist on first contact."

I tried to look as though I found gladii an interesting subject on what might be our last night together, but my expression must not have been convincing.

"Why did you wear your infula the night of Bona Dea?" Nesreen shifted subjects quickly.

"It is what we wear. The infula, the palla, the suffibulum." I shrugged and stole a glance at the flame. I had to crane my head to the left in order to keep it within my sightline, but we were close enough that I was not actually worried. Checking the flame was a reflex, much like anything else.

"But your sisters did not wear their infulas. It was not required."

"Caecilia wore hers," I said, feeling strangely defensive. "But no, it was not required. There were no men present. But many years ago, a man snuck into Bona Dea, and a woman suffered because of it. Her husband argued that she must be above suspicion. It is the same for me. I must be above suspicion."

Nesreen giggled—a new sound for me that made my chest tighten with exhilaration and incredible sadness. She lost control of the sound and began to thump the ground with her palm in a manic frenzy.

"Nesreen?"

But my query only made it worse. She paused between fits of laughter, and I could see her lips begin to form a word and then it was as though the idea that had taken hold of her reasserted itself, and she was laughing helplessly once more. I wanted desperately to laugh with her.

"What? What, Nesreen?"

"You must be … ." That was as far as she got, and then she was laughing uncontrollably again. I grabbed my infula from the floor.

"I will put this back on," I threatened. She did not look as scared as I would have liked, but she managed to sit still for more than a handful of seconds.

"You must be above suspicion, so you are on the ground with me hoping no one sees you. You are below suspicion." She started chuckling again.

"That is what you were laughing about?" I shook my head, wondering what passed for humor in Cyrene that my venatore was so tickled by my admittedly pompous assertion that I must be above suspicion.

And then, without warning, I understood that it was funny. I began to laugh as loudly and helplessly as Nesreen had moments earlier, and after a few quiet seconds, she joined me. It would not have been humorous with anyone else, but that was what I prized most about Nesreen: the layers she brought into my life, the questions and doubts, the salty taste of the sea she had crossed unwillingly but still shared with me.

Our laughter saved us from having to cry, but it came at a price. We fell asleep, facing one another with Nesreen's arm beneath my head. I had never allowed myself the luxury of sleeping in the temple before, but the danger in laughter is that it deludes you into thinking the world is kinder, merrier, than you know to be true. With happiness coursing through my veins and the jocular aftertaste of laughter on my lips, I forgot my troubles, and Nesreen's, and plunged headlong into a sleep that did not care about oaths and consequences and flames.

Until something woke me. It was not Nesreen, still beside me and as peaceful as I could have hoped. I placed my veil over her and tried to listen. I half stood for a quick glimpse of the flame and thought I saw the door to the temple close. I considered panicking, but that meant acknowledging that Nesreen and I would both die and be one another's cause of death. Silly as it may sound, that also meant waking Nesreen, who was comfortable and warm, and I wanted to rejoin her. It was still dark. If someone had visited the temple and seen us, they would not have left quietly. There would be yelling—accusations and threats we could not deny with our clothes strewn about the temple floor.

So I did the easiest thing. I rejoined Nesreen on the floor, holding her hand tightly in case someone arrived in the night and tried to take her away from me.

A crashing storm tore me from sleep. I sprang from the ground and circled the temple twice before it occurred to me to check on Nesreen. Still sleeping. It occurred to me that it was not a storm that woke me, but a furor. But the temple was as peaceful as it had ever been. Quieter, actually. With great dread, I looked for the flame that protected Rome. It was not there.

The closing door in the middle of the night had an added, ominous significance.

"Nesreen! You must wake!"

I gathered clothes and piled them on her as she began to move. There was no thought behind anything I did; I was riding on pure instinct and terror, not for myself, but for my hunter.

"O Vesta, please protect her!" I wrung my hands in front of the hearth, forgetting there was no fire and that I was probably not in the best of standing.

Nesreen rose more slowly than I would have liked, but when she saw me standing in front of the flameless hearth, her eyes went wide with fear. She tried to hug me, and though I would have appreciated the gesture under any other circumstances, terror had blocked out all affection.

"Get dressed." I pushed her away. "I think someone was here. I think they saw us. Maybe they saw the fire. Maybe they put it out to make this look worse. How could this look worse?" I was wailing now, and the only thing that calmed me was the sight of Nesreen putting on her clothes.

"When will they come?" She was steady as ever, but I could see that her hands were shaking. As well they should be. They would bury me alive, but she would be whipped to death in the Comitium, and the crowds would not be kind.

"I do not know. Soon. I thought I saw the door close hours and hours ago. But I went back to sleep! Nesreen, I am sorry. I thought if we had been found out, we would know. If I had acted more quickly, you would already be back at your school."

"I would not," she said sharply. "Are we sure they are coming? There might be time to light the fire, and perhaps you did not see the door close. You were tired, and the temple was dark."

Dark. What time was it?

I opened the door just the tiniest fraction and was

relieved to find darkness waiting on the other side. The moon was slender and new, and I was grateful for the cover it would provide Nesreen as she snuck back to the school. I opened the door wider, hoping for a cold draft to restore my reason. If there had been some air, it probably would have, but instead I heard the distant clamor of voices raised and angry. They came from the direction of the house, and I knew what they meant for me. It was in the wind, and all of Rome sang with it: justice. No one ever speaks grandly of justice when the defendant is found innocent. They like to see the guilty punished. That is the meaning of justice.

They would be coming, if they were not already.

"Run!" I ordered, holding the door and gesturing toward the night.

"No." Nesreen was fully dressed, but did not step any closer toward the door.

"You must."

"They will kill you."

"They will kill me either way. If you are found here, I have no defense. If you leave and I can restart the fire, I might have a chance of defending myself." I gestured to a small stack of branches from a felix arbor—the only type of wood we were allowed to use when igniting the flame. I almost believed myself, almost believed that there was time to put on my palla, start the fire, and conjure an explanation for what someone may have seen. Which was an unpleasant trail of thought I had not yet visited: Who had it been? A servant? A vestal? It must have been a servant; the vestals were all too frightened to leave the house.

I took a deep breath and prepared to deliver the most important speech of my life, which also happened to be a lie. And a farewell.

"If you leave right now, I believe I can save myself. But for that to happen, you can never mention this to anyone. Go defeat your enemies in the Coliseum, and I will defeat whoever came to spy on me, and we will meet again in more peaceful times." I could feel myself choking up at the end, knowing there would be no reunion, no peaceful times. But I forced back my sorrow. There would be time for tears, but if I wanted to save Nesreen, I had to make her believe what I was saying.

She still did not budge, just stared at me with giant brown eyes and glistening cheeks that made me gulp back tears once, twice, until—

"I will leave. For you."

I exhaled and almost smiled in relief.

"If you promise to really try," she added, still watching me.

"Of course I will try. It is my only chance of seeing you again."

I gripped her shoulders and walked her to the door.

"Run," I instructed her. "Do not stop, whatever they say. They do not know who you are. If you run fast enough, they never have to." I remembered her running in the Coliseum and knew she could do it.

The din from the house was considerably louder, which meant they were outside now and our precious minutes had dwindled to nothing. Like the fire.

She started to say something, and more than anything I wanted to hear her say anything, even if it was nonsense, even if it was in a language I could not understand, but there was no time.

I kissed her, for myself, as fortification against what was coming. As kisses go, it was not fantastic. It was trying to say too much with far too little time. But I knew I would never regret it.

I gripped her shoulders, looked into her eyes one final time.

"*Te amo*," I told her for the first time. Then I flung her outside the temple and closed the door. I waited several seconds, but there was no knock. Then tears came, bursting from me as though a dam had broken—hot and salty and endless.

I raced to the relic room and wrapped my palla around

me as best I could under hasty circumstances. Then gathered two sticks from the felix arbor, knelt before the hearth, and frantically attempted to light them. I did this knowing there was very little chance of success. I had never had much luck lighting the fire on my own, but I had promised Nesreen that I would at least try. Maybe they would find me here alone, desperately trying to relight the fire, and assume I was merely crying because the flame had died. Maybe the servant had not seen Nesreen at all. Maybe she had merely spotted me asleep on the floor and the flame gone and reported that I fell asleep on my watch. Commodus would whip me until I fell unconscious, and I could resume my life as a vestal virgin.

It was pathetic how quickly I kindled a brief flare of hope where my efforts in regard to Vesta's so-called eternal flame failed miserably.

I heard them outside: a chorus of death and fear. They flung the door open less violently than I imagined they would, but then, this was still a temple. Vesta's name still had some power, even if mine no longer did.

Fulvia was with them. When she walked through the door, she was stern and proud, but her eyes fell on me—only partially dressed and obviously struggling to light the fire—and she wilted. Grief and disappointment clung to the turns of her face, and I saw the weight of my crimes in her shoulders. It occurred to me then that perhaps she had heard and refused to believe the allegations against me, that she came with the intention of protecting me. But the evidence of her eyes suggested I was not as innocent as she hoped.

Cloelia was the last to enter the temple.

"They were there." She pointed to the relic room. "On the floor."

Now was the time for me to muster some defense, however paltry. Fortunately, I had collected my discarded infula, which was gathered at my feet. There was nothing in the relic room to suggest everything was not precisely as it should be.

I held up my hands in what I hoped was a gesture of

innocence. "There is no one here. And now all these profane men! I cannot imagine what crime you imagine I have committed that is worth defiling Vesta's temple by allowing men to enter!"

The men scowled to hear themselves referred to as profane, and it occurred to me that if there were going to be a trial, I might need them to vote in my favor.

"As you can see, the fire is out. As I told you." To my surprise, Cloelia did not sound at all smug. She sounded … unhappy. Was it difficult, then, befriending someone with the intention only of spying on them? I shot her a spiteful look.

"I am not denying the fire is out, though it gives me no pleasure to admit it," I said reasonably. "That is a matter for the Pontifex Maximus to address."

"We are all going to see the emperor. He knows we are coming and is aware of the nature of our business," said one of the men, none too assuringly.

"Search the temple," another man ordered. "We need to find her conspirator. He will be tried as well."

I spared a glance at Cloelia to see if she would correct him, but she did not. All I could think was *run, keep on running, and do not stop until you are somewhere even Rome cannot reach you.* The treasonous bent of my thoughts surprised me, that I should long for a corner of the world where my beloved empire could not find Nesreen, even if that meant there was a chance I too could not find her.

They did not try to touch me as we exited the temple, and I marveled, as they marched me to what I presumed would be my trial, at how young the night was—barely half over, by my estimation. Then I marveled at how much damage I had managed to inflict in a few short hours—on myself, on the order, on the flame, possibly on Nesreen.

"I am sorry," I told Fulvia, knowing I owed her much more than three of the most frequently spoken words in the world. She said nothing in return, but then I had not expected her to.

The court—more than a dozen senators; Commodus;

seven flamens, three major and four minor; and at least as many of the emperor's favorite advisors—was already assembled when we arrived at the imperial palaces on Palatine Hill. Until I saw them, I had not been certain where the trial would be held, or whether I was going to be tried at all, or merely buried in the Evil Field on the strength of Cloelia's word. I was the greenest of dupes for trusting her. She had seemed so genuine in her concern for me. I now recognized that she had merely identified me as the vestal most likely to betray her oath and therefore the worthiest of her time.

And I began to have some understanding of why it had taken them so long to detain me. A guard gripped my arm roughly—the first time anyone except Nesreen or a fellow vestal had touched me without permission in more than a decade—and placed me directly in front of the Pontifex Maximus, where they could all look down at me with derision that almost masked their fear. Fulvia was staring at the guard with unconcealed horror, but she did not reprimand him, which was perhaps the greatest indication of the thoroughness with which I had tumbled from Vesta's good grace.

Commodus saw her grimace and directed his first comment of the evening to her.

"It was generous of you to accompany your fallen vestal, but now that she is here and safe, might your energies be better directed toward your other lambs to ensure they do not follow her here?"

Fulvia looked wary, as well someone might if she were about to ignore what may have been a command from the mad emperor.

"Members of this order have been found guilty before without any opportunity to defend themselves." Fulvia spoke quietly, but the court hushed to hear her words, so perhaps she knew what she was about. A quiet, contemplative court was less likely to condemn a woman to death than a loud, disorganized, angry one. I hoped.

"Then we will begin the trial to return you home as quickly as possible." He smiled as if he really liked her, as though he was not disturbed that she showed more backbone than the others. He made no mention of the possibility that I would return home with her, reminding me of my words to Nesreen earlier in the night. Domi ego sum. I wanted to return to that moment.

"Servant from the house, come forward and tell us what you saw and heard. Do not lie, on pain of death." Commodus wore a smile. The other members of the court were grim.

Cloelia stepped forward and stood opposite me, so I could watch her as she told the court that I was an unfaithful bride to Rome. She had a welt on her right cheek, and though it was young and pink and angry, it would probably be as purple as the emperor's robes within a day's time. Was it because she reported me? I looked over at Fulvia for some indication of passionate temper, but it seemed unlikely.

She obediently began speaking. I should have listened carefully for any mention of Nesreen. I should have listened for inconsistencies I could exploit in my defense. But I was tired and guilty. One vestal—I could not remember her name—successfully carried water in a sieve to prove the charges against her were false. Perhaps Vesta would overlook my failings and enable me to do the same. I regarded my hands, trying to determine whether they looked capable of playing a crucial role in a miracle, but they felt disappointingly ordinary. Weary. They felt weary, like the rest of me. Saying goodbye to Nesreen had drained the fight from my bones.

If the flame had not been extinguished, maybe they would have forgiven me. Maybe I would have lived a day, a week, a year more, possibly in exile. Which was as good as a death sentence. Or so I thought growing up. I would love to see those tigers and elephants and exotic beasts outside an arena, possibly in Africa. But there is no place in this world for a runaway vestal. As I looked upon the hard, eager glint of Commodus' eyes, I knew my only future would be confined to an underground tomb. Everyone else seemed to know it as well. Yet it was difficult to work up bitter feelings when I knew

I was guilty.

Cloelia finished her story. A priest—the Flamen Dialis, who served Jupiter—questioned her. She answered. The Flamen Martialis, who served Mars, posed still more questions. She answered. They seemed genuinely determined to unravel her tale, but it did not budge. She had told no lie.

I could not discredit her. I did not want to lie about Nesreen as though ashamed of her. So I said nothing. I did not answer their questions, did not ask the assembled men if any of them had a sieve with which I could prove my innocence. They read my guilt in my silence as much as Cloelia's words, and after numerous proclamations and arguments, I was declared guilty.

Reus. It did not sound like the kind of word that could end a life, but, as my sisters liked to say, I had always been special.

Commodus wanted to beat me, which was the punishment when any vestal allowed the fire to extinguish on her watch, and which I expected. The others seemed horrified by the emperor's proposal and insisted that being buried in the Evil Field was sufficient punishment. How could they know for certain that I had died from being placed in the chamber rather than from the beating?

Commodus did not understand why it mattered.

Because it was forbidden to spill a vestal's blood. If they buried me alive, they could at least argue that they had not actually killed me. Semantics. But what is a government for if not quibbling over the most honorable way to kill someone?

Commodus relented. Perhaps he reasoned that he had his vestal virgin, and insisting on further concessions might damage his cause.

Fulvia beckoned, and I went to her. We did not speak. Her face had the most terrible expression of grief I had ever witnessed, and that included my mother's face at Junia's funeral. My mother had been sad for us because we could not keep Junia, and a little for Junia because of the years she had been robbed of. But Fulvia was sad for Rome, because she knew it would suffer from my infidelity. She was sad for herself and my sister vestals, because I had betrayed them, lied to them, likely brought increased speculation down upon them when they were already so careful and afraid. And I believe she was sad for me, even though most Romans would say I did not deserve her compassion. I was 17. What better age is there to be a sentimental fool?

My Virgo Vestalis Maxima began wrapping me in funeral linens, shielding me from the emperor's view as best she could. She was slow in her work. Meticulous. That is when the fog began to lift, and the panic returned. These were the last clothes I would ever wear. Fulvia seemed to note the flicker of life in my eyes, because she continued her task, her eyes now welling with tears, but her hands grew gentler, if that was possible. Her thumb briefly brushed my cheek, and it might have been an accident, but I chose to believe it was not. Then she handed me to the priests.

There was more linen—so much linen I had to struggle to breathe, enough to smother any sound I might consider making. That was the point, I suppose. They had to carry me outside, because I could not walk, and through the haze of linen and fear I saw a distinctive shape waiting for me: a human-sized box on top of a platform.

Two of the priests lifted me into the box and produced thick leather straps, which they used to bind my wrists and ankles. My face became hot, and I realized I was panting in great, terrified gulps, but the gusts from my breath had nowhere to go. The linen was meant to muffle my pleas. When I had heard the stories before, it sounded so humane: silencing the vestal virgin so the people of Rome could pretend she was already dead and begin to remember her at her finest rather than for her sins. But being dead and not dead simultaneously is impossible and cruel beyond the proportion of my crimes.

Post mortem is after death and ante mortem is before death, but there's no term for hovering between life and death, still breathing, still suffering as humans do, but without any hope of life. I had no idea it would be like this.

But I did not cry out, nor would I have if such a thing were possible. The trial had lasted the better part of the night, and they carried me into a dawn freshly made by the gods.

It was to be my last sunrise. I was lucky. Most know not the day or hour of their demise, and so fail to appreciate those final gales hastening into their lungs. My final breaths were sweet, for they drank in ambrosial Roman air. And I, in my final hours, had known and cherished Nesreen. To love and be Roman is to be doubly blessed by the gods.

I kept my peace, from the vantage and prison of my funeral bier. On either side of me, the streets filled with mourners, and I could hear the terrible heartache in their silence. They carried me through the forum for a final view of the splendor I had endangered. The city was as beautiful as it had ever been; the hour was one of giddy promise rather than sepulchral melancholy, for which I was grateful. The Evil Field lies just outside the Servian Wall, between the gardens of Sallust and the Colline Gate. This was to be my final resting place. This is where they are carrying me.

I shall die and lie dumb in a silent tomb.

I could not distinguish any faces I knew among the crowd that lined our path. My family was probably out there—watching, marking our progress, hoping that there had been some mistake, and it was not really me cocooned in a small mountain of fabric. I desperately wanted to see them. It was probably for the best that I was already separated from the rest of them, the living who would go on living.

But I wanted to see my parents' faces, to apologize for the foolish things I had done, to hear my mother lie to me that it would all be all right somehow. And Aemilia needed to know how special she was, that she had a flame within her that made sacred fires seem modest by compare. I worried about Liviana, who seemed so unhappy of late. All she ever wanted for herself was to become the emperor's mistress, and now she was carrying his child as well, and all of Rome lay at her feet. But it was not what she had hoped. She would know that he had given the order against me, but she already knew that he had given the same order—reus, guilty, death—against his own sister. Few people saw it, but Liviana was quite practical beneath her gaudy exterior. She would see a lesson in my foolishness, and she would profit by my example.

The priests stopped abruptly, and my feet struck the bottom of the box. They began to lower my coffin to the ground, and I wanted to ask for one more trip around the city, perhaps along the Tiber, which was not at its finest during the warm months of summer, but I could overlook that. I could gaze out over the river and remember the wild rush of it when we fed the Argei to it. I truly do love this city. I never intended to betray or disappoint. I was 17! I had fallen in love! Why could they not understand that?

The coffin reached the ground. A priest removed the straps from my wrists and ankles and instructed me to stand. A second caught the linen that encased me, freeing me from my unwieldy cocoon. There was a rupture in the earth several yards from where I stood, and a small segment of ladder was just visible over the top of it. I tried to pretend I did not know what it was. I could see the crowd more clearly—not a hostile mob gathered in condemnation bent on vengeance, but a confederation of Romans united by sorrow, gathered to bid farewell to a vestal virgin who had served them, if not perfectly, to the best of her ability, for 10 years.

I could not have endured it if they had met me with hatred or disgust. I was grateful for my infula, bound securely around my head once more. But I knew that they saw me as no more than a condemned priestess. I wanted to shout at them: "Please do not remember me like this! If it is this or nothing, please do not remember me at all!"

A priest handed me a small bundle and a lamp and gestured toward the ladder. He turned his back, and the men with him turned as well. I considered running, only to spare myself having to descend into the tomb by a handful of minutes. But tradition and pride spared us all the embarrassment of a runaway vestal. None of the others—

guilty or innocent—had run when they faced the empty tomb, and neither would I.

They began by removing the ladder as soon as I was done climbing down. I wanted to grapple with them for it, but I would buy myself only a few seconds and be remembered as a coward who attempted to trade her good name for a ladder. Of course, if the ladder was all that stood between me and freedom, I would have swapped my good name a dozen times, but matters were a good deal more complicated. Then they took away my light—filling the hole in their ground and my ceiling with dirt. If you have ever wondered what it feels like to go mad, climb in a deep, dark space and watch as someone takes away your only exit, one humble piece of dirt at a time. If you can speak after the experience, then your grasp on sanity must be stronger than my own. I could only cower with my arms tightly wrapped over my head, so I could not hear the flow of dirt funneling in or have to know the final moment I would never again see sunlight.

I cannot describe the darkness of such a place. Or even determine whether it was the tomb that was exceptionally tenebrous, or the knowledge that I was to die there. And soon. My rations consisted of some bread and water and the lamp the priest had given me. Neither the food nor the water were meant to sustain me for more than a day, and it seemed unlikely that my light would last half as long. There was a small bed in the corner, and I could not help but wonder where it had come from, whether it belonged to someone else before it found its way down here or if it was crafted for this sad purpose. Neither seemed cheerful, but rather than pity a piece of furniture that had never known the sorrow of bidding permanent farewell to the sun, I saved my empathy for the truly afflicted: myself.

There is a certain calm in knowing the worst has happened, the hour you feared most has struck but there is nothing you can do; you are beyond helping, beyond salvation. Unfortunately, that peace was a tide that swept in and out over the course of my time there. At first I tried to measure time's passage in my head, to bind myself in some small fashion to the world above me and all the people I loved. But I could see that there was no point in it.

When the first pangs of hunger struck, rather than rationing the bread, I placed it in a far corner of my tomb and hoped I would not be able to find it when the light died. I positioned myself on the bed in the same shape my body had formed when sleeping with Nesreen. I did not have to close my eyes against the murk, but I did anyway because it was easier than panicking because it was dark. Nesreen's arms were around me, and all I had to do was trust them to protect me, trust her to take me to wherever I was supposed to be.

Domi ego sum.

XVI

To find myself trapped once more, hostage to the will of a man who felt no more sympathy for me than for the Turkish rug that hung above the entryway, was sufficiently frustrating that I wanted to kick myself for my stupidity in coming here. When I said as much to Aemilia, she advised me to actually attempt kicking myself before making any other rash statements.

"It's a lot harder than it sounds," she said. I waited until she left the room and attempted to kick myself to prove it wasn't as difficult as she made it out to be, but I found that my options were limited by my mobility. I managed a few blows to my calf, which was pointlessly thick-witted but at least enough to prove that it was possible to kick myself.

After more than a week trapped inside Basilio's contemporary mausoleum, my only goal at the end of each day was to retain my sanity. I wasn't even allowed in the yard, where the promise of authentic air and a sky that wasn't merely a secondhand reproduction would have done wonders for my flagging morale. Ilium had its share of windows, but they were mostly situated too high on the wall to be accessible to anyone who wasn't a professional basketball player. After announcing that I was no longer allowed to leave Ilium, Basilio activated the house's security alarms so he would know if anyone attempted to enter or depart.

Aemilia was proving to be no use, despite her fancy war notebook and our earlier talk of finding, and defeating, whoever hunted me. It was true that we'd been vague about what we planned to do with them once we figured out who they were; our options seemed limited in a foreign country, and neither of us had packed a weapon in the traditional sense of the word. I had theories about the stabbing potential of some of Aemilia's high-heeled shoes, but hadn't been given the opportunity to test these theories. Aemilia was very protective of her shoes—more than she was of me, her hunted big sister, as it turned out.

Aemilia was out with Adamo the night Basilio announced his intention of keeping me here, and though I didn't yet know how he meant to go about it, I also knew that I couldn't leave Rome without my sister. I went to bed believing that I would hear her come in when she returned, and we would leave immediately. Instead, Basilio waited up for her and summoned her to his study. I don't know what he said, though I suspect it was along the lines of arguing that I was mentally unstable and there was the potential I might fall into some harm if left to my own devices. It's what I would have told her, anyway, were I the type of person who does things to people under the guise of helping them.

The worst part was, Aemilia seemed to have accepted whatever it was that Basilio told her. When she finally came to our room, I insisted that our safety depended on our leaving that very night, having already packed our luggage while I waited for her.

"We can't leave, Rhea. I've talked to Basilio about it, and it's going to be OK. You have to trust me." She said this in the tone she used when her mind could not be changed. And then she pulled her suitcase from where I had sat it in solidarity beside my own and began to remove her clothes.

"Aemila, Basilio knows who I am. He won't let me leave the house. We have to get out of here before he does something even more psychotic! I'm not sure how much further the situation can escalate before we've entered horror film territory."

"You shouldn't call me Aemilia," she said in a low voice. "If he hears you, it's going to mean more trouble. And besides, what do you know about horror movies? You're always too scared to watch."

I recoiled at the realization that she was asking me to revert to calling her by her new name. No, not asking me. Telling. It was as though all the moments I'd thought had mattered this summer were being swept away, and I didn't understand why. I didn't want us to go back to being near-strangers whose occupation of the same house seemed more happenstance than intentional.

"All right, *Emeline*. You remain here with Basilio. I'm leaving."

"I'm so glad I brought this," she mused, holding up the ivory disco dress she'd worn on the all-day church marathon. "You know, Mom was a little horrified at the idea that I would wear this here, but it just works. It really shouldn't have been crammed into my luggage. It belongs in a garment bag."

I ignored her lunacy, gripped my suitcase, and headed for the door. I'd been a captive once before and found it did not suit me.

"Where will you go?" she asked reasonably just before I reached the door. "You can't leave the country without your passport."

"Then I'll go to the embassy and apply for a new one. What I should have done months ago."

"He has friends at the embassy. They'll alert him as soon as you arrive. And it takes a couple days, long enough for him to come up with some new way to keep you here."

"Then I'll find an embassy somewhere else."

"There are four in Italy: Rome, Florence, Milan, Naples. Five if you count San Marino. If you believe Basilio's influence doesn't extend beyond Rome, well, that's just wishful thinking. What if he has them detain you on some trumped-up charge? And don't ask me if he would, Rhea, because you know better than I do what he's capable of."

"Then what do I do? Find another hole to fling myself into while the rest of the world marches on without me?"

"No! You should unpack your suitcase, find something to occupy your mind and time, try not to provoke a direct confrontation with Basilio, and trust me." Her voice had a desperate edge akin to panic. It turned out that was all I needed: some acknowledgement that I was not alone in this. I unpacked enough of my suitcase to fool Basilio if he looked through our room and tried to imagine some pastime that would take my mind off my situation.

At first it had seemed a poor man's confinement. There were plenty of people who would scoff at the notion that being locked in an elegant, spacious villa with plenty of food and reasonable treatment even qualified as imprisonment. But however many bowls of Raisin Bran I might eat and whatever the thread count on my sheets, I did not have my liberty and when so key a component of happiness is absent, luxuries won't caulk the gaping wound.

Emeline still came and went at her pleasure, though she tried to stay a little more often to help combat my restless anxiety. She didn't tell me where she was going, and I never asked, partially out of fear that she was hatching some dangerous plot to free me, and partially out of fear that she wasn't. After a couple of days, I could speak her name without stumbling over the old one—an accomplishment that should have filled me with relief, but instead produced a sense of wrenching anguish only relieved by long bouts of dreamless sleep that bore an uncanny resemblance to death.

I wanted to play knucklebones, but worried that Basilio would confiscate them if he found me playing, and that would produce exactly the kind of confrontation Emeline was so eager for me to avoid. It also might prompt questions about where the knucklebones came from, and, lacking any lie that sounded plausible, I might be cornered into telling the truth. How to tell the truth (that the knucklebones were a gift from

Emeline) without also revealing certain prejudicial information (Emeline spoke Latin, Emeline was once Aemilia, Emeline should probably be detained and forcibly drugged with antipsychotics) were questions too difficult to navigate without the possibility of physical retreat. So I kept the knucklebones in my pocket and contented myself with a few tosses every night before bed, when the door was locked and I was reasonably certain Basilio would not come barreling into the bedroom.

Basilio's relationship to Abri caused me to think about my parents in a context I had never before considered: as people. It was disconcerting, for some reason, to think of either of them having siblings. My father was an only child, and the fact that Abri's only brother lived on the other side of a large ocean had created an insular family unit—and within that unit I tended to operate as my own insular being. But to think of my mother as the younger sister to this commanding, all-knowing bully had me wondering what she'd been made to endure in her childhood, which parts of his personality she had already been made aware of, and whether she had any doubts about sending us here alone.

It's the primary responsibility of a mother to protect her child, but life's greatest dangers don't always come emblazoned with a skull and crossbones. She knew Basilio as a respected psychiatrist, and perhaps she considered her eldest daughter's apathy and antisocial tendencies a greater threat than whatever she knew of Basilio's penchant for intimidation and cruelty. Perhaps my uncle was a villain disguised as a lesser evil. Perhaps my mother thought I was a damsel in distress disguised as a sullen teenager … or was it the other way around?

Two days before we were scheduled to fly home, Emeline and I agreed that we'd have to come up with a way to retrieve my passport. She insisted it was best for her to act as my ambassador and negotiate with Basilio on her own, and I was so reluctant to talk to him that I didn't put up any kind of fight about it. Armed with youthful confidence and an irresistible smile, my younger sister sallied forth to fight my battles. It wasn't a proud moment for me, but pride was one of the few luxuries my present circumstances would not allow.

She was gone for a very long time, and the prospect of following my week of hanging around the house with another hour of sitting around our shared bedroom wasn't terribly appealing. Though I knew it was foolish, I walked to the closet where Emeline's wardrobe had made itself at home, sprawling lavishly with a full six inches of space between each garment. I stole one last glance toward the bedroom door, then crept low to the ground and crawled to the back of the closet, the longer of Emeline's dresses fluttering against the top of my head as I passed them.

I was glad they couldn't speak; doubtless they'd have found it strange to have a girl crawling below their extremities. If Basilio wanted evidence that I was mentally unhinged, he only need consult my sister's clothing. Fortunately, a man like Basilio lacked sufficient imagination to converse with objects that gave the appearance of being inanimate. Something crimson and silk caught the top of my head, and I brushed it away with one hand while the other reached for the black marker I'd left there a couple days before.

It wasn't something I planned, or even necessarily understood. One minute I was standing beside the bed, and the next thing I knew I was in a closet with the thick black marker Emeline liked to carry in her purse in case she ran into anyone famous and wanted an autograph. I was writing on the walls in big letters, and the more I wrote, the calmer I felt, the less I needed to fashion my words into a spear and heft it through Basilio's pale beating heart.

Ab irato. From anger. *Absolvo.* I acquit. *Amor vincit omnia.* Love conquers all. It didn't conquer Fulvia or the Pontifex Maximus. But it conquered death, and death conquered them, so I have won. *Fiat lux.* Let light be made. The vestal virgin has paid for her sin with her blood. The sun can rise.

I was undoubtedly tempting fate—or at least risked provoking Basilio, which was worse. I had painted graffiti in a dead language across the walls of his precious Ilium, and Basilio was not the careless sort of man who disregards his home's nooks and hideaways. But it worked, because it was destructive, because it was a violation of his home—not an entirely just recompense for depriving me of my liberty, but a good start.

I even scrawled "Aemilia" onto the wall, figuring that even if Basilio found it, he would never know to whom I was referring. I briefly considered putting Nesreen's name on the cornsilk-colored paint, but it felt too personal. If we left this place, *when* we left this place, I did not want to supply my enemy with any essential information.

"Rhea? Rhea! I swear to all the gods past, present, and future, if she snuck off while I was talking to that pig, I'll—"

I emerged from the closet as casually as it's possible to crawl out from a small space you're not actually supposed to enter, somewhat disappointed that I would not get to hear what she had planned for me if I'd escaped. Emeline was so preoccupied with the task of angrily stomping around the bedroom that she forgot to ask what I was doing in her closet. If it had been me stomping around the bedroom and her wriggling out of the wardrobe, it wouldn't occur to me to bother about it, but Emeline was as fiercely protective of her clothes as a mother honey badger—a creature that could claim vicious and territorial tendencies by dint of its species even before you accounted for maternal instincts.

"Did you get my passport?" I figured, based on the fact that she was now kicking the bed, that the mission had not been successful. But I didn't want to make any hasty assumptions.

"No! Not yet, at least." She slumped on the bed, not quite mollified, but too tired to carry on with her tantrum.

"You need to fly home in less than two days," I said quietly. "Whatever happens."

"Of course I'm flying home in less than two days," Emeline replied. "Don't tell anyone I said this, but I'm actually kind of looking forward to the first day of school. I haven't seen some of my best friends in more than two months, and now that I've gotten over Soren, I'm eager to dive back into the dating pool."

"Good. I just wanted to make sure we were clear on that point."

"Oh, I understand what you were saying, but I'm not sure you understand what I'm saying." She sat upright, spine rigid and unyielding, and gave me a stern look. "We're both leaving. At the same time. And I'm not missing school because of some weird, petty family drama."

"How?"

"I'm going to get your passport back tomorrow. Your job is to make sure our bags get all packed up without attracting Zio's attention."

"How can you call him that?"

"Call him what?"

"Zio. Uncle."

Emeline shrugged. "He's our uncle. It's factual. I'm not nominating him for Uncle of the Year or saying I haven't considered calling the police and reporting that he's essentially kidnapped you. But he is our uncle."

"I guess. I just don't really see him as an uncle."

"Yeah, but you don't really see Mom and Dad as your real parents, either," she pointed out. "And if I wasn't also Aemilia, you wouldn't see me as your sister."

"It's not that I didn't consider you my sister," I hedged. "It's more complicated than that."

"Look, you spent most of your last life living in a convent with a bunch of holier-than-thou priestesses. It stands to reason that you don't know how to be a sister, even if you had five of us to teach you. We just didn't get enough of a chance. I think the isolation from your family wrecked you as much as that rotten execution." She barely hesitated before she said the final word. We'd come a long way.

"It doesn't mean I didn't love you," I said. "Or that I don't now. It just … makes things a little harder. And listen to you! We might just have another psychiatrist in the family! You

232

could specialize in reincarnation adjustment disorder."

Emeline snorted. "Go to sleep. For tomorrow, we flee this elegantly designed coop!"

I obediently turned out the lights and shuffled through the darkness to my bed when I heard her whisper, "Vesta willing."

*   *   *

I awoke to discover that something was blocking out the sun—a trembling aquamarine presence that fluttered but did not disappear when I tried to sit up. I licked my lips to assure myself that I had not been gagged, before reaching to my forehead. Something peeled away, leaving a sticky trail I did not want to think about.

A Post-it Note. That did not confirm my first theory, which was that I'd been bound and gagged while I slept. At least the tacky sensation on my forehead wasn't blood. On the other side, it said "STAY" in Emeline's careless scrawl, and the word was underlined three times. As I followed her orders from the previous night, showering, getting dressed, packing my luggage, I wondered: What sort of person sticks a Post-it Note to someone's forehead?

My sister.

I was so distracted by the note that I failed to realize something unpleasant and startling. Emeline's luggage was gone, along with her clothing, hair dryer, toiletries, purse, and war notebook. It took more than half an hour and four thorough room searches before I could believe it—and even then, I was not certain I understood the implications of this discovery.

Had Emeline abandoned me? Did Basilio catch on to our plans and kick her out of the house? Or was she being held somewhere else, separate from me, so we couldn't plot? Nothing made sense, least of all that Emeline would leave me here. And then an idea crashed into my head as tumultuously and painfully as though it had been shot from a cannon. What if Emeline woke up early to begin the first phase of her plan and started to clear out the closet to begin packing and found my markings on the back wall? What if they scared her enough that she started to worry that maybe Basilio—Zio—was right about me, and she went to him with her concerns? What if he convinced her to leave without me?

Figuring that Basilio might come looking for me and discover my packed bag if I never left the room, I went to the kitchen and spent 20 minutes rifling through the cupboards as though I really cared what I ate for breakfast. Eggs? Not unless I could spackle the walls with the regurgitated contents of my stomach. Cereal? Any other day I'd say yes, but I was beginning to feel that I'd fallen into a food rut, and it felt important, on what I still hoped would be my day of liberation, that I establish a new precedent. Leftover spaghetti? I'd be all over it if it weren't for the message that might send to Basilio. I could just hear him arguing, "She doesn't know what year she's supposed to be living in. She doesn't even know whether she's supposed to be eating breakfast or dinner. Irresponsible, reckless, mentally unfit!"

All over a plate of spaghetti. Then again, he was Italian—an observation that isn't so much a stereotype as just plain truth, though I suspected he fancied himself too cosmopolitan to be boxed into a stereotype perpetuated by a corporation that produced marinara. He loved Italy. Of that there was no doubt. But he loved himself more, and you can't make room for 61.5 million countrymen on a pedestal. In order to be genuinely impressed by himself, he couldn't believe that his many admirable qualities were an accident of blood, that there were as many Basilios wandering the world as there were educated Italian men. I really hated him.

Toast it was. It might not have been exciting, but it was benign.

I was starting to feel like I was trying to run down a clock, like the games my dad and sister sometimes watched on television, when one team had a much higher score than the other, except that I was fairly certain I was on the losing team right now. Still, I trusted Emeline, and the sad fact is there are times when waiting is the only and best option—even if you're so impatient you'd almost rather try and fail.

By the time Emeline did finally return, it was well past dark, and I'd already made a grand show of pretending to decide what to eat for lunch and dinner. My luggage was packed away in the rear corner of the closet to conceal my adventures in indoor graffiti, and I'd even tossed the bulk of my toiletries trying to make my pack as light as possible for my escape. I regretted that I wasn't carrying a large backpack—the type we'd seen frequently during our brief stay in the hostel, with so many pockets and straps you couldn't imagine a use for half of them. I'd pictured our flight from Ilium over and over in my head, and the sight of my suitcase clacking rapidly over the stone driveway didn't capture the urgency of the situation.

Maybe, just a little bit, it was the kids carrying the backpacks that I envied—a whole generation of confident world travelers equipped with languages that real, living people still spoke. I was wary of them at first, and I realized it was because they made me ashamed of the fact that my younger sister had to practically drag me out of my hometown and beyond my comfortable borders. I wasn't entirely certain that visiting Italy wasn't a mistake—and my present circumstances validated that opinion—but there were still nearly 200 other countries I could visit. Excluding the 30 or so nations with high travel risks, I was still left with more than one 150 options, not to mention the entirety of my own vast country.

What had happened to the curious, brave Rhea of my former life? She'd have hassled her parents for a travel pack for Christmas by the time she was 16 and accumulated enough money for a plane ticket anywhere by the time she graduated from high school. I'd always thought I was ahead of my past-life self simply by virtue of being alive this long, but Rome had forced me to reconsider. Yes, I'd lived longer, but what had I accomplished? Maybe I was actually behind.

Unfortunately, I couldn't begin to vindicate myself until I left Ilium. As long as I remained in this house, I would continue living as I had spent the past 18 years: cowering, fearful, bent only on survival. But if Emeline's plans for our escape were successful, well, that would be a different story entirely.

She came barreling into the bedroom, breathless and frantic. There was no sign of her luggage, and she was wearing a backpack I remembered seeing somewhere, but which I knew did not belong to her. She was wearing her smoky high-waisted cotton linen pants with pleats that produced an old-fashioned flair somewhere between her calves and ankles, accentuating a pair of simple, brown leather shoes that might have passed for men's footwear half a century earlier. There was a black smudge on her chin, and the right corner of her lip was swollen. None of it added up to a narrative that made any kind of sense.

"You weren't starting to doubt me, were you?" she asked with a quick smile. Even behaving as though she were being pursued by Cerberus—the three-headed watchdog of the underworld—Emeline couldn't help but pause to gloat.

In response, I rolled my suitcase out of the closet.

"How come I didn't hear the alarm?" I hadn't been expecting her, because the agitating noise of the alarm, which resembled a sci-fi arcade shooter at high volume, hadn't sounded as it almost always did when anyone left or returned to the house.

"Adamo called Zio and asked him to turn off the alarm because he was coming home."

"Where's Adamo now?" For the past couple weeks, I'd been struggling against a growing sense of concern that Emeline would not want to leave Adamo when the time came. I didn't have any doubts about whether Emeline would or would not come home, but I was concerned that she might be planning to spring a houseguest on my parents.

"Don't worry about it," she said, not meeting my eyes. But I saw her tongue press tentatively against the fat part of her lip, and things started to fall into place.

"All right. What happened to your mouth?"

"Pass," she said, sweeping through the bedroom one last time to make sure we weren't leaving anything important behind. When she got to the back of the closet, I heard her inhale sharply, followed by several seconds of undignified laughter that mostly sounded like snorting.

"You don't get to pass on two questions in a row. I want to know what happened to your mouth. And if Basilio's errand boy had anything to do with it, then I want to know where he is, too, so I can bid him a proper goodbye."

"Adamo's ... not coming back," she said vaguely.

"Did you kill him?" I whispered in fascinated horror. That would certainly explain her urgency.

"No! I didn't kill anybody! I just left him in a tough spot. We won't be seeing him again, and the less you know, the better." Though she was trying to sound casual, I watched her face while she spoke, and it was grim.

"Okay," I relented. "I trust you, of course."

"You'd better. In fact, I think you're going to need at least three more lives to repay me for being such a good sister." She waved my passport at me.

My knees buckled against the intense rush of relief. I hadn't mentioned it because I was afraid of what Emeline might say, but in a matter of seconds, an entire continent of worry and doubt tumbled away to be replaced by a sense of confidence and well-being I hadn't experienced in nearly 2,000 years. If Basilio was all that now stood between me and the new life I wanted to claim as my own, he was going to need the entirety of the Italian Armed Forces to keep me here. Emeline and I were strong, capable, and angry. Why did it take so long to realize?

"We need to leave quickly and quietly. If Basilio sees me, he's going to know what's going on," Emeline said urgently.

"Why? Your plane isn't supposed to leave till tomorrow."

"He thought it would be best if I left sooner rather than later. He even put me up in a hostel for tonight because he was worried about your reaction when I left for the airport and you weren't allowed to leave." She sounded apologetic, which would make sense if she were actually planning to leave me here, but considering everything she'd done, it didn't make much sense.

"I knew he was trying to keep me here! I almost wish I could see his face when he wakes up and realizes that I've gone." I thought about our previous conversations and his calm expression when he tried to manipulate me into doing something I didn't want to do. Predictably, I smelled black licorice as my stomach twisted into a hard, angry knot. "Almost."

"Just don't forget that we're not past him yet," Emeline whispered. She slowly eased open the bedroom door and gestured for me to walk through ahead of her. She would walk behind me with my luggage. We made it safely beyond the second set of guestrooms and kitchen before the gentle scuffle of a turning page betrayed our uncle's location and occupation.

"Uncle. In the library. With a book," I whispered to Emeline with a giggle, because it reminded me of when we were younger and our parents would play *Clue* with us.

"What do we do?" she whispered back. Somehow her uncertainty bolstered my resolve.

"We leave. If he chases us, we run. If he tries to stop us, we fight."

I felt Emeline's nod of agreement from behind me.

We marched into the open and toward the door. Basilio let us take several steps before he interrupted.

"Emeline, I must say I'm disappointed in you. We agreed it was better for you to say goodbye to your sister over the phone after you were at the airport."

"That's what you told me to do," Emeline responded cautiously, neither agreeing nor disagreeing.

"Forgive me if I sound simple, but that does not appear to be what is happening." Though he addressed his conversation to Emeline, he kept his eyes on me.

"No, Uncle, that is not happening."

"Why not?"

"Because I don't agree with you. Rhea belongs at home with her family. That's where she wants to be. And we want her there, too."

"That's a rather selfish view of things. It's natural for you to want to please your older sister, but that is not what she needs. In time, she can return home. She'll be ready to live her life by then—go to college, get a job, all the things young women her age are supposed to do."

"I will do those things, Uncle. If I decide that is the best path for me to follow." I was tired of listening to them discuss my future as though it belonged to someone else.

The many wrinkles of flesh that comprised Basilio's face folded into a severe frown. We'd all been dancing around so politely, and I decided it was time to draw first blood.

"But you will never be given any say or consideration in determining my future. Goodbye."

I started for the door, the loud, rumbling roll of the suitcase behind me indicating that Emeline was following. Basilio didn't leave the couch, which surprised me a little. I'd been expecting more of a fight, but perhaps he simply did not know that I had my passport back and thought he could catch me at the embassy. Still, I walked as quickly as possible without making a show of my haste.

I tried to twist the doorknob, but it wouldn't turn. There were a half-dozen locks and bolts on the door—a fact I'd considered somewhat paranoid when I first saw it, but now that I knew my uncle better, I could understand why someone would want to harm him—and I flipped and twisted them in various combinations. Nothing worked.

"You've noticed the double cylinder deadbolt." Basilio's matter of fact voice came from the other room.

"We might have to use a window," I muttered to Emeline. We returned to the living room to make one final plea for reason. At least, that was my intention. Emeline seemed to have other ideas.

"Congratulations," Emeline said in a voice that was

droll and furious and superior all at the same time. I was convinced only 12- to 18-year-old girls were capable of speaking that dismissively, and Emeline was a master. "You made a trip to a hardware store to purchase equipment most people don't need because most people are sane and nice enough that they don't have to lock people into their house to keep them there!"

"I'm a psychiatrist, Emeline. Many of the people I help are a greater danger to themselves than the rest of the world. I bought the lock for the same reason I went into psychiatry: to help people. Now, Rhea ate the last of the spaghetti in the refrigerator for dinner, but I'm happy to make more if you're hungry. I won't ask you to apologize for disobeying me. I know it can be difficult to make the right choices at your age."

"Uncle, we have no desire to argue with you or damage your property, but if you refuse to allow us to leave this house, that is exactly what will happen." I tried to sound calm rather than threatening, but I saw a hard glint in Basilio's eyes when I mentioned the possibility of property destruction. He loved Ilium, and though his furnishings and possessions were spare, they were carefully curated.

"When the two of you have calmed down a bit, we'll have a discussion about increasing your medication. It's clearly not having the desired effect," he responded.

I turned to Emeline and looked her directly in the eye. "Find the first window you can reach and smash it open using anything you have to." I didn't whisper. I wanted Basilio to know what was going to happen.

Emeline dragged the suitcase into the kitchen where we could hear her rifling through the cabinets. There was a loud thud.

"It might take a couple hits, but I think I can break this!" Emeline's voice was high and excited.

Basilio stood and took a step toward the kitchen. I grabbed a small statue of a robed woman from the table beside the couch. Basilio looked undecided. There was another crash from the kitchen, indicating that Emeline was moving forward with her demolition project. It was not the sound of breaking glass, but it sounded expensive and destructive, and I could feel Basilio inching ever closer to losing his composure.

I'm not going to pretend I didn't derive joy from the pain I knew the noises were causing him. If he walked over to the front door and unlocked it, we would leave without causing any further damage, but he would not. He could call off the entire skirmish whenever he liked, but we had no such power. The only power within our grasp was to disfigure the thing he loved best, and I was a little disgusted with myself for not thinking of it sooner. Of course, he'd always had Adamo, so we were evenly matched—Emeline and me against our uncle and his assistant.

And how could we have known that it would ultimately come to this? Deep down, I'd figured that Basilio would relent when the time came. Instead, he sat comfortably on his couch and offered to make Emeline one final dinner before her departure. While I was never meant to leave at all.

I heaved the statue toward a window settled on top of an alcove above the door. The sound the impact produced was heavy and brief, not at all like the sound of breaking glass I wanted to hear. I shrugged.

"It was probably too high for me to climb out of anyway," I observed with a friendly smile.

There was a third crash from the kitchen, accompanied by a volley of imprecations I would never have guessed Emeline knew.

"*Smettere di farlo!*" Basilio howled, striding toward the kitchen. He didn't run. Perhaps he felt sprinting around his house chasing teenagers was undignified. But I would have been less scared for Emeline if he moved more quickly.

"Run, Emeline!"

"Don't worry about me! He said to keep breaking everything in his house!"

I thought for a second about my life leading up to this moment—both of them, actually—and the horror and shame of what I had allowed to be done to me paralyzed me.

I tried to mobilize my limbs. Emeline needs me! My sister needs me!

But Emeline didn't need me. She was far more self-sufficient than I had ever been. In that moment, I realized that the best thing I could do to help Emeline was to help myself, to free myself from Ilium, to tear myself from this cycle in which I found myself at the mercy of powerful people offended by what I had done or the prospect of what I might do.

To claim redemption, I had to sacrifice Ilium. Nothing had ever been clearer. If I did this right, I could atone for all of it: my broken vow, the flame that had ceased to burn, my lackluster performance as big sister, the 18 years I'd mostly wasted being afraid.

As though I'd stuck a key into a very particular lock, my limbs were free. I darted to the nearest alcove and tore everything from the cabinet built into the wall. Books, several of them written by Basilio. Geodes. More statues. I flipped the table, then picked up one of the chairs by the leg and began smashing it against the wall. It was a flimsy geometric design—nothing more than two triangles facing one another, really—so it didn't break so much as collapse into an unimpressive heap.

There was a painting on the wall, a half-dozen pink naked figures, their curves broken into a complex series of triangles. Using both arms, I pulled it from the wall and flung it like a disc across the room.

I didn't waste my sympathy on the possessions that fell victim to my spree.

I didn't consider the cultural, intellectual, or artistic value of what I had destroyed.

I didn't plan my course or consider how best to avoid or antagonize Basilio. I merely acted. Everyone else ceased to exist. I made a ballet of my fury, arcing a leg as I spun a pillow and released it toward the moon, flinging an arm wide like a triumphant discus thrower. Before I flipped the second table, I did my own version of a tap dance: a series of jumps and stamps that would have looked meaningless to anyone else, but felt beautiful and graceful to me. My heart pounded fiercely, and the sound of my own breathing was so loud I would have been embarrassed if I had believed there was anyone nearby to hear it.

It was in the middle of one of these jumps, when I hung suspended in air, an expression of intense concentration and pleasure on my face, my hair whipping freely in a shape and manner that resembled nothing but itself, that something swept my leg from beneath me, and I landed with a crash that sent a single, sharp surge through a rib on the right side of my body.

Something tugged at my arm, jerking me from the wreckage of my collision.

"I knew you were crazy … such meaningless destruction … never going back to America … see you locked up like an animal … ."

There was a second voice, which did not agree with the first voice and seemed insistent on the point that someone needed to be taken to the hospital immediately. I decided I did not care for either of the voices. It had been better when they weren't there at all, and I could do what I felt was best.

I let the arm tug me upright, and when I was certain I would not fall, I wrenched myself free with a mighty tug and pushed the thing that had called me crazy to the ground. The other voice pounced on him, clawing for something in his pocket.

"Give me the keys!" the voice demanded.

Free from their loud, uncivilized squabble, I sprinted through the living room, ripping apart two decorative throw pillows that had survived the last round of destruction, then making my way to the study. It was always locked, unless already occupied by Basilio, but I wasn't following any logical course of action at that point. My instincts told the rest of my body what to do, and my legs and arms obeyed.

But when I twisted the knob, and the door actually swung toward me, some logical part of my brain quietly witnessing the takeover knew enough to be confused. All it accomplished was a momentary pause, less than a quarter of a second, and then I was rummaging through the drawers of Basilio's desk, raining important documents like confetti through the office.

"Ferragosto! Ferragosto!" I cried to no one in particular. My uncle was so charmed by the notion of the end-of-summer festival, I couldn't imagine that he would be anything but pleased by the prospect of end-of-summer revelry being brought to his beloved Ilium. Perhaps it would help ease the sting of our long overdue departure.

There were several bottles of pills in the bottom drawers, and I popped them open and began throwing miniature cylinders in all directions, the way costumed celebrities on floats throw candy during parades. The rainbow pharmaceutical hailstorm delighted me to such an extent that I found myself questioning why I'd been so bothered by the idea of my medication.

A shadow materialized beneath the festive pellets, sweeping over my feet the way a determined tide overtakes an inattentive beachgoer. I danced backward as though my feet really were at risk of getting wet, then looked up to find Basilio staring in the doorway, incredulity blossoming across his features.

"Uncle! Ferragosto came to Ilium while you were fighting over the key!"

I wanted him to understand what I meant, but I was out of pills, so I turned to the desk to search for more. If this was what they meant when they called me mad, I didn't mind it so much. I felt free.

There were several seconds of silence while Basilio observed every corner of the study. There were the uneven scraps of white paper that had fallen like a peaceful snow and contrasted nicely with the exactly identical blue, green, and purple cylinders scattered across the floor. For a brief second, I believed that he might surrender his righteous outrage and laugh or dance or something equally constructive. Instead, he threw himself at me with enough force to displace one of the life-sized statues on Palatine Hill.

I dove to the other side of the desk, slamming my hip against its sharp, wood corner and dislodging several shelves of books and framed certificates. With the desk between us, and the pain in my hip now competing against the throb of my rib, I watched as Basilio attempted to fend off a small avalanche of paper and glass.

"Now, now Uncle! This isn't the Coliseum!" I chided him. He responded with a deep-throated rumble that was not quite a growl or a roar, but just as angry, just as threatening.

"Rhea! Get out of there!" Emeline was at the door, waving me toward her. When she saw the pills on the ground, she began to laugh, the top half of her body tilting toward the wrecked room and convulsing. She took a few steadying breaths, and as soon as she was able to speak, she announced, "You did this to yourself, Uncle! You really had this coming!"

Then she took my hand, and we fled the study. Something about the sensation of another sweaty hand clutching mine flipped a switch in my head, and my priorities shifted. I wasn't romping through the house like a first-time performance artist. I was trying to escape.

"Did you get the key?" I asked.

Emeline shook her head. "Almost. It's in his pocket, though." She held up her other hand to show a bloody gash trailing across her palm.

"That doesn't make sense. What does that mean?"

She made a grappling motion with her hands. Then she stabbed at her wounded hand. She had obviously been too swept away by the urgency of the situation to take the time to explain, but she forgot to keep moving while she mimed so we actually wasted more time that way.

"Where's my suitcase?" I was willing to leave without it, but would really prefer that it didn't come to that. An idea was beginning to take root in the quiet depths of my brain, and though I didn't yet recognize it, I knew my suitcase was important.

The kitchen window, I was surprised to find, was shattered. Emeline smiled proudly when she caught my surprised expression.

"It turns out that when you hit a window repeatedly with a large sauce pan, it eventually breaks." She took a pretend swing. "It's heavy, though. I don't think I have the strength to do it again."

The window was a single, long, horizontal panel, which would be wide enough for us to fit through, though not by much. There was another problem as well.

"There's still some glass," Emeline admitted guiltily, pointing to the largest shard, which jutted more than halfway across the window. It would be impossible to make it through entirely without getting cut, but so long as we didn't sever any major arteries, it seemed likely that we would be able to escape the house, get to the airport, and catch our plane in time. It was all pointless if we didn't make our plane.

I handed Emeline a broom.

"Start knocking as much glass loose as you can. Don't worry about the whole window. Just focus on a patch large enough for us to squeeze through." I heaved my suitcase onto the counter behind her. Not that I was worried about forgetting it. But seeing it there, so close to the broken window, I felt like I had spotted a buoy after far too long at sea. We could make this happen, my sister and I.

I turned to assess the location of our enemy and found him leaning against the kitchen counter, watching us with an eerie expression. His lips had twisted into a wry smile—not terrifically unlike my own, I was forced to admit. But placed beneath eyes that coldly spoke of dispassionate violence, the smile was an alien gesture by an alien being.

Emeline correctly interpreted my silence as fear and handed me a sliver of glass from the window. She clutched the broom. That it should all come down to a standoff in the kitchen made a certain kind of sense. It had been here that my uncle had rebuffed my awkward attempts at a kind of friendship and announced his plans to use psychiatric drugs to chisel away the parts of me he deemed problematic.

Basilio had no weapon that I could see, but didn't look like he required one.

That's when my nose picked up something foreign and yet … familiar. It had an impatient, rustling quality that spoke of wind and wood and felt heavy on the back of my tongue and throat.

Basilio seemed to sense something as well—or heard it.

"Adamo?" he called hopefully.

"He's not here," Emeline replied, with no small degree of glee. "In fact, the only way he's coming back is if you go get him. And the only way you're going to know where he is is by letting us out of this house."

"There's a fire in here," I announced, now certain. The prospect frightened me, but it also made me incredibly happy.

Basilio rushed into the living room, and I noted that he was moving much more quickly than he had been when he was following us earlier. Emeline shrugged and jumped down from the window, still clutching the broom. I gripped the handle of my suitcase, and we followed our uncle into the living room.

Basilio was waving pieces of the pillows I had destroyed at moderately sized flames that were rapidly consuming his couch and the bookshelves behind it. The entrance to his study was no longer visible through a thick plume of smoke.

"That's a fire, alright," Emeline announced, her face pale.

"Flagellum dei!" Basilio hurled at me for a second time. He was walking closer to the fire, and I could see from the corner of his face that was visible that there was no longer anything cold in his expression. The fire had burned that away, leaving grief as burdensome as the smoke now glutting the hallway. I racked my brain for a reasonable explanation for the fire and remembered sweeping through the living room with my arms wide. There had been candles, but I didn't remember whether they were burning when I ran past.

Emeline was staring at the growing mark on the wall, looking alternately delighted and horrified. It was like watching one of those clowns that sweeps its hand over its face, grinning one moment and grimacing the next, except with a greedy and dangerous blaze set before it.

"It shouldn't have grown this quickly," Emeline whispered to me. "You must have done this! Vesta must have done this for you! Unless fire is faster than I thought." She frowned.

Basilio seemed to have the same idea.

"Flagellum dei! Flagellum dei! This is my home! What gave you the right ... ?" He had finally stopped moving toward the fire, but the flames now reached greedily toward him. I'd never seen his suit in any condition other than pristine, but now it wilted, and the soft, luxurious gray was smeared a deeper, more primal shade. He was sweating—something I'd never seen him do, even on the hottest of days. Ilium was always cool: a dark, orderly cavern within which no detail was too insignificant to fall beyond Basilio's control.

"We have to go," I told them as they stood staring, transfixed by the fire. Part of me wanted to stay with them and watch the conflagration play out its natural course. If I found myself before the three judges on the other side of the river Styx, I might argue that sacrificing myself to feed this inferno was penance for failing Vesta's fire those many years ago. They would send me to the Plains of Asphodel, where I could reunite with my family ... if they accepted my account of my life, of course. Most fallen vestals don't expect to join their families in meadows of tall, blooming flowers. They might set me their own penance and send me to Tartarus until it was repaid.

But even the Furies of the underworld didn't terrify me as they once did. Their dominion was impermanent. Though their reign might be long and terrible, eventually I would meet my debts and finally be free to find them— Nesreen, Mater, Pater, Liviana, Junia, Decima, Hortensia,

Caecilia, Vibiana, Maximiliana, even Valens. They'd have been dosed with water from the River Lethe to make them forget their past life, so they need not remember me as the oath-breaker who had brought them grief. And Aemilia would be right there beside me, as she had always been. We might not know each other, but at least we could be there together. We could be happy.

For some reason, that reminded me of Basilio's pills and my overwhelming fear of falling asleep and never properly waking up again, forgetting my family, losing myself, losing Nesreen. I wasn't ready to settle into a passive, peaceful existence.

I grabbed my uncle's arm in my left hand and Emeline's in my right and spun them away from the blaze.

"You're not dying here, despite your best efforts," I said sternly. "Emeline, fetch my suitcase." She blinked twice, then turned to obey me, wheeling it toward the entry.

"Zio, I need the keys." I spoke gently, trying to penetrate the fog of desperation and confusion enough to be understood but not wanting to surprise him sufficiently that he remembered his hatred and possible desire to kill me.

He looked at me briefly, and when his eyes focused on my face, there was a momentary flash of recognition and rage, but it was followed by the pained, confused expression he'd had after exclaiming that I was the scourge of god.

He shook his head no.

"Yes, we need to leave so people can come in and put out the fire. There's still a chance you can save Ilium." I spoke slowly, as though he were a very young child.

His hand twitched indecisively, then darted for his pocket. He withdrew a brass chain with several keys and held them in mid-air. I took them from him, slowly, then steered him toward the front door.

"If one of these doesn't work, we're going to have to try to make it through the kitchen window," I told Emeline.

"I don't know if he can fit through," she objected, pointing to our uncle.

"We'll cross that rickety bridge when we come to it," I said grimly, knowing I needed to get her out of the house, but not certain that I could leave someone behind to die. I had no fond memories of starving to death, but the more I considered the prospect of melting into the fire, the less power the memory of my own violent hunger pangs held over me.

There were four keys on the ring, and the second one I tried clicked neatly into place. I wasn't expecting it, and I could tell from the whoosh of Emeline's breath when she heard the key click that she hadn't expected it either. I thought there was a very good chance some or all of us would die trapped inside Ilium, because I knew from previous experience that hope is often baseless, even when it's necessary.

Despite the fact that hope is often baseless; despite the fact that just half an hour earlier Basilio was doing everything in his power to keep us inside; despite the fact that we had engaged the enemy on his own territory (and without recognizing that he was, in fact, the enemy far longer than we should have); despite the fact that there was space for us in pastures rife with asphodel; despite the fact that I had spent the greater portion of this life determinedly not succeeding at anything, when I turned the handle, the door opened, and we stumbled into a night just as rich in beauty and wonder as the one that had been my last 1,824 years earlier.

Emeline found Basilio's phone and called for fire services. I don't know how she knew who to call, but I marveled at the efficiency of her Italian and marveled that anyone else listening would think they were hearing a woman all grown up.

Once she'd finished conveying the necessary information, she made a second call, which was much shorter.

"That's the best I can do, Uncle," Emeline told Basilio, pressing his phone into his hand. "We're leaving now. We need to catch our plane, and I'm afraid we won't be able to do that if we're answering questions and filling out paperwork and all those other useless things that happen when there's a fire. So you're going to have to say that your nieces went back to their hostel and had nothing to do with the blaze."

Basilio was staring at the front door with the same dazed, empty expression he'd had inside the house when he almost stepped into the flames. He gave no indication of having heard Emeline's speech. She shrugged.

"Goodbye, Uncle," I told him, fighting the unexpected impulse to shake his hand. The overwhelming odor of smoke had drowned out the stench of black licorice, and I attributed my almost reconciliatory impulse to this fact alone. "It has been downright awful knowing you, but if you go your way, I'll go my own and make sure they don't intersect ever again. I hope you're well … for Mom's sake."

Emeline was waving me along as I spoke, and we began walking down the long driveway together when she suddenly stopped and turned back.

"You should know, if you decide to go after Rhea again, I've put some calls in to the American Psychiatric Association, and they seem to find it highly unethical and suspicious for a man to prescribe drugs to his niece against her wishes and without the consent of her parents and another psychiatrist. My conversations with them were purely hypothetical, of course. But if you follow her, I will take this information to them, and not only will your career be over, but you will likely spend time inside a prison."

She jogged back to where I stood and put a protective arm around my shoulder as we hobbled down the path toward the main road. Neither of us looked back.

"We have to hurry," Emeline said softly. "A taxi is going to meet us at the bottom of the hill, across the road. I gave him the address of the nearest neighbor, because I figured he might get suspicious if it looked like we were running away from a house on fire."

"But we're not running away from a fire. We're running away from Basilio." I spoke more for my own benefit than Emeline's—and not because I felt guilty, but because I felt cleansed of everything, and I wanted Emeline to feel the same way.

The taxi arrived as planned, and the driver was either exceptionally blind or made a habit of driving foreigners who looked like the chimney sweeps in *Mary Poppins*. In either case, he made no special note of our appearances and, at Emeline's orders, drove us to a hostel.

I'd been expecting The Mauve, but Emeline insisted that Basilio might think to look for us there, though it seemed unlikely to either of us that he would bother to come looking ever again; the fire had a dignified tone of finality, like the gentle sweep of the last page of a book.

The hour was late when we checked in, and we were long past any reasonable expectation of sleep. Instead, Emeline collected the luggage she'd been storing there, and we used the time to wash away the physical evidence of our strange escape. My side seemed to ache more with each breath, and I was beginning to suspect that I had seriously damaged at least one rib. Looking in the mirror and seeing a pale creature with knotted hair and a shirt that was torn from catching on any number of possible items in Basilio's house, I felt like a victim—something I'd never intended to become in this new life. And I liked to think that I was unburdening myself of every grievance, petty or otherwise, that had plagued me. I was shedding an entire skin, and with it, shifting my identity. In addition to the bucket or so of sweat and dirt I had accumulated over the course of the night.

Our checkout was at 11 a.m., but we left well before that, too restless and exhilarated either for sleep or exchanging polite chit-chat with our neighbors. Instead, we seized our luggage and made our way to the nearest palazzo and found seats outside a café that was still mostly empty.

We had an hour before we needed to leave for the airport. Emeline ordered us cappuccinos, but after the waiter left, neither of us wanted to break the silence. I could see the city's beauty now, at last—enough, at least, that my chest felt heavy with the knowledge that we were leaving. There we sat, two incendiaries from another country and another era, accompanied by large, overpacked suitcases that proclaimed to all the world that we would soon be leaving.

"What's next?" I looked up to find Aemilia staring at me anxiously, equal parts trepidation and curiosity. It was funny how quickly she was Aemilia again as soon as we were away from Ilium and beyond Basilio's grasp.

"You mean after I get this cracked rib fixed up?" I joked with a wince. She looked worried, and I knew she was going to offer to delay our flight to give me time to see a doctor, so I stopped her with my serious answer.

"I think I'm going to Libya," I replied. Though I wasn't really sure when I had made the decision, Libya now presented itself as the only option available to me.

"To Cyrene," Aemilia murmured softly. "What if she's not there?"

"Then I will find her."

My voice hadn't carried such resolution for more than 1,000 years. Aemilia might have thought she missed it and had spent years pushing me to fight for something, but now she was being reminded of what it was like to be left behind to worry.

"So that's why you were so insistent on hauling that suitcase out of Basilio's damn house," she said. "You're not coming home. Rhea, she might not be here. I know you are, but you have to prepare yourself for the idea that you might be the exception. You've always been the exception. You committed the gravest sin against the empire of Rome, and you're being punished for it. That's why you're here."

"You're here." I tilted my head, fishing for Rome's not-yet-ripe rays of morning sun.

"Being punished for sins of my own."

My eyes shot open, the sun and the palazzo forgotten.

"What sins? You lived a long and prosperous life. You married Valens. You had four children: Domitius, Gratianus, Otho, and Rhea. Your sister was the emperor's mistress." It was difficult to believe that just two months prior, I had envied Aemilia each of these accomplishments. But it seemed important somehow, that one of us, at least, had discovered happiness in her past life. It gave me hope for the future, now that my life expectancy had shot up rather dramatically over the course of the last 48 hours.

"Valens and I weren't quite your saviors, the way I may have made us out to be." Aemilia wasn't looking at me, and her knuckles were white from clenching her coffee cup.

"I know you didn't succeed in saving me, but the fact that you tried means everything," I insisted, patting her hand. "You've been the hero in all this. You got me out this time. And that's more important than what happened last time."

"I hope you really mean that," Aemilia said nervously, her voice now shaking. "Rhea, Valens wasn't trying to dig you out because he loved you. Well, he was. Why does the truth always have to be so complicated? But he was also there out of guilt."

"What guilt?" Somewhere in my subconscious, I realized that I might not want to be holding anything that might break, so I set aside my coffee cup.

"The servant that betrayed you?"

"Cloelia." I would never forget that name, no matter how many life cycles I endured.

"She was Valens' servant. He placed her in the house to spy on you for him. When she found you, you know, in the temple, she went immediately to Valens, and she told him what she had found. She left it to him to decide what to do with the information. He could have not said anything. He could have protected you. But he was so ... I'm not saying his love for you was healthy, but anyone could see it. And he couldn't stand the idea of you loving anyone else, so he went to the emperor that very night. Of course, it wasn't an easy thing getting an audience with Commodus. You remember how paranoid he was?" She caught my expression and averted her eyes, hurrying on with her story.

"Once Commodus realized that Valens was there to report a fallen vestal, he allowed him in and heard his tale, spoke with Cloelia, and began rounding up the court. That's how it happened so fast. But Valens regretted it immediately.

He tried to convince Cloelia to say that she had lied to him so you could at least receive a proper burial. He hated himself. And he never forgave himself, Rhea. Never."

"And you married him? You married the man who reported me to Commodus?"

"No! I didn't know then."

"When did you know?"

"When he died. It took … well, it didn't happen quickly or painlessly, we'll leave it at that. He knew what was coming, and so did I, so he asked everyone to leave the room, and he told me."

"What did you do with Cloelia?"

"Valens couldn't stand the sight of her, and the Virgo Vestalis Maxima didn't want to keep her at the house after what she'd done to you, so he granted Cloelia her freedom on the condition that he never have to look at her again."

"He blamed her? After ordering her to stalk me and report to him? He blamed her!" All this time, I'd believed that my mistake had been trusting Cloelia, but really it had been trusting Valens.

"Don't speak against the sun," Aemilia whimpered in reply.

"How can you say that to me, knowing what you now know?"

"If I had known what he did before I married him, I wouldn't have gone through with it. As much as I loved him, I'd banish him before I willingly married the man who killed my sister. But I didn't know. I spent a lifetime with him as my husband and the father of my children. That's how I knew him, Rhea."

Aemilia was doing something I'd never seen her do before: She was crying in public, sobbing, not seeming to care that anyone might see her. It was, somehow, the obliteration of the final barrier between us, and I couldn't simply sit there and let her do all the work on her own.

"*Amor et melle et felle est fecundissimus,*" I said gently, patting her hand. Love is rich with both honey and venom.

"Yeah," she agreed, laughing and trying to blow her nose surreptitiously into her napkin. "Yeah, it really is."

"So what's next for you?" I asked, not even bothering to try to be subtle about the change of subject.

"I dunno. I think I'm gonna finish school, go to college, maybe major in Spanish."

"Spanish?"

"Yeah, I think it will give me a solid professional edge."

"That's so … practical."

"Yeah, y'know, I think I actually am a practical person. I just always fought against it because I mistakenly thought you were the practical sister. You know, older, quieter, more boring than me. But it's so obvious to me now that you're not at all practical. You're the dreamer. I'm the one that puts my brain to the grindstone and gets things done." She grinned reluctantly at me.

"I'm not sure about brains and grindstones pairing well together," I said doubtfully, "but other than that I know exactly what you mean."

"So I guess this means you won't be joining me on the plane?" Aemilia asked wistfully.

"No. I don't think I will. I'll accompany you to the airport and stay with you until your plane leaves, maybe help you pick out a trashy novel or two for the trip. But I think I'm going to take the train to Sicily, and then catch a ferry to Malta, and then another one to Libya." I spoke as though I'd been planning the journey for a very long time. Maybe I had. I'd just been doing a very good job keeping it secret, even from myself.

Aemilia pursed her lips, and I realized she was trying to stop herself from crying again. With her pink nose and long, shiny tear tracks down her face, she finally looked like a little sister to me—not the kind I could always protect, and not the kind that could always protect me, but someone I loved more dearly than anything else in this world: a reason to go on learning and growing and fighting to the furthest reaches of my abilities.

I dipped my fingers into the pouch at my waist and withdrew five warm, smooth knucklebones. We had a quarter of an hour left. I threw them on the table with a dramatic flourish and smiled what I hoped was an irresistible smile.

"Best out of three?"

ABOUT THE AUTHOR

Ashley Schwellenbach is a Seattle resident, author of the young adult fantasy novel *Scourge of the Righteous Haddock*, reader of just about everything under the sun and moon, vegetarian, caregiver to two ungrateful cats, feminist, hothead, captain of sinking ships, and likely a few other things besides.